ELIZABETH'S HEART

BOOK TWO
THE 1929 SERIES

M.L. GARDNER

TABLE OF CONTENTS

For Lisa
With special thanks to Monica Haynes

Soften your eyes toward the sad and the broken—for you never know what might have come before . . .

I WILL TELL THE STORY FOR HER

They say I was born with the sight. The people who admire me also question and fear me. I don't know what I call what I have, what I see. But I have no choice when the visions come. I am a captive audience. There are those who say I am cursed, and that much I do believe. My name is Simon, but that doesn't matter. This isn't my story. I tell the story for her.

PROLOGUE

THE FIRST TIME I saw Elizabeth, two orderlies carried her in. She screamed, terrified. Her brown hair whipped around her face as she kicked and fought them every step of the way. She hissed, spit, and cursed. I watched, pressing myself against the cold, white wall of the corridor as they drug her past me to the wing where they kept the women. Most of us came here heavily sedated, barely aware of where we were, or who we were for that matter. She came here awake and aware. Even in her violent panic, she must have sensed my eyes on her. She stopped fighting, her entire body flaccid in the arms of the orderlies. She looked right at me, huge brown eyes suddenly sane.

"*Help me*," she whispered and then arched her back with a primal scream, fighting again to get away. There was something in her eyes in that single lucid moment that haunted me. For days, it was her eyes I saw when I closed mine. They came with the visions and dreams. They became part of them. It was then, before I ever spoke my first words to her, that I knew I would love her. I must tell her story for it deserves to be told.

DREAMS

I STOOD AROUND the corner, waiting for my turn with the doctor. He was an old, crotchety bastard who twisted everything you said, contorting and perverting it so there was no right answer to his questions. He held the keys to get out of here, and he held them high. Muffled voices behind the door grew louder and more insistent until there was a loud shriek, and then a crash. I hung my head and sighed heavily. I was hoping I was wrong, and she would make it through this appointment without an incident. If she did, they would let her into the commons area, for a brief period at least, and I would have a chance to talk to her.

Two orderlies pushed past me into the room, followed by a nurse with a needle. No chance to talk to her today. The door flew open, slamming into the wall behind it, and they carried her out while she screamed and cursed. The nurse jabbed the needle into her hip as they passed me, and before they were to the end of the hall, she was limp in their arms. They disappeared around the corner as the doctor called my name.

I sat down in the chair, not too fast, not too slow. He was the kind to pick everything apart. If I sat too fast, I was nervous, scared or hiding something. If I sat too slowly, I was tired. He would suspect I was kept awake at night with visions. And that I was hiding something. Always that I was hiding something.

"Hello, Simon," he said without looking up.

"Hello."

"How do you feel today?" he asked, now looking me over carefully.

"Fine."

"Really?"

"Yes." I stared at him, trying desperately to pull off an unreadable face. He hated that.

"Have you had any more visions?" he asked, narrowing his eyes at me. There was no right answer. If I said no, I was a liar, hiding something. If I said yes, I was still crazy, and they would shock me again, shove pills down my throat that made me forget who I was. Even those didn't stop the visions. They came in dream form, always proving to be prophetic snippets of what was to come. Today, I went with lying. My head still ached from the last therapy session.

"No, not today. Or yesterday."

"Nothing? Not a single one?" he asked in amazement.

"Yes. I think the new medicine you gave me is helping. I don't even dream anymore," I lied with a convincing shrug. I had dreamed a lot lately and always about her.

"Really. We didn't start you on a new medication, Simon," he said with a smirk. "So you're lying."

"I'm not lying. I haven't been seeing things, and I don't dream anymore."

He sat back in his leather chair, smiling at me, deciding. I knew what he would decide, so I wasn't as worried today. What *was* awful was knowing he would decide to send me for treatment regardless, and even then, I would try to word everything carefully in hopes of avoiding it. It never worked. But this morning, while brushing my teeth, the room went black, and I saw myself walking back to my room under my own power. I saw her strapped to her bed, so I knew today would be uneventful. No painful shock therapy and no speaking to her. One good, one bad.

"Are you *sure*, Simon? You've had no visions? No fortune-telling dreams? You're not hiding anything?"

"No," I said tightly. "I'm not hiding anything."

"Why are you getting so agitated, Simon?" he asked with a twitch of his lips. I could tell the bastard was intent on finding an excuse to shock me today.

"Well, Doctor," I said, composing myself quickly. "I get tired of you asking me that. You may think I'm crazy because I used to see things, things that sometimes turned out to be true, but I'm not a liar," I insisted, lying. "Wouldn't you get tired of someone picking your brain every day, your every thought, emotions and feelings, and then calling you out on your answers? There's no trust. Without trust, there can't be progress."

"You speak well beyond your years, Simon."

"And how does that make you feel, Doc?" His eyes flashed, and I backtracked quickly to avoid angering him. "What am I supposed to say to that? Is there a right answer? How is a twenty-one-year-old *supposed* to sound?" I sat back in the hard metal chair, struggling to control my temper. Bastard still wouldn't answer my questions. He just sat there with that smirky educated smile of his.

"It was an observation, Simon, that's all. Why are you so tense?"

"There you go again." I blew out a long breath and looked down at my crossed arms. "I really need to use the bathroom. Are we finished?"

He ignored me and scribbled on his notepad. That sound grated on my nerves. I always wondered what he was writing about me, what he really thought, and more importantly, when he would be convinced I had stopped having visions and let me out of here.

"Yes, Simon, we're finished. Come to me right away if you have any more visions or disturbing dreams, all right?"

Yeah, right, I thought to myself. "Of course," I said aloud. I would damn myself to hell, for time and all eternity, before I ever spoke of my visions again. To anyone.

"Have a good day, Simon."

I rose from my seat, walked to the door, and then hesitated.

"What is it, Simon?" he asked impatiently, not looking up from his incessant scribbling.

"I was just wondering," I stopped, thinking twice, and then curiosity got the best of me. "The new admission. The girl. I was just wondering about her."

"Have you been thinking about her? Are you interested in her?"

Shit, I thought and glanced at the ceiling. *You brought this one on yourself, idiot. If you get shocked, it's your own fault.* I wondered briefly if the outcome of my premonitions could be changed by my own stupidity.

"No, no." I shook my head. "She just seems really..." I

decided to let him fill in the blank.

"She's someone you should stay away from, Simon. Your problems, we might be able to cure those if you do your therapy and are honest with us about your thoughts and feelings. But Elizabeth, well, I doubt that she can be helped."

So that's her name, I thought.

I looked out into the hall and back to him. "How can you say that? She's only been here a week."

"Trust me, Simon. Just stay away from her. She's not your type of girl anyway," he said with a mocking smile.

"And I suppose you know what my type of girl is, Doc?"

He opened his mouth to say something, but then closed it quickly, probably wanting to reference something about one that rode brooms and fancied black cats. I left before I could get myself into trouble and walked down to the commons area.

~ ~ ~

I SAT NEXT to Ronnie, who appeared to be in a good mood.

"Hey, Ron," I said, sitting down on the couch next to him. The vibration spilled his drink into his lap, and he came up swinging. His fist met my jaw with a loud pop, and my head bounced off the back of the couch. He looked down, screaming with fury at the water running down his white hospital gown, and then, taking a deep breath, he screamed again as he lunged at me. He had both skinny hands around my throat before I could blink.

"He's gonna kill me! Now, he's gonna kill me!" He seethed with wild, bulging eyes, spittle dripping from his clenched teeth. I tried to pull his hands away from my throat as he threw my head back and forth, but this

bastard was strong, and it took three orderlies to get him off me. They pried his fingers from my neck, and I rubbed it, catching my breath as they dragged him out, screaming paranoid delusions of how the king was going to behead him for his sins.

"Well, I didn't see *that* coming," I said aloud. A nurse jerked her head toward me with suspicious eyes.

"Joking," I said as I held my throat with one hand and the other up in honesty. "I'm going to my room. I think the party's over." The other patients cowered in the corners of the room, laughing, crying, and chewing their nubby nails. The nurse nodded for one of the orderlies to accompany me to my room.

My luck it was David, a tall black man, wide as a doorway, menacing-looking as hell. But he had the kindest eyes, and most importantly, he knew I wasn't crazy.

When I first arrived in the land of the delusional and deranged, I did as most of the others did. I fought. Angry at being trapped and out of control of every aspect of my life, I frequently fought. Our friendship, if you can call it that, began with a bang. More specifically, a punch. His fist to my stomach. They had called David after I had managed to fight my way out of the holds of three smaller, less influential orderlies. If I hadn't been flooded with adrenaline, I would have turned and run to my bed, tucked myself in and blown him a kiss goodnight. But I was stupid. I swung and hit his jaw. He didn't even flinch. In fact, I think he smiled. I dislocated three fingers on his iron face. I was more than willing to comply at that point, but lacked a white towel to throw. He let me know, in one convincing blow, my fighting days were over. I lay on the floor, curled up in a ball, holding my stomach, crying like a grade-schooler. He let me writhe for a few moments and then held a hand out.

"Now, don't make me have to do that again," he said in a deep voice as intimidating as his stature. I nodded, and he pulled me up, then walked with me to the infirmary, shooing away the other orderlies. Since coming to our understanding, we'd become the closest thing to friends as you can have in a place where you trust no one.

"So, David," I began as we walked down the sterile hallway, "what's up with the new girl?" I asked in a hushed voice, keeping my eyes on the floor.

"Crazier than the day is long, Simon," he said as he leisurely strolled beside me. "She got two of her. Up here," he said, tapping the side of his head and then shaking it in pity. "Why do you ask?"

I shrugged, trying to play it down. "Just wondering. Haven't had a new one for a while."

"She's cute." He elbowed me, teasing.

"She's crazy."

"She might be in the commons area soon," he said intuitively. "If she stops trying to crawl across the desk to kill the doc."

"Have they got her pretty sedated?" I asked, knowing the answer. He nodded, almost grimly, and then stood next to my door, waiting to lock it behind me. I waited as another disgruntled customer, screaming and spitting, was dragged past us and then turned to David. I trusted him, mostly. But I always stayed just this side of paranoid, and I feared I had said too much.

"I won't say a word," David whispered. I nodded and then turned away, worried to give away more of myself. I heard the loud metal clink of the lock as I lay down on my thin mattress with my hands behind my head. There was a small window with bars on both sides high on the wall.

Too high to reach, even though it was so small a toddler would struggle to squeeze through it. I watched the light fade from the room before closing my eyes and dreamed again about Elizabeth.

~ ~ ~

THE SUN WAS warm and spring was in bloom all around us. I could smell the colors. Pink buds on cherry trees and tiny, new leaves sprouting out of thin brown branches, and fresh green moss on the trunks of the trees. Suddenly, the sky darkened and nervous fear enveloped us. The forest fell away, and we were on top of a seaside volcanic mountain, its top glossy black, flat, and slippery. We skidded to a stop, looking down over the dizzying cliff in front of us. Small rocks tumbled off the razor sharp edge, bouncing off the jagged overhang and then disappearing into the darkness. We could hear the ocean crashing against the rocks below but couldn't see it in the darkness. There was no moon. Black clouds swirled above our heads like a whirlpool in slow motion, and small pebbles and sticks poked at our bare feet. Dogs barked in the distance, and I knew they were coming for us.

She turned toward me, her back to the cliff. She never took her eyes from mine as she backed up slowly toward the edge. I called to her desperately, eying the edge she was so dangerously close to begging her to stop. She did, and only her toes clung to the ragged edge, her heels bouncing lightly over nothing. Her long, curly hair spilled over her shoulders and she stretched her arms out wide.

"Come with me," she whispered, and then tilted her head back and dropped out of sight.

I woke with a loud yelp, my face covered in sweat.

The expressionless face of the nurse loomed in the small window of the metal door. I didn't need a premonition to know what would happen next.

~ ~ ~

I FELT WELL enough three days later to walk into the commons area. I had a mild lingering headache. Deciding not to risk upheaval over spilled water, I leaned against the wall across the room from everyone. They were huddled around the radio. It sat against the wall, encased in a wire cage. Our only link to the outside world. Was it October? Or November? I'd have to ask David the next time he was on shift. I kept my eyes on the floor, humming along with the radio show. They liked it when you hummed. It showed you were coherent enough to follow along, but not quite enough to sing. I was slightly off tempo. The buzzing in my ears hadn't stopped yet.

Ronnie let out a howl of excitement, and I looked up, tucking my chin to my neck instinctively. That's when I saw her. She sat in the circle with the other partygoers. Curly brown hair fell around her face, hiding it as she stared at her hands in her lap. She wore the same white gown we all wore when we first got here. If she were good, they'd upgrade it to a baggy white dress.

She didn't look up when Ronnie yelled or even as they dragged him off. I ironed my face straight and argued with myself for several minutes. Susan rose and stumbled away, sobbing into her hands. Apparently, the staff forgot show tunes upset her. That freed up seats on both sides of Elizabeth. Curiosity overrode caution, and I casually limped, thanks to overly tight restraints, over to her. I slipped smoothly into the chair.

She didn't acknowledge me, and I hesitated to speak.

An orderly and nurse stood just ten feet away. I studied her from the corner of my eye.

Her hair was matted and tangled, hanging in clumps off her scalp. She tapped her thumbs together lightly, and I could see dried blood along the cuticles and under the edge of her nails. Most of them tried to claw their way through metal doors and concrete walls. No one had succeeded yet. I saw her lift her head very slowly, tilting it enough to steal a sideways peek at me. Then her eyes rose up from underneath the tangled brown mass, and she met my stare with eyes that dared me to break it as we studied each other curiously.

~ ~ ~

I SAT ACROSS from her at dinner the next evening. She had washed her hands, but not yet her hair. I cursed the nurse under my breath for letting her wander around in such a disheveled state.

"Even crazy people deserve to be clean."

Her eyes twitched up briefly, and I hated myself for letting her hear it. She picked at her food, so I decided that was a good place to start.

"You should eat." I kept my eyes on my metal plate as I spoke.

"What?"

"Keep your head down," I said. "They don't realize we're talking to each other that way. They think we're talking to ourselves."

She dropped her eyes back down to carrots that had been boiled to mush.

"You should eat," I repeated.

"I'm not hungry," she whispered to her plate.

"Doesn't matter. You have to stay strong in a place

like this. Besides, if you don't eat, they'll notice and force feed you."

I hated to lie to her like that, but it would draw attention if she started to lose weight. I watched one die of that. Just stopped eating. It took several months, but she died. And they didn't do a damn thing to help her. I wouldn't let that happen to Elizabeth. She took a bite of carrot mush and I smiled at mine.

"Who are you?" she asked, stealing a quick peek up at me.

"Simon. Who are you?"

"Elizabeth," she whispered just before an orderly walked by.

"Just Elizabeth?" I asked. She shot me a lightning-fast angry look.

"I meant, what's your last name?" She knew what I originally meant and ignored me.

"How long have you been here?" she asked after an awkward silence. Ronnie had started a commotion across the room, and I used the opportunity to look up at her fully.

"Five months. Give or take a few weeks."

Beautiful, but dark and tired eyes looked up at me.

"That long? My daddy said it would only be a few days, maybe a week at the most." Her eyes brimmed with tears.

"Maybe for you," I said, trying to give her some hope. "Just be good and do what they say. And for God's sake, don't try to act too sane."

"I'm not crazy," she said quietly through her teeth.

"I didn't say you were. But obviously, someone thought there were enough... issues to bring you here. I'm just saying don't try to get better *too* quickly."

"I didn't ask for your advice," she said, glaring

hatefully at her fork.

Ronnie screamed, flipped the table over in one fast movement, terrifying the other diners. He had three orderlies on him in seconds. She glanced over at the commotion and then looked back at me.

"I'm sorry," she said without dropping her eyes this time. Preoccupation with Ronnie gave us a few moments to look at each other.

"Don't worry about it," I said. I wouldn't have broken from her eyes even if it meant another shock treatment. Let them blast me into oblivion. I'd just sleep for two days with those eyes in my mind.

"No. You're the first person to be nice to me here. I shouldn't have. That's not like me."

It killed me to look away, but with Ronnie removed, the orderlies were breaking up to patrol the room.

"Yeah, well," I stood with my tray and tossed her a smirk, "this place can make you nuts."

I carried her smile with me to my room and studied every detail of it behind my closed eyes so I could have it always. It was the first time ever I had tried to will the visions. I needed to see more. I paid for that need the next day.

~ ~ ~

THEY FOUND ME sitting on the edge of my bed staring at nothing. I wasn't aware, of course, the world blacked out as I watched the white portal of pictures that played out in front of me.

I came out of it strapped to a stretcher. I lifted my head as they rolled me toward the familiar doorway that led to days of confusion and pain, and it took all my strength not to put up a futile fight.

We passed by David, who refused to look at me, his jaw clenched tight, his fists balled up at his sides. I banged my head on the pad several times, growling in frustration and worried for the first time that I would lose something. I knew I wouldn't lose the visions. They never left me for long. But I might lose something more important.

The paintings of her in my mind, images and snapshots from both visions, and the reality I had studied and committed to memory. I might not be able to remember so clearly the little indent above her lip or the exact shades highlighting her hair. I might forget her smile or the perfect shape of her eyes. There were flecks of black in her brown eyes. I had to remember that. Small flecks of black spiraling outward like a pinwheel, surrounded by a dark burnt brown. Black lashes drooped in sadness. I willed myself to remember as they shoved the bit in my mouth. I didn't fight it, but I breathed hard and fast in anticipation and fear. I closed my eyes tight as they strapped the prongs to my head. Her eyes were the last thing I saw before the blinding white light. Then nothing.

~ ~ ~

"WHERE IS SHE?" I asked David groggily two days later as I entered the commons. I was woozy and the bright light hurt my eyes.

"They took her up to the clinic," he said, sizing me up, no doubt trying to decide if I could continue to stand under my own power. He took a step closer, just in case. I rubbed my aching eyes and cleared my throat.

"Why? Is she sick?"

"No. You know why, Simon," he said quietly to the

floor at my feet. My head cleared so fast it made me nauseous.

"They didn't." David just nodded inconspicuously. "Why, David? She's not crazy," I said through my teeth, glaring at one of the nurses. "You said you saw two of her, but I didn't see any of that. I know crazy. She's not. And you know it," I seethed.

"No, Simon. I have seen it."

"I don't believe you." I glared up at his six and a half feet and got a blank expression in return. I felt my whole head vibrating with rage. I turned and beat the wall with my fist several times. It got the attention of everyone in the room before he could grab me and their eyes flashed from me to David and back.

"You'd best get yourself under control. Don't force me to do something I don't want to do," he whispered, his hand covered my entire fist, suspending it midair. He spun me back around and held it up over my head, pressing me against the wall. I closed my eyes and took several deep breaths to calm myself.

"I can't do another treatment," I growled through my teeth. It was the signal we used that I was under control and wouldn't be a problem.

"She'll be back in a week or so," he said, barely moving his lips as he let me away from the wall.

He turned to the other orderlies and nurses. "He's fine," he assured them, and they slowly pulled their eyes off me.

I pulled my aching fist out of his and shook it, glancing around at the others who watched me cautiously. Most of them had never seen me violent. The ones that had were gone. Either died or moved on. A lucky few had found their way home. I didn't look at them. I just found a chair by the barred window and stared through it the better part of the evening.

I couldn't stare at one spot for too long. I could feel them watching me. I moved my eyes and head often, letting them know I was still there. But I wasn't looking at the courtyard outside, the tall fence in the distance that encased us, or the dried orange leaves in small piles that nature would rearrange with wind gusts to her liking. I tried to see her across the open space in front of me. I sighed in relief when I began to recall the perfect shade of her hair, the exact shape of her lips, and then the black pinwheels set in her brown eyes flashed before me. I was so grateful to still have it, my own eyes closed and misted. With everything important accounted for, I turned my thoughts to where she was. What they were doing to her. It wasn't fair, and I wanted to kill them for it. I had never thought of doing bodily harm to anyone before. But I could have, I think. Killed each of them, and it still wouldn't be enough to make it up to her. I should have warned her. I'd seen it done a dozen times. But what could she have done? I shrugged helplessly, and then answered myself. *Nothing. Just be afraid until they came to take her away. No,* I decided. *Not knowing what was coming was better. I should know.*

~ ~ ~

I HAD NO appetite the week she was gone. I had two more visions that I didn't understand and one more treatment. How sick was I becoming in my own head not to mind it this time, knowing it would make the days go faster? In fact, I had spent the better part of the last three days she was gone recovering.

I opened my eyes and squinted at the bright light. I had heard someone say her name, and it jerked me from my fitful sleep. David. David had said her name, right by my door. I swung my feet over and swayed on the edge of the bed for a moment, my head pounding. I wiped the drool from the side of my face and felt my ear. Something dried and crusty covered it. I scratched it and saw flakes of blood floating down onto my leg.

Great. I never hear right for weeks when it bleeds, I thought. The only reason it mattered now was that I might miss something she said. Maybe something in a whisper. Then I remembered Elizabeth.

She's back. She'd lived. One hadn't.

For everything they did to us here, there's always one who wouldn't make it. I held the wall for support until the room stopped spinning. When the nausea passed, I shuffled my way out of my room.

David saw me and gave the tiniest nod toward the commons. I blinked my thank you and sped up my shuffle. My legs would start working properly in an hour or so. That much I knew from experience.

She sat in the same chair I had sat in before. She sat staring out at the courtyard. I wondered when they would let us all outside again. How wonderful would it be to walk along the path with her, free to talk above a whisper? To have even the thinnest veil of privacy. I pulled up a chair with a long metal scraping sound that pierced my brain and sat a few feet away from her. I crossed my arms and followed her gaze out the window.

"Are you okay?" I asked eyes forward. She gave a small nod. "What did they do?" I asked, even though I already knew. I wanted to make sure she knew. Sometimes, they didn't tell them. I got no answer, she just cried. Silent tears rolling one after another down to her chin told me she did know. Anger flared up, hurting my head and making my hands tremble. She knew and she cared. It mattered and it made her sad. Crazy people don't have that depth of emotion. "I know you're not crazy," I blurted out. I heard a shuffle at the door and turned. David was relieving the other orderly for lunch. I glanced at the clock on the wall. It was early for that. He looked at me briefly and winked. I was free for the next few minutes to talk to her like a normal person.

Before I could decide what to say, he tapped the table twice with his knuckles, and I looked back. A nurse rushed in the door, dropped something on the table, and left again. I knew that would be the signal.

"We can talk now," I told her. "If someone's coming, he'll knock twice. Face forward in the chair and stop talking if he does." I watched her and wasn't sure if she heard me or not. She stared forward with dull eyes. I started getting impatient to hear her voice again. The clock's hands moved swiftly, reminding me how we only had minutes. I relaxed a little as she spoke, finally.

"How do you know I'm not crazy?" she asked.

"I just know. I, ah—" I glanced around the room. "I've spent a decent amount of time with 'em and I can tell. You're not."

"You're the only one who believes that."

"For now. It will be seen, eventually, whether they like it or not. And they'll let you go." I hated myself for lying to her again.

"They won't," she said with fresh tears. "Do you know what they did to me?" she asked, looking at me for the first time. Her eyes were swollen and red, but the brown was just as I remembered with the pinwheels.

"Yes." I wanted to look away, anywhere else to escape the pain in her eyes, but I couldn't.

"I can't have kids now. Ever." She put a hand on her stomach and looked down.

"I know." I clenched my jaw and nodded.

"Why did they do that, Simon?" She looked at me as if I should have the answer. I opened my mouth with no idea what to say when David knocked on the table. I turned to face the window, still watching her out of the corner of my eye.

"I don't know," I whispered with a hoarse voice. "I don't know why they would do that to you."

Of course, I knew why they did it to the truly crazy ones. They didn't want nuts breeding nuts. Or bearing the consequences of those who take advantage of them. But they shouldn't have done it to her.

~ ~ ~

WE MANAGED LITTLE pieces of conversation over the next week, mainly at mealtimes, but it was never enough. David went out of his way, without being obvious, to give us a precious few moments when he could. He would arrange patients in group meetings so we could sit next to each other.

At night, when we stood in line for our pills, he would control the excited rush of patients toward the narrow door so I would end up standing by her.

I talked to him one evening as he walked me to my room, almost as freely as I talked to her.

"Why?" I asked simply. He knew what I meant. He thought about it for a moment, and I watched the floor tiles as we walked.

"She's better when she's with you."

"How is she better?"

"The other one doesn't come out when she's with you. Not that I've ever seen anyway." He looked at me with eyebrows raised, wanting confirmation.

"No. Never."

"The only time she smiles is when you two are having your secret talks. It's the only time she—" He paused and I grew anxious as we got closer to my door.

"What, David?"

"It's hard to explain, Simon. She's just better with you. That's the only way I can explain it." He shrugged in apology. I stopped at my door with disappointment. If I couldn't talk *to* her, I at least wanted to talk *about* her. "Weather should be nice tomorrow. Little Indian summer before it turns nasty," he said as he swung the metal door open. I liked how his eyes could say everything his tone and facial expressions couldn't. I trusted him more every day. I smiled at the floor and then at him briefly before turning into my room.

I lay restless on my bunk for a long time. The idea of getting out into the courtyard the next day kept me awake. I thought about the mossy cobblestone path and smiled. I had seen it two days earlier, the two of us walking in the sunshine on that path, breathing the fresh air. Talking freely like sane people. Maybe we could laugh, just a little. Laughter was seen as a side effect of insanity here. I missed laughing. Maybe if we could get just out of earshot.

I had to stop thinking about tomorrow or I would never get to sleep. I shoved my finger into the little hole in the corner of my mattress and dug out the piece of chalk I had stolen when the nuns came to do art projects with us. The wall was a dingy, tan color from years of neglect, and the white chalk showed up well enough, even in the shadows of evening.

I rolled onto my side, facing the wall and then peeked over my shoulder to the door. I wondered briefly if drawing on the wall was a *shockable* offense. As I drew the outline of her face, it mattered less and less. I was a good artist, but it was a crude drawing. I could never capture the perfect details of her with a small cracked piece of chalk. My mind filled them in, and it came to life before my eyes. I traced it with my finger when I finished, smudging the hard line of her jaw into softness.

I tucked the chalk away into its hiding place, feeling it was my most prized possession. I laid my head on my arm, looking at her on the wall. I smiled, touching her forehead and nose. I felt cold concrete under my finger, but I imagined her skin much softer.

When the light had almost faded from the room, and I could only see the outline of her, David coughed loudly outside my door, signaling a room check. I sighed heavily.

"Goodnight," I whispered to her and then, with my open hand, I rubbed her off the wall just before the nurse peered in. I stayed on my side, breathing slowly and evenly, my hand flat against the concrete where she had been.

~ ~ ~

I WOKE AT the first light of dawn and paced my room, waiting for breakfast. I had to suppress any hint of happiness when the orderly brought me the small mirror and stayed with me while I washed my face, shaved, and brushed my teeth. I brushed them especially well this morning. I hadn't foreseen a kiss. *But then again, I don't see everything,* I thought, smiling with a mouth full of foamy toothpaste.

I saw her sitting at breakfast and had a warm surge of energy race through me. I consciously willed my legs to pace themselves. I sat down and waited until the nurse set my tray in front of me. Elizabeth stole a peek and gave me a small smile when the nurse turned her back.

"Morning," I said to the biscuit as soon as it was safe.

"Good morning," she whispered back. I could see her struggling to kill a smile. "They say we get to go outside today," she said, disguising the words with her chewing.

"That's what I heard." I glanced at the window to the courtyard—overcast gray skies. That was good. They would wait until the fog burned off and the sun came out. I had seen David in the distance as we walked, and he didn't come on shift until after lunchtime, so I knew I had the whole morning to kill. "Will you walk with me? Out there?" I nodded toward the window.

"I was hoping you'd ask." She smiled up at me again, eyes shining. Out of the corner of my eye, I saw the nurse watching and my blood ran cold.

"Look down," I growled. She did, a little too quickly.

We were silent for several minutes while we ate. The nurse still glanced at us more times than I was comfortable with, and I knew what I had to do to take the attention away from us.

"I'm sorry," I said softly to her as I gathered my tray. "I can't risk losing this," I said. "No matter what happens, keep a straight face," I whispered before I walked away. Her eyes followed me and then, remembering herself, she looked back down at her food. I could see her straining to watch me as I sat down across from Ronnie. I took a deep breath and then blew it out in guilt.

"I'm sorry to have to do this to you, Ron," I said. "But you have no idea how important this is to me." He looked up at me, oatmeal hanging from his chin, in confusion. He rarely spoke. He mostly yelled amid outbursts. He was so far gone, it made it a little easier to do what I was about to do. I leaned forward and lowered my voice.

"I don't know if you can understand, but when something is really important to someone, it's amazing the lengths they will go in order to protect it," I said, casually glancing at Elizabeth. The nurses didn't think anything of me talking to Ronnie and went about their business, leaving me to talk freely. Even yesterday, I couldn't imagine myself doing something like this. He continued to stare at me.

"How's the king, Ron?" I asked. His eyes twitched and he swallowed hard. "You haven't done anything to make him angry, have you, Ron?" I whispered. I hated myself for this. But I cared for her more. "I heard he's here to talk to you about the water. The water you spilled. He's not happy with you, Ron." Ronnie's eyes grew wide, and he breathed fearfully through his nose. He didn't snap though. I rubbed my forehead in frustration. Ordinarily, it took literally nothing to set him off. Today he was making me work for it.

"I would hide if I were you, Ron. Hide until he's gone." His eyes twitched and he whimpered.

Christ, I hate myself and I hate you, you crazy bastard. Would you flip the table already! I tapped my fingers on the table, thinking. It seemed to irritate him, so I kept it up for several minutes. They didn't give us much time to eat and breakfast was almost over. The nurses were collecting the trays. I saw he was holding on by the thinnest of threads. I only had seconds to snip it. I leaned forward and whispered, holding the proverbial scissors open.

"I heard he's brought the queen."

The scissors snapped and so did Ronnie. He screamed, and when he flipped the table away from him, my tray flew into my face. I tried to roll away before the table came crashing down on top of me. Several orderlies restrained him as two nurses lifted the table off my head. I had a small cut, not deep enough to stitch, but it bled like hell. I looked around frantically for Elizabeth. She remained in her seat, staring at her plate. She had never even looked up.

Good girl, I thought and smiled. I felt a heavy hand pull my head back by the hair and press a cloth to my forehead. It was David.

"Was that really necessary?" his husky voice demanded. I tilted my head back and looked at his upside down face.

"Would you let that crazy bastard come along on a date with you?" I asked, my eyes glancing toward the outside.

He couldn't help but give a smile and a grunting laugh. "No, I guess I wouldn't." He pulled me up and walked with me to the infirmary to get the cut cleaned.

~ ~ ~

LATER THAT DAY, all the male patients sat around in a circle while the good doctor and his student quizzed us. After he had asked you a few questions, he would turn to his student and talk about you as if you weren't even there. I tuned him out as he tried to explain some of the more complicated mental disorders. I watched out the window as the clouds slowly cracked and the sun began to filter through them. It lit up the courtyard, making the colors of fall vividly beautiful. The few shrubs that clung to their green seemed to burst alive, and even the dead trees of autumn took on an illusion of beauty.

The visions always came when I least expected them.

All of the light disappeared from the courtyard, and the room went dark before I had time to panic. I saw the angry waves of rough seas—skies as black as pitch and violent flashes of lightning. Everything was spinning around and around, and I could barely make out the rocky shore in the distance. There was a bright light, like the flash of an exploding sun, and then a deafening noise ripped through the air as a boat split in two in front of me, sending shards of wood and cloth in every direction. I jumped in my seat when I came back to myself—scared and beginning to sweat.

Please, sweet Jesus, don't let them have seen me, I prayed. My hands shook and I crossed my arms to hide them. I hesitated to look up for fear the doctor would be staring at me. He would call for an orderly and send me away. I would fight them this time. I would fight with everything I had. They weren't going to take this day away from me.

"Are you all right, Simon?"

My heart lurched, but I raised my head with a clear face. "Fine."

"You look odd, Simon," he said, tilting his head in examination.

I rolled my head away and then back to him. "I'm bored," I said with dull eyes and a hint of juvenile impatience.

"Simon is one of our more interesting patients," the doctor said to the intern, still staring at me. Finally, he turned away, and I exhaled slow and long. "Except for the disturbing visions that haunt him and keep him from leading a productive life, he is rather sane." He looked back at me in approval. I could tell he was trying to credit himself for every ounce of the sanity I had walked in here with. I'd let him take it. But he could not have today.

"That was close," David said under his breath as I walked past. Dead serious eyes met his own at the truth of his statement.

"What are you doing here this early anyway?" I asked.

"Working a double shift, lucky for you. If I hadn't been here, you know they probably would have thrown you in *the* room," he nodded down the hall at the small empty room where they took you when you really went nuts. "When I saw you, I called the doctor and asked him a few questions. Kept his attention for a few minutes."

I shuddered, more at missing a chance to talk to Elizabeth than the thought of them locking me in that cold, dark room.

"Thank you." He nodded. "What month is it, David?" I asked.

"October."

"October...?"

"It's October twenty-fifth, nineteen and twenty-nine," he said.

"Halloween is next week," I realized aloud. It didn't matter. Just an interesting fact. "What time is it?"

"Ten-thirty," he said, glancing at his watch. He held open the door to the bathroom. "Just two more hours," he teased. There were no locks on the bathrooms here. An orderly simply stood outside and waited for you. He crossed his arms with his back to the door.

Sometime later, I blinked hard several times and a dark blur flashed in front of my face. I realized David's hands were on my shoulders, throwing me back and forth. He was hissing my name. I coughed and choked from spit that flew down my throat with the violent shaking. He looked nervously at the door and back at me.

"Shh! They'll hear you," he said, almost as scared as I was. He let me go and I fell forward, elbows on my knees, trying to catch my breath. I felt very tired.

"What happened?" I gasped, rubbing my eyes.

"You had another one," he said quietly. "After five minutes, I got worried and looked in. You were sitting here, staring. I couldn't think of what to do besides shake you," he whispered apologetically. I glanced at the door. We heard neither voices nor footsteps. "I think it'll be okay." He stood straight and brushed bits of dirt off his white pants. "Pull your pants up and get back out there," he said.

"I've never had two that close together before," I panted. I felt like my head was swimming, full, and it started to hurt.

"Maybe excitement," he whispered, holding his hands out in suggestion. I would be so glad to be able to have a conversation in something other than a whisper one day.

"No," I said and looked at him while buttoning my pants. "David." He looked at me and waited while I waged war with myself inside my head. "Don't take the staff bus to the gate tonight," I said through my teeth, closing my eyes and damning myself to hell.

His eyes narrowed in question. I tried to convey the importance of what I was trying to tell him without telling him anything more. "No. Just don't take the bus." I turned and left the bathroom, fast.

He didn't ask more, thankfully.

I had seen two things. One I spoke of. One I kept for myself. The pieces were beginning to fit together now. Visions and flashes that started days before she arrived were knitting themselves together and just as I knew I would love her before I saw her, I knew she would love me, too.

Sitting in the commons area later, I casually looked around for her. She sat across the room by the window, looking out with another girl. By her description the day before, I think the girl was her roommate.

"Sane enough to have a conversation with," she had told me.

"What do you talk about?" I had asked. Her cheeks reddened and she looked away, fighting a smile.

I realized I had been staring at her for too long and looked away, fighting a smile of my own. *If this second Elizabeth never came out when I was around her, and I never had visions when she was around me...* I looked back at her as she pushed her hair behind her shoulder and smiled at something her roommate said. *Then maybe we're each other's cure,* I thought, this time unable to pull my eyes from her.

~ ~ ~

THE CLOCK SLOWED just to torture me. I pushed off my bed just as the hand struck noon and waited at my door for it to be unlocked. I hated naptime. Why did they have it *before* lunch? No one was tired before lunch. I tapped my foot impatiently until I heard the hollow clink of partial freedom. It wasn't David. It was a different one, and I dropped my smile before he could see it.

This one took his job of ensuring order and compliance to a personal level, and I felt instantly tense. He turned away without a word at the door of the commons, and I saw David standing by the food cart. He gave me a slight nod and I returned it discreetly. As I passed him, I said another silent prayer that he would heed my warning tonight.

I looked around and was disappointed when I didn't see Elizabeth. I sat down with a frown, and the nurse set a tray of unappetizing food in front of me. I hovered over it, picking and pushing it around the dull metal plate, looking up every few minutes at the empty doorway. Finally, she walked in, and I straightened in my chair. She walked to an empty table and sat down without looking up at me. My heart deflated a little as she began to pick at her food without even acknowledging me. I caught David out of the corner of my eye. He wiped his fingers across his mouth, reminding me to scrub my own face. It dropped into blankness. Still, I glanced up every few minutes to look at her.

They opened the metal door leading to the courtyard. I lingered in the back of the small crowd and watched her from behind. A few overly excited souls in front of me started whooping and hollering at the illusion of freedom. They pushed to the front, trying to get out, and I took several steps to put myself between Elizabeth and the oblivious. Hard as it was, I walked away without looking back at her.

The cold autumn air bit the edges of my nostrils as I noticed the faint smell of wood smoke. A strong breeze stung the tips of my ears and picked up a handful of dried leaves, swirling them a few feet in the air before scattering them again. I watched for her out of the corner of my eye. She walked with her roommate across the grass, squinting up at the sun. I looked up and it was an odd sensation with the heat of the sun on my face while my ears burned cold. When I righted my head and opened my eyes, she was waiting there for me on the old cobblestone path. I looked around apprehensively and saw David across the courtyard. Another orderly read a magazine by the door and one of the nurses from the women's ward sat in the grass, reading a book. I noticed the absence of the real troublemakers—the loud, violent ones. I think even the staff wanted to enjoy some time in the sun today without incident. I looked back and smiled as I walked toward her. I stopped a foot away and that was still too far from her.

"Hello," she said.

"Hi." I couldn't keep the ridiculous smile off my face. "You'll still walk with me?" I asked.

"Of course." We turned together and faced away from the courtyard.

After a few paces, I turned to look at her and then turned away with a nervous laugh. Now that we were here, I had no idea what to say. I had only rehearsed this conversation with her a hundred times in my mind. But now, as I finally walked beside her, free to say anything, I was stupid and mute.

"Why are you here?" she asked, breaking the silence. "I've always wondered." She looked down as if she'd asked something wrong.

Great, I thought. *I was hoping to start with something easy—the weather or the food at hotel le manic.* I had already admitted a vision to David because I had to, self-damning as that was. I guess it was time to add the eternity part. I was taking forever to answer her, and she looked over, waiting.

"I see things," I blurted out, not sure how to clarify.

"Things that aren't there?" she asked as casually as if she was asking the time.

"Not exactly. I see things that haven't happened yet." I had never said those words aloud, and I steeled myself for her reaction.

"So you're a fortune teller," she said, nodding her head slightly.

"Not exactly."

"Well, explain it to me. I want to know." She looked over at me with genuine curiosity. I glanced over both shoulders to make sure no one was near.

"I don't see it coming, and I don't have any control of it. The room just goes dark and I see images. Sometimes they move, like a picture show, and I watch like a fly in the corner of a room."

Her eyebrows knit together as she thought. "So what types of pictures? Good things? Bad things?"

Now it was my turn to frown. "Almost always bad things," I said.

"What type of bad things?" She had stopped walking and turned toward me.

"Accidents, deaths." I paused and thought back to one I didn't understand, "explosions."

"Never good?" She started walking again.

"Only recently." I smiled at the ground. "Until a few weeks ago, they were never good. Until you came." I glanced at her with a nervous smile, and she looked away, embarrassed. "Sometimes, no, more times, the good comes in dreams, not visions."

She nodded as if she understood before asking her next question.

"How do you know then? If the good is going to come true or if it's just a dream?"

"I don't." I shrugged. "I just have to wait." I looked around the serene courtyard. "And hope."

A few birds chirped loudly as they did some last minute work on their winter nests.

"How did you get here?" she asked. I didn't mind telling her these things. In fact, it felt wonderful to talk to someone without that deep paranoid feeling. I knew she would take what I said for what it was and not twist it into something else.

"My father brought me," I told her.

"Does he come to visit you?" She stopped to pick wild weeds that were the closest thing to flowers we had. I shook my head.

"Your mother?" she asked.

"She's sort of the reason I'm here," I said hesitantly, and she looked at me curiously. "It's not her fault. That's not what I mean." I sighed. I really wanted to talk about her, ask her questions that required long answers so I could commit her voice to my memory. Store it safely to pull out later when I needed to hear it. I decided to give her the condensed version so we could move on to the subject of her.

"I saw something, and I told my father to keep a close eye on my mother that day. He was always suspicious when I tried to warn them of things. I hadn't for a long time." I shrugged and stared at the other end of the courtyard. "It was my mother. I had to."

She stopped walking and turned to face me. "What happened?"

"I told my father not to let her out of his sight. I told him that she shouldn't go anywhere near the horses, no matter what." There was a long, ominous pause. I squirmed under her concentrated gaze.

"What happened?" she repeated.

"I learned that I couldn't change the outcome of the things I saw. Even when I warned someone." My heart sank as David came into sight. "I still try," I said with a sigh. "So, with what happened to my mother, and the fact that I foretold it, my father thought I was crazy. Or possessed. It was the same difference in his mind. He wanted me gone before I could bring any more bad things to his house."

"I'm sorry," she said, squinting at the sunlight behind me. I shrugged and changed the subject.

"So, besides me needing someone more beautiful to look at than Twitchy Tamera or Sobbing Susan, why are you here?"

Her amused smile had lingered for a moment before it faded. "The last time you asked me that, I told you I didn't know. I still don't, for myself. But I can tell you what they tell me," she said with a nod toward the building.

"What do they say?"

"They say that when I get angry or sad, another person comes out. I talk in a different voice and I act strangely. I don't remember doing it, so it's hard to believe them."

"Did they tell you what you say?"

It was her turn to squirm. "I talk about my father's work."

"What does your father do?" I had to find questions with lengthier answers.

"He runs a tannery on our property."

"A tannery?" I played dumb.

"We raise cows and then we," she hesitated and swallowed, "we turn the hides into leather."

"Ah."

"We sell the beef, too. What we don't use, anyway. We eat a lot of beef," she said with bugged out eyes.

"Why would your other voice talk about that? Seems boring to me."

"I don't know. They tell me what I talk about, but not what I say exactly. Then they demand to know what I meant. What the other person meant. How can I know that, when I don't remember what it says? They say it's me, but it's not. It's all very confusing," she said, exasperated. I resented the few moments of silence that followed.

"Maybe they think you're faking?" I suggested, feeling immediately stupid.

She confirmed that with a hard look. She took a deep breath and then faced me.

"I've been looking forward to today," she said.

I smiled self-consciously. "Me, too."

"I wanted to ask you something." She avoided my eyes now, and I moved my head to try to see hers.

"Anything," I said, meaning it.

"Have you ever seen it? The other me?" she asked as her bottom lip quivered.

"No," I said, leveling my eyes with hers. "Never."

She nodded in relief and we started walking again. "Have you ever seen me see things?" I knew she hadn't, I just wanted her to feel less strange.

"I wouldn't know what that looks like." She laughed and I loved hearing it. I took a moment to replay it in my mind, cementing it in.

"They say I stare off. I don't answer when they call me and I drool." I looked away, slightly embarrassed. "For a few minutes, I guess I look like I belong here."

"I've never seen that." She smiled.

"Good."

We had made a full circle around the courtyard, and David winked at me discreetly when we passed.

"One more time around?" I asked. She nodded. I tried to remember jokes, any jokes to hear her laugh again. I came up blank.

"So what do you make of that?" she asked. "Neither one of us has ever seen what the other is here for." Her eyes touched on a few patients who were cautiously picking and poking at a shrub as if they had never seen one before. "We can certainly see why the rest of them are here."

"I don't know why that is," I lied. I didn't *know* exactly, but I had thoughts on the matter. It was far too early to suggest them to her, though.

"Have you ever seen me? In your visions?" She stared at me intently, and I had a feeling she was studying me for lies.

"I have." Her smile dropped and I could see fear replace happiness. "Not bad," I assured her and had to hold my own arm to keep from reaching out to her. "Remember what I said. It's *almost* always bad. But with you, it's good. I promise."

Her smile returned. "What do you see?"

I looked away and scanned the courtyard.

"I don't know that I should." I was grateful it was cold. It lessened the reddening of my face.

"You don't have to." She looked away. "Did you know what they were going to do to me?"

I shuddered at the dark turn the conversation was taking.

"I knew, but I didn't see it or anything. I just knew. They do that a lot here." I looked away again. Anger flashed in her eyes as she glanced back toward the hospital.

"It's not right," I added. Not that it helped much. David coughed in the distance, and my head whipped around just as the door started to swing open.

"Go over to that bush," I told her, "and act like you're studying it." I took several steps in the opposite direction, sat down quickly and began picking at the half-dead grass.

The doctor appeared and scanned the grounds. I watched his eyes roll over me and then, after seeing the patient he had come for, he called him over. I watched from under my lashes until the door closed behind him.

"It's okay now," I called. I craned my neck to see her turning from the bush.

"You're good at this," she said. She sat across from me on the cold grass, tucking her legs behind her and her white hospital dress neatly around them.

"Good at what?"

"Avoiding getting caught by them. Playing their game." She waved her hand at the staff, now huddled together and talking near the birdbath. I prayed they weren't deciding to bring us in.

"Not David," I said in defense. "He's not like the others." I picked at more grass and prayed again for just a few more minutes with her.

"You trust him?" she asked sounding rather shocked.

"Yes. I do now. Not always. When we first met, well—" I smiled. "We had to get some things straight. But since then—" I looked back up at him and threw up one more silent prayer he could avoid what I saw in the bathroom. "I think he likes me. He knows I'm not crazy, at least."

"What do they call what you are, then?" she asked in a teasing tone.

I studied the detail of her teeth when she smiled. I would add that to my painting tonight. I shrugged.

"Depends on who you talk to. Old people say I'm touched. Superstitious people say I'm cursed. Our good doctor in there tends to believe I am *so* brilliant I notice finite details and fabricate the visions. He doesn't think I do enough to consciously control them, so they try to shock it out of me. I don't know if they're trying to shock away the ability or the will."

"They do what?" Her eyes were horror-struck, and I hated myself for talking so casually about it. I shouldn't have said anything.

"It's a form of therapy. It's nothing." I tried flicking the grass away with the topic.

"I know what it is." She glared at me, a horrified look

still on her face. "I saw them do it to a woman in our wing." She looked away and then back. "It's horrible."

"Yeah, but it's okay."

"How can you say that?"

"Because I've gotten through several of them and kept what's important." I smiled, tapping my temple.

"Like what, the ability to speak?" she said with a sarcastic tone.

"No. Pictures."

"Pictures of what?" she asked.

"Important pictures," I said, not certain if I wanted her to press for more or leave it alone.

"From your visions?" She instinctively lowered her voice with the word. I smiled, dropping my eyes and shaking my head.

"What then?" She held her hands up and then dropped them in her lap in a fluster. I glanced over her shoulder at the staff who had all of their backs turned. I took a deep breath.

"Like this." I reached up to touch the small indent above her lip, and she sucked in a small breath of surprise. She watched me, but I couldn't read her expression. "And this." I ran my finger along her jaw line. "I've gotten good at drawing this." I smiled and touched the ends of her hair before reluctantly pulling my hand away. "I have every single one of these shades of brown memorized. There's no blonde or red in it anywhere. But there are six shades of brown." I dropped the lock onto her shoulder. "You can count them yourself if you don't believe me," I said with a smile. I had added one last thing before she found her voice. "But mostly..." I couldn't help but touch her one more time, and if they shocked me for it, I'd smile with the bit in my mouth. "Your eyes." I touched her temple and committed to memory the warmth and texture. "The black explodes out from the center in tiny fragments and the brown matches—" I paused, searching for a strand of hair. "This one." I held it up for her to see, and she took it from my fingers. She pulled it with a little yank, looked at it, and then held it out to me. I took it with a smile.

"Thank you." I wrapped it several times around my finger and could easily see the color. I glanced up at David. He was looking over the courtyard. *Not yet,* I thought. *Please, not yet. Just a few more minutes.*

"Why are you frowning?" she asked. I shook my head. "No, what is it?"

I sighed. "You know at breakfast this morning, when I moved to the other table?" She nodded. "The nurse was watching us. I got nervous, and I didn't want to ruin today, so I went to sit in front of Ronnie. But as soon as I saw him, I worried that he would ruin this, too." I looked up at her, almost ashamed. "I pushed him. I said things that I knew would set him off, so they would throw him in his room for the day."

"I don't understand how he would ruin this." She watched my fingers as I played with the brown grass.

"Every time we've gotten some time out here, he goes nuts. It upsets the others, and we end up having to come in early. I couldn't let that happen," I said.

"Why?"

"I'm waiting for something," I said softly as I watched David begin to gather the others in. I mumbled and then closed my eyes. I opened them a second later with a rough laugh.

"What's so funny?"

I watched David's every move. "I just thought it was odd, what a praying man I've become lately." He looked over at us, and my heart sank as he waved us over. I was so distracted that it was almost a shock when she slipped her hand into mine.

"Will you pray for me?" she whispered. I looked down at our entwined hands. It was what I was waiting for. What I saw would happen, the day before.

"*Yes*," I promised her, not able to take my eyes away from the sight. David called out, loud and direct. I stood without letting go of her hand and pulled her up carefully.

"Maybe they'll let us out again soon."

"Maybe." I smiled. I could feel the distance growing as she walked ahead of me with her head down. *To hide a smile?* I wondered, hoped.

Once inside the door, she went left to the women's wing and I turned right. We acted as if we didn't know each other. As soon as she was out of sight, I turned to my memories. I replayed her laugh several times and felt the single hair wrapped tightly around my finger. I laughed to myself, thinking that perhaps sane people would consider a single strand of hair a strange gift. But I didn't. I loved it. David waited for me by my door. Only the gleam in his eyes gave him away.

"And how's your day going, Simon?"

I smiled as I walked past him into my room.

"Wonderful, David. Just wonderful." I saw his grin through the small glass window as he locked the door on the other side. I lay on my bed with my hands behind my head.

If it weren't for being caged up like an animal with insane people, having to eat flavorless overcooked hospital food, alternately shivering or sweating at night, and having a suspicious doctor pick through my every thought... my life would be perfect.

I closed my eyes so I could find hers.

~ ~ ~

LATER THAT EVENING, I didn't draw her on my wall. I was too preoccupied with other things. It was so uncomfortable, the feeling of impending doom and being unable to do anything about it. I had to lie in my tiny room of metal and stone and wait. And hope. I heard voices growing louder outside, talking and laughing.

Shift change, I thought with a grimace. My stomach lurched, and I sat up, too anxious to lay still.

It had begun raining a few hours earlier and slight pecks of icy rain quickly turned into a downpour. I knocked loudly on my own door, letting them know I needed to use the bathroom. One of the nurses unlocked it and swung the heavy metal door wide. She stayed close but didn't hover. I looked down the long hallway and saw David walking toward the exit with the other staff. He stopped, let others go by, and then turned away.

"I've got to do something," he called to them. "I'll walk to the gate later." He waved off their protests and looked up. He saw me and gave a small nod. I sighed in relief and went into the bathroom.

After I had returned to my room, I heard it, and then the sirens started. They grew louder as they grew closer. Flashing red and white lights broke up the darkness of my room. Outside, I heard panicked voices and disbelieving shrieks mingled with the chaotic madness. The light from the hallway disappeared, and I looked at the small window in my door. David's face filled the small space. He stared at me, his face somewhere between nothing and serious.

"*Thank you,*" I whispered to the ceiling.

The staff took a bus to and from the guarded gate of

the hospital grounds each day. No one had noticed the century-old tree jarred loose in the wild windstorm from the previous week. The roots, rotten and soggy, chose that moment as the bus passed by to give way. It fell, crushing everyone in the back half of the bus.

~ ~ ~

I SAT WAITING anxiously for Elizabeth at breakfast the next morning. It was hard to keep the smile off my face. She would appear soon to brighten my world, and David had listened. He believed me, and somehow, it had changed fate. I had kept one bad thing from happening, and the feeling was exhilarating.

I didn't have a lot of time to enjoy it, though.

In front of the entire morning staff, my eyes fixed. The vision brought heavy black clouds, which took my sight, loomed above the brick wall that shook violently, and then crumbled in front of me. Pieces of it flew in every direction, and money burned in piles along the sidewalks. People ran along busy streets with desperate faces, dodging the bodies that rained from the sky. I stared at the back of a man's head, his hair black as night as he knelt in defeat in the middle of an enormous and busy room.

I woke up slowly and tried to lift my head, but my neck was stiff and pain shot down my spine. *I must have really arched this time,* I thought. I moved my legs, and there was something hard and unmoving next to them. I squinted in the dim light of the late afternoon and saw David sitting on the foot of my bed.

He leaned forward, elbows on knees with the fingers of his massive, dark hands laced. His fingernails gleamed clean, and for the first time, I noticed a thin gold band on the left hand. He didn't speak for several moments. I closed my eyes, comforted by his presence, and took the time to account for all of my memories of her.

"*Still there,*" I whispered in relief and opened my eyes.

He didn't turn but took a deep breath before he spoke.

"You saved my life, Simon," he said quietly. I stared at the side of his head, unsure of what to say. "You saw something. And you trusted me enough to tell me. I know how much you hate the treatments."

I nodded. Hating them was an understatement. They terrified me, they hurt, and they made me angry. They were punishing me for something that wasn't my fault. Something I couldn't control, something that never hurt anyone. I glanced at David. In his case, they might have helped.

"You listened. That's what saved your life." I tried to keep my thoughts from those who hadn't.

He shook his head tightly. "I would have gotten on that bus, same as I do every night." He stopped with a short laugh. "Did you know I always sit three seats up from the back? Always. Same exact spot, every night. Two nights ago wouldn't have been any different." He sat back now, flexing his fingers. He pulled a wet cloth from his side and put it to my ear, wiping away dried blood.

"I'm glad you listened," I said as he cleaned me.

He nodded in full agreement, put his hand on my arm, and squeezed lightly. He still wouldn't look at me but stared at my ear with a frown.

"If there's ever anything you need, anything that's within my power, as God is my witness," he paused and swallowed hard, "if it's in my power," he whispered.

There was only one thing I could ask for.

"I want to see Elizabeth," I said. He smiled and moved his hand down my arm, gripping my hand and pulled me up to a sitting position.

"I am curious. More curious than ever," he said with a smile. "What did you see two days ago at breakfast? Before this." He waved his hand over my tired and bruised body. I stiffened and unconsciously pursed my lips shut. "Simon, I'm not going to tell anyone. You can trust me completely."

"At least, now you know I'm not crazy."

"I never thought you were."

"Really?"

He held up his right hand. "I swear on my child," he said. "I never thought you were crazy, and I will never tell anyone what you tell me."

"Well, that's a relief," I said, smirking. "Think you can convince the good doctor I'm not nuts?"

"What did you see?" He bent at the knees in front of me, his eyes level with mine. I sighed in resignation and then explained my vision to him in all the detail I could. His eyes grew wider, and he sat back suddenly, looking very disturbed.

"Dear God in heaven," he whispered and wiped his face hard with his hand.

"What?"

"What you saw, Simon... it happened today." His voice was shaky, and it distracted me to see him shaken by anything.

"The stock market crashed. They're still adding up how much was lost. It'll take days. Millions, gone. It's on the radio. Folks lost everything they had. People jumped off buildings, killin' themselves because of all they lost. It all happened, Simon, just like you saw."

"What is today, David?"

"October twenty-ninth."

~ ~ ~

I SAT ACROSS from Elizabeth at dinner. It made me nervous how she didn't attempt to hide her eyes, and she spoke to me directly, instead of to her food.

"They did it to you again, didn't they?" she asked.

"I'm fine." I assured her with my eyes. "Really, I am."

"You've been gone three days."

"That's the usual amount of time." I glanced at the supervising nurse. "You'd better look down," I told her quietly.

"I won't," she said through her teeth. "It's not a crime to talk to you, and I won't look down, and I won't whisper! We're grown adults and should be able to have a conversation!"

The nurse stared at us now.

"If you aren't quiet, they'll take you away from me," I pleaded, my head safely down.

"Well, I won't *let* them take you from me," she said.

"Elizabeth, please," I begged. The nurse was walking toward us. "Please, just look down."

"It's not a crime to talk to you," she repeated, glaring right at me. "It's not a crime to walk along the path together! Or laugh! Or hold hands! It's not a crime how I feel!" she hissed loudly.

"It is here!" I shot back. I turned my head away, and she must have caught a glimpse of dried blood in the crevices of my ear because, as soon as the nurse approached her, she came up out of her seat with her tray, swinging it.

"What did you do to him!" she screamed, flinging the tray at her head. One nurse blew a whistle and another ran in a moment later with a needle.

"Elizabeth!" I stood up and tried to get her attention. "Please, calm down!" Even through all the chaos, I looked for the other one. She said it came out when she got angry or sad. I watched helplessly as she got the best of both nurses in her rage. If it were going to come out, it would come out now. Nothing. Just Elizabeth raging in my defense until the shot took effect, and she went limp on the floor. Her eyes rolled and found me. They stayed locked to mine until she slipped into a deep sleep.

I swallowed against the hard lump in my throat and turned around, closing my eyes. I couldn't watch them carry her out. When they were gone, I pushed my tray, hard. It slid off the other end of the table with a crash. I didn't ask to go to bed or wait for an orderly to walk me. Half the staff was dead. They would be working on a skeleton crew so I would have been waiting for a while. *To hell with them,* I thought of the living and the dead. *Except David, to hell with you all, because she's right. It's not a crime.*

~ ~ ~

I WAS IRRITABLE the next morning from a fitful sleep. I had lost track of the days, and I prayed I didn't have an appointment with the doctor. Even though I hadn't foreseen a treatment, it didn't mean I couldn't bring one on. I was foul and everyone avoided me. I sat alone at breakfast with a frown. David told me Elizabeth hadn't woken up yet.

"Maybe by lunch," he said with a hand on my shoulder as he passed by.

She didn't wake up for lunch but did before dinner. She was still groggy when she sat down carefully.

"I'm sorry," was the first thing she said to her plate.

"It's not your fault," I said.

"It is. If I had looked down, like you said. If I hadn't raised my voice." She looked around with tired, swollen eyes. "They know now," she whispered.

"It'll be all right," I told her. She shook her head with tears in her eyes. "No, really, it will be all right. David talked to them. He straightened it out. They don't suspect anything."

"Really?" She looked up with a little hope.

"Really." I smiled at her. "Just don't do that again. I know it's hard," I said before she could interrupt. "But don't do it again." I smiled.

"I won't," she whispered and lowered her eyes to her plate.

I scanned the room as David came in to relieve the nurse on duty. He settled into a chair to supervise and gave me a small nod. The room was relaxed as the biggest troublemakers were locked in their rooms for meals due to the sudden staff shortage. I slid my hand across the table and held it open. She looked up and then around in a panic.

"It's fine. David's watching out for us," I told her.

"He knows?"

"And he's on our side."

She pulled her hand from her lap and slowly placed it in mine. I relaxed instantly at her touch, and we were free to look at each other and ate dinner single-handedly, not willing to let go or look away, for anything.

~ ~ ~

I HAD JUST rubbed out my chalk picture of her when I heard the lock on my door turn. David stood in the doorway and waved me out with a hand. I stepped into the dim light of the hallway.

"What's going on?"

"I have something for you," he said and pointed to the commons area.

"What is it?" I asked.

He smiled wide and toothy. "Some time with your girl." I looked at him, confused. "Go in there." He nodded toward the commons area. "If she's not already in there, she'll be along shortly."

"How?" I asked. I was suddenly paranoid. "How can we do something like this, David?"

"I'm the only one on this wing tonight. Loretta is taking care of everything on her end."

"How did you manage that without giving us away?" I asked.

"I just did. Now, go enjoy some time with your girl," he said, pointing.

It was too good to be true.

"No, David. You'll get in trouble. They'll fire you, or worse, they'll take me for a treatment. God knows what they would do to Elizabeth." I stood, shaking my head. "I can't risk it. Me, you, her. No." I turned into my room, but he grabbed my arm.

"I'm keeping your secret. Can you keep mine?" he asked in a hushed voice. I nodded, looking him up and down. What secrets could he possibly have? He touched the ring on his left hand. "Loretta is my wife," he said. "No one in this building knows that, but you."

I was failing to see how this helped me until I remembered what Loretta looked like. She was tall with long blond hair and skin fairer than mine. He saw my eyes flash as I made the connection. He put his hand on my shoulder and leaned close.

"I know a little something about having to hide your love," he said. I understood then, why *he* did, and why he helped us. "I've talked to her about you."

My eyes flew open and I stepped back in a panic. "No, Simon. Not about that." He tightened the grip on my arm. "Just about Elizabeth. She sees it, too. How Elizabeth is better with you. *Because* of you. She thinks that she might be able to get out of here if she keeps getting better. The other one hasn't come out in days. Even when you were away from her, recovering."

"She will get out of here someday. I've seen it," I said. I looked down the hall at the dim lights of the commons area.

"It's all right, I promise. I would never do anything that would risk another treatment for you, Simon."

I took a deep breath while deciding. I thought about being with her, not worried about watchful eyes, really truly free for a few moments. And then my mind touched on the consequences.

"It would be worth it," I said before turning down the hallway.

She wasn't there yet, so I sat on the sofa that faced the radio. The room had been cleaned for the night, and there were only two lights on, one in each corner of the room. There was a dull glow from the radio in front of me. I smiled at all of David's preparations.

All of the tables were against the wall except one. There were two chairs, close together on one side of it, and I squinted to see what was on the table. There was a small plate of cookies. I got up and walked over, noticing a small note next to it.

Thank you, David had written. I smiled and ate one. Saving a person's life had its benefits, I decided. I turned to see her standing in the doorway. She looked nervous to come in.

"It's all right," I said, taking a step toward her. "There's no one here tonight that can ruin this for us." I prayed I spoke the truth. She took a few tentative steps and I stopped. She wore a dress. A normal dress, not a hospital gown, with normal shoes. Her hair was shining, falling in perfect curls around her face. I tried to commit every inch of her to my memory.

"Loretta loaned me this," she said, touching the skirt of the dress.

"It's beautiful. No," I corrected myself. "You're beautiful." She looked down with a shy smile.

"Come sit with me," I said, holding my hand out. She took a few steps and took it, walking with me to the couch. I sat close to her, but not quite touching. I turned a little so I could watch her. After weeks of stealing peeks and glances, I was going to enjoy every minute of watching her freely.

"Why did they do this for us?" she asked. Obviously, Loretta hadn't explained much.

"They understand," I said. "And David sort of owes me a favor." I smiled. She eased back on the couch, letting herself relax a little. I scrambled for something to say. "David says you're doing better," I said for lack of anything more intelligent.

"That's what they told me. The other one hasn't come out in a while. Even when I was so upset over you," she said, looking over at me. She started to turn away and I touched her chin.

"Don't. Keep looking at me," I said.

Her face flushed, but she kept her eyes on mine. "I started feeling hopeful that I might get out of here soon."

"You will. I've seen it," I said softly.

"You have?" Her eyes flew open.

"I've seen you out there. Happy."

"Are you with me?" she asked.

"Yes. We're near a lake, walking along the edge, and trying not to get eaten alive by mosquitoes," I said and laughed.

She thought about that for a moment and smiled. "That would be nice. Bites and all. I know just the place. I wonder..."

"You wonder what?"

"The place I know of, where you saw us walking together. I wonder if it will be there?"

I shrugged and she went back to her wondering. "They think they know why the other one comes out," she said suddenly. "And why it doesn't come out."

"Why?"

She took a deep breath, straightened in her seat, and looked away. "They say I'm weak—"

"You're not weak," I countered. "They don't know what they're talking about."

"Just listen," she said. I crossed my arms and sat back as I grew angry at the things they were feeding to her, trying to make this her fault. I had no patience for that. "A fragile mind, they said. Like glass, even." I made a disagreeable snort. "I told you my father operates a tannery. When he was away fighting in the war, I was a small girl, and my mother had to take over the business. I tried to help her, even though I was just a kid. She hated it, but she was strong and carried the business until daddy got home. When he finally returned home, everything was wonderful for a while, but then my parents started fighting a lot, always over his medicine. I thought we couldn't afford it, but that was ridiculous. The tannery made plenty of money. It made my head hurt when they yelled at each other. I would hide in this small cove in the back of my closet until they stopped. A few years passed and they stopped fighting about his medicine. Things seemed normal again. Then my daddy said it was time I learn the business so I could take it over one day since he was obviously never going to have a son. I didn't want to—" She paused and looked away.

"Go on," I whispered. I couldn't stand it any longer and moved my arm to rest my fingertips on her shoulder.

"There are parts of this business that are scary. Disgusting and messy," she said, looking back with tears in her eyes.

"What parts?"

"Killing the cows," she said quietly. "Skinning them, butchering them up. Scraping their stretched skins. The smell is..." She closed her eyes and huffed out her nose as if trying to blow away the smell that haunted her. "It's horrible," she said, opening her eyes again. "They say that the stronger one comes out when something upsets me. When I can't stand it, the other one takes over to do what needs to be done."

"Interesting," I said and almost slapped my own face. The doctor said that, often, bobbing his fuzzy white head. I never knew what he meant. I didn't mean it like that with Elizabeth. It truly was interesting. "What do you think of all of this?" I asked her.

"It makes sense, I guess. When I got too big to hide in the cove, and when I got scared, I guess I created another me in my own mind."

"But you're still in there. You're just not talking or having to see and smell."

"I'm in there, hiding. When whatever I'm hiding from goes away, I come back." She crossed her arms and sat back with a sigh. "That's what they tell me anyway. I don't realize it."

"You don't see it? Or feel it?"

"No, and I don't have a choice. It just takes over."

"What if you do have a choice?" I suggested. "You've never done that in front of me. It's never interrupted us. Maybe that's you, choosing to stay in control."

She sat quietly for a moment and then a smile spread across her face. "I've thought about that."

"And what did you decide?" My heart pounded lightly in my ears, hoping she'd say it was me. Or us.

"I feel safe with you," she said, meeting my eyes again. My heart did a hard *thump* and then beat fast and thin, making me dizzy.

"I'm glad," was all I managed to say.

"I wish I could do the same thing for you," she said with disappointment.

"You do. I don't have visions when I'm near you."

"But they aren't gone for good."

"They never will be," I whispered from habit. "They're part of me. They always have been." I lifted her chin up. "It's okay, Elizabeth. I don't mind them so much. Especially, when I get to see you in them, and how happy we'll be when we get out of here."

"Soon, Simon? Will we get to leave soon?"

"I think so," I said as I took her hand. I thought back through the last few visions I had seen.

"This is nice. It's so quiet," she said, leaning her head back.

"I can turn the radio up if you'd like," I said.

"No, it's fine. I like the quiet. Usually, this room is so loud."

"Between Ronnie's screaming, Tamera's seizures, and Susan's crying, I'm amazed we've been able to hear anything we've had to whisper to each other."

She laughed beautifully. "I like this much better," she

said, squeezing my hand. It was odd to enjoy the quiet since that's all we had between us during the day, but I did. I listened to her breathing and memorized the different look of her face in the glow of the radio. "How long will they let us be here?" she asked, sitting up to look at me.

"Not nearly long enough," I whispered. I got an idea and smiled. "We really are going to have to hire less intrusive staff," I said. She looked at me with raised eyebrows, confused. "House staff," I said with a grin. I stretched my arm around her shoulders and leaned back with her on the couch.

"See, this room is our grand parlor," I said, looking all around. "And that doorway, that leads to the staircase. The workers will be here tomorrow to knock out these small windows," I said, turning to the small panes behind bars on the opposite wall. "I'm having them put in a *massive* one for you, so you can see for miles." Her eyes followed my finger as it pointed. "Do me a favor and pick out light curtains, not those heavy ones that block out all the light." I grinned as I watched her eyes make the shift, and she began to see the world around us reconstruct itself. "This couch," I said, running my fingers along the faded fabric, "belonged to my grandmother. It's very old and expensive." I saw the fabric change from tattered brown to red velvet, and the mahogany framework rose up out of the arms and along the back. "That glow in front of us." I nodded to the steel caged standing radio. "That's a fireplace." She smiled, and I saw her imagining a brick fireplace with a matching mahogany mantle drop down into place in front of us. "It's a small fire tonight. Usually, it's bright and warm." I looked around again. "There are beautiful pictures all around, expensive art and sculptures. See that marble pedestal in the corner?" I pointed to the corner, its gray walls empty. "I had that bust made special."

She grinned, straining to see what wasn't there. "A bust? Who of?" she asked.

"You," I whispered, leaning my forehead on the side of hers, trying to see what she saw. "We sit here every night after putting the kids to bed," I continued and felt her stiffen. Her face lost the magic of what she saw. I turned her face to mine before she could lose it all. "We'll adopt," I said, her eyes so close they were a blur.

"Are you sure you don't want someone who can have kids?" She looked down, and I prayed I hadn't ruined our evening.

"You're not the only one, Elizabeth," I said. It was true. They did it to almost all the women here.

She was shocked, and her eyes flickered from my eyes to my lap and back. She blushed slightly. "You mean, you, *too*?" I couldn't say yes and lie. But I could let her believe it if it helped her.

"We'll adopt," I repeated, letting her believe what she would. Her face softened. I felt our time was growing short. I closed the space between us with one slow, careful tilt of my head and kissed her. My eyes closed, storing the feel of her lips and the taste of her tongue to my memory. That was now my most prized possession. My lips twitched into a smile, mid-kiss, and I almost laughed. I thought of the treatments, odd as that timing might be in this moment of earthly bliss. The voltage they shot through my head was nothing compared to the surge of energy that made my every hair stand on end, my mind fill with a deep hum and every fiber of my body tingle. It was all the sensation with none of the pain. *I wish this were my treatment,* I thought and did laugh this time, a short amused grunt that broke the kiss.

"What?" she whispered breathlessly. She looked worried.

I moved my hands to the sides of her head, not letting her move more than an inch away from me.

"Nothing," I whispered and kissed her again.

Our imaginary world moved fluidly around us, and we were the center of it, holding each other as tightly as we held to the illusion. It popped to life with vivid detail, and I saw every inch of it behind my closed eyes. I would have given my soul to stay there forever.

A soft knock on the door shattered our world. The brick fireplace crumbled in upon itself. The window with the sheer curtains shriveled up and disappeared as it shrunk, and the black bars grew back. The paintings bled, fading into the gray walls and the coldness returned.

I sighed at the perfection and the frustration of it all and glanced back at the door. David was there and gave a small wave, signaling our time was over. Glancing at the clock, I saw it had been an hour.

I looked back, still holding her, and she laughed this time.

"What?" I asked.

"I was just thinking about this." She looked around and back at me.

"What about it?"

"We're talking about our house and our furniture, adopting children...that doesn't seem normal for a first date." She laughed.

"Well, we're not normal people, now are we?" I smiled.

She shook her head with a smile, and I took one more kiss—short, deep, and thorough.

I carried it to my room and slept as it remained on my lips.

~ ~ ~

THE NEXT MORNING, there was a new orderly at breakfast. He looked nervous as I walked up to introduce myself. I always thought it was better to get off on the right foot and make a good impression.

"Hi, I'm Simon," I said, holding out my hand. He looked at it warily. "Don't worry." I leaned closer. "I'm not crazy," I added with a smile.

"They say it's always the ones who act sane that are the most nuts." He shook my hand briefly.

"Ask David," I said with confidence and found my seat for breakfast.

She was late and that always made me nervous. I worried that the other one had come out, and they had sedated her. I replayed our evening together in my mind to pass the time. I sat with a crooked smile, lost in my daydream. I relived the kiss repeatedly in a continuous loop, could pull out every detail. Hands grabbed my shoulders and I looked up, stunned. Then I realized what they thought, and what they were doing. "No! I didn't have one!" I yelled up at the nurse and new orderly.

"The doctor says we're to take him to treatment immediately when he has one of these delusional visions," she told the orderly as she helped him drag me out of my chair. "The quicker we administer treatment, the better," she said, grunting as I fought her.

"But I didn't have one!" I screamed. "I was daydreaming, that's all!"

She ignored me and blew the whistle for help.

Elizabeth stood looking scared in the doorway. I tried not to fight, for her sake, but I dreaded what I knew was coming. She covered her face with her hands while they pulled me past, still trying to convince them. I begged and pleaded until the white-hot pain shot through my head, and everything went dark.

~ ~ ~

IT WAS LATE evening, and I woke with the usual headache and tingling legs. Something sat in the corner of the room. Even if my vision wasn't blurry, it was too dark to make out what it was. It made no noise and stayed perfectly still, watching me.

"Simon."

I sighed at the sound of her voice. "How did you get in here?" I asked, trying to get up on one elbow to see her.

"David," she said as she let go of her legs and stood up. There was barely enough room for her to turn around to sit on the side of my bed. "My roommate," she paused, looking at the door. "She hasn't come back from the clinic yet, so Loretta propped pillows under my blankets, and David snuck me down here to wait for you to wake up." She took my hand and held it tightly. "I just got here a few minutes ago."

"I'm glad you're here," I said, meaning it. "But he's going to get fired." I meant that even more. "He's taking too many chances."

She ignored the warning and turned to lie down beside me, molding her body to the side of mine. "I wish I could take these treatments for you," she said. "I'd take every single one of them."

I could tell she was close to tears. I shook my head. "I'd never allow that." I smiled and pulled her closer with what little strength my arms had. "Besides, after one, you'd decide I wasn't worth it. I'm not *that* great a kisser," I teased.

"Yes, you are." She put one hand on the side of my neck. Her head rested on my shoulder, and I could feel her smile. "We're going to be free together one day. And the other night, we were free. Just for an hour, we weren't here. You took me to a world all our own, and I still see it clearly every time I close my eyes."

"I do, too," I said. I didn't tell her that remembering our evening had led to this last debilitating treatment. "How long has it been?" I asked. My mind began to clear. I put my hand on my forehead, willing away the last of the headache.

"Three days," she said and moved her hand to replace mine, pushing it out of the way as she massaged my temple, forehead, and scalp. I closed my eyes, enjoying it.

"I have to go soon," she said after a few minutes. "David has to get me back before the other orderly finishes dinner." I nodded, hating the fact. She kept massaging my head, sending the softest shivers down my neck and shoulders.

David knocked so lightly we almost didn't hear it. I opened my eyes, and more reluctantly, my arms, releasing her. She kissed me quickly and walked to the door without looking back.

David told me later that the other one came out, right after I left. He said it wasn't pretty. The others were afraid of her now.

~ ~ ~

I WAS A few minutes late for breakfast, having nicked myself while shaving. I walked in slowly, taking stock of patients and staff. Only one nurse with her back turned. She was in deep conversation with Sobbing Susan.

I took the golden opportunity to put a hand on Elizabeth's shoulder and kissed the top of her head as I passed.

"Good morning," I said.

"Good morning." She smiled and I noticed how alive her eyes were.

"You look beautiful today." Noticing the nurse turn out of the corner of my eye, I looked down resentfully.

"Thank you," she whispered.

I looked past her at the other not so lively patrons and noticed that many of the excitable ones were present. They must be re-staffing quicker than I thought.

Great. A bunch of new, nervous orderlies means less freedom for me. For us, I thought. It had taken months to prove myself and get a little leeway and extra privileges.

"What's the frown for?" she asked.

"Just thinking," I said, stabbing at my congealed oatmeal. "I'll just be glad to get out of here."

"Have you seen when?" she whispered.

"Not really," I frowned. I didn't have time to tell her that I had seen frostbitten trees, light snow along the lake and a fireplace. Ronnie stole the show. I watched him look up, staring past the nurse's shoulder and start whimpering. His imagination was in full swing, and he started babbling to the king he desperately feared. He threw his tray, and it flew by the nurse's head, narrowly missing it.

"Just another day in the happy factory."

She glanced at Ronnie and back at me. "I feel sorry for him," she said. "All of them. They won't get out of here, will they, Simon? Not like us."

I shook my head without looking up. I knew what would happen to Ronnie, and I tried not to look at him.

~ ~ ~

THE NEXT DAY, I had a meeting with the doctor. I hadn't seen a treatment, but I hadn't seen myself walk out either.

"How are you feeling, Simon?" he asked. The scratch of the pen tip on paper nearly drove me crazy enough to belong here.

"Fine."

"You always say fine, Simon."

"Because I am."

"I heard from the nurse that you had a treatment last week, and for the first time in a long time, you fought it. You tried to deny having a vision and fought the nurses. That's not like you, Simon." He stared at me intently.

I met his gaze head on. "Because I didn't have one that time," I said, trying to relax my jaw.

"Really? The nurse said you did. You were staring off into space and didn't answer to your name for three calls." He sat back and crossed his legs.

"I was daydreaming, Doc. Have you ever heard of daydreaming? Even the sanest people do it."

"Well, you have to understand, it's hard for us to tell."

"Apparently."

"I wonder what we can do about that?" he asked almost mockingly.

"How about listening to me when I say I didn't have one? You said yourself that I never fight it when I've had one. When I say I didn't, I'm being honest."

"But that would give you leave to lie to us, Simon. To avoid treatment. How would we know you weren't lying?" I sighed in frustration. There was no right answer and I gave up. "What do you daydream about, Simon?"

My eyes flashed up, angry and defensive before I could mask them. *No. You fucking bastard, you can't have that.* I looked down, stuffing my memories deep inside my mind and looked up, composed. It was too late. He already saw it. "Lots of things," I said, thinking fast. "Vacationing on the beach, sailing, and painting. Normal, sane things, Doc."

He nodded and I tried in vain to read him.

"It wouldn't have anything to do with your new friend, would it?"

I felt a cold shiver and had the urge to jump up and hit him over the head with his paperweight. It took everything I had not to panic.

"Which friend would that be, Doc? I'm pretty well-liked around here."

"Elizabeth," he said with a tiny twitch of his lips.

"No," I said too quickly. "I've talked to her a few times. No more or less than any other patient." My mind raced at who might have seen us, read between the lines, and told the doctor. I looked up at him with calm eyes. *I will kill you before I let you take her away from me,* I thought. I took a slow even breath.

"Do you remember what I said about her, Simon?"

"Yes."

"It might serve you well to keep that a little closer to the front of your mind. She was doing better for a while, but she's had a setback recently. Ronnie said it was because of you. She was upset over you needing a treatment, and that tells me, Simon, that you are indeed friends. Good friends."

My hands shook so I folded my arms to hide them. I tried to shrug casually, but the movement came off choppy. "No more than anyone else."

Please, God, please let him believe me. Let him leave it alone, I prayed.

"Let's just keep our minds on you getting better, shall we, Simon? There really is no room in your life for friends. Concentrate on getting better so you can leave one day," he said, looking down and scribbling with the last few words.

"Getting out," I repeated. "Sounds good, Doc." I stood, anxious to leave his office.

"Yes, you can leave now, Simon."

I kept myself up all night with worry that bordered paranoia. I filled spurts of fitful sleep with nightmares. Some I didn't understand. But the ones that terrified me always involved Elizabeth being taken away from me. The others involved someone who had become a regular in my dreams. A woman who cried and painted. I couldn't see what she painted past her blonde hair, but her grief was so deep and poignant, I couldn't help but wonder what her grief was for.

~ ~ ~

THE NEXT MORNING was miserable. I walked into breakfast looking a mess—bleary, bloodshot eyes, hair sticking in every direction and I hadn't bothered to shave. I didn't acknowledge her but sat across from Ronnie, it being the only open seat other than in front of her. I slumped in my chair, crossed my arms, and waited for my food. I could feel her eyes on me, and it was so hard not to look over at her. I closed my eyes and looked at her in my mind.

The nurse set my food in front of me with a metal *plunk*. I hovered over it, barely eating. I had no appetite. Ronnie made disgusting snorting noises as he ate. He looked up at me every few minutes and then nervously over at Elizabeth. *I wish he'd stop doing that,* I thought. *It's not fair that he gets to look at her and I don't.* He stared at me while he chewed his oatmeal with loud smacking sounds. I grimaced and kept my eyes on my food. I heard her cough once, then twice. I knew she was trying to get my attention, and I leaned my elbow on the table, put my hand on the back of my head, and gripped the hair, forcing my head to stay in place. I had to put distance between us, which was the very last thing I could ever want. But I had to take some attention off us. I argued with myself at just how long that would take. A few days, a few weeks.

Christ, I can't make it a few weeks without touching her, I thought with despair. Ronnie started making weird noises, and I looked up to see if he was choking. I turned, unable to help it, and saw her staring at me, a question in her eyes. I looked away quickly and decided to try to get a message to her through David later when he came on shift. Ronnie reached across the table and started pushing my tray closer to me until it was nearly dumped in my lap.

"What are you doing, you crazy bastard?" I asked, pushing it back with an irritated shove.

"I don't want you here," he answered. I had forgotten what his normal voice sounded like.

"Well, guess what, Ronnie, I don't want to be here," I said with a huff and loomed over my flavorless food. I wasn't even sure why I had come here this morning. I should have faked sickness. *But then she would worry. She'd think I'd gotten shocked again and she would worry. Or worse.* I was distracted from my thoughts when Ronnie's skinny arm tried to sneak across the table. It was ridiculous how he tried so hard to be covert, but I could see every move he made. He started pushing my tray again.

"Would you stop that?" I yelled. "Shit! Just leave me alone!" Two orderlies looked up. One started walking over toward us.

"You go sit with *her*," he said and crossed his eyes and lolled his tongue in the best imitation a crazy person can make of another crazy person.

"Piss off," I growled and shoved my tray back, slamming it into his. I shrugged off the indecisive orderly who tried to take my arm and stormed out of the room. I turned and looked back, right at the last second. Her eyes watched me, and I saw hurt and confusion in them.

I stopped at the nurses' station on my way to my room.

"Can I have a piece of paper?" I asked impatiently. I didn't look to see which nurse it was. It wasn't David so it didn't matter.

"What for?" she asked.

I looked at her then, fully irritated. "To make a paper airplane," I said sarcastically. "I want to write a letter," I added quickly, remembering that these people had no way of discerning sarcasm from truth.

"Be sure to let us read it before you send it," she said.

"Can I have a pencil?" I asked. I ground my teeth.

She unlocked the desk drawer and dug around in it. "You'll have to sit here and write it. I can't let you wander around with a pencil."

The complete and utter lack of privacy or freedom had taken its toll on me, and I grew dangerously close to exploding. I threw the paper back at her.

"Forget it," I growled and turned toward my room.

After lunch, which I skipped, choosing hunger over heartache, I pulled David aside and explained what happened at my appointment the day before. Then I detailed my miserable Elizabeth-less day.

"I don't know who could have said anything, Simon. I haven't heard anyone say or suspect anything. They all know you two are the sanest of the bunch, and they assume that's why you sit together. But they don't know about you."

I nodded, reassured. "Can I get a piece of paper? I need to tell her why I'm doing this. I don't want her to think..." I closed my eyes. "I need her to know I still feel the same way."

"Not a problem," David said. "I'll give it to Loretta, and she can give it to Elizabeth."

"Don't let her keep it," I said in a panic. "They'll find it."

"Don't worry, Simon, I'll take care of it. It'll go home with me and I'll burn it, I promise."

"Okay. Okay. Thank you," I panted, feeling some of the weight lifted.

He left and then returned with a piece of paper and a pen. He handed it to me secretively, and I tucked it under my shirt. I retreated to my room and tried to think of what I would say. I scribbled nervously, not for writing to her, but for someone finding it, reading it. I was risking everything and my hands shook.

Mid-letter, I slammed my fist on the table. *I'm a goddamned grown man! I shouldn't have to sit here and be afraid to write a letter to the woman I love!* I seethed inside my mind. I wanted to write that so badly. More than anything. *I love you.* I couldn't, though. I couldn't risk them finding out, and I wanted her to hear it from me. I wanted to see her eyes when I said it, not have her read an emotionless scribble on cold paper.

And I didn't know if she loved me. I thought she did.

I was almost certain, but not completely. I wondered how I would find out and whether I should take the chance of saying it too soon, which might scare her or too late, and by then she might think I didn't and would never say it first. That's not how it worked. It all made my head spin, and I realized I had wasted ten minutes. I scribbled the rest of the note and stuffed it down my pants just as the lock on my door turned.

~ ~ ~

Seven long days. One hundred sixty-eight hours. Ten thousand eighty minutes. I swear, at one point, the clock hands moved backward, making me relive them again and again before I was able to see her again.

Then, I sat across from her at breakfast one morning, exhaling as if I'd been holding my breath. "I missed you." I leaned forward and then looked around nervously.

"I missed you, too," she said. "I got your note."

"Good. David promised me he would get it to you."

"Thank you for letting me know. I was worried."

I nodded to my food as an orderly walked by.

"I thought you changed your mind about me," she whispered.

I looked directly at her, to hell with the consequences. "No. Don't ever think that." She smiled, nodded, and slid her foot across the floor, nesting it close against mine.

~ ~ ~

DINNER CAME AND nearly went before Elizabeth walked in. She looked ragged and weak. She pushed her hair back and slumped, holding her own head up with her hand while she began to eat.

"What's wrong?" I tried and failed to keep the concern out of my eyes.

"I'm tired," she whispered and then blew on a spoon of cold soup out of habit.

"What happened?" She shook her head. She looked like she would nod off at any minute. She had been fine after lunch. I stared at her, waiting. She ate slowly and kept her head down.

I rubbed my knuckles over my mouth impatiently. "Damn it," I grunted, not at her. "Elizabeth, please. If you don't tell me, I'll worry." She knew the feeling well, and she wouldn't want it for me.

"They pushed me," she said quietly.

I lowered my head, kept my eyes on her, and waited for her to clarify. I bounced my knee under the table. "Elizabeth," I hissed.

"The other one hasn't come out in a while. They were pushing me to see if they could make it come out, or if I could stay in control and keep it away. They said there's a chance it's gone. But we won't know unless they push me."

I hated the thought and had to push the mental image of what that looked like out of my mind.

"They shouldn't have done that."

"I did well, Simon. It didn't happen. No matter what they said or did, I never lost control. Not even when they—"

"I don't want to know what they did," I interrupted. She recoiled and dropped her eyes. "It's not that I don't care. Elizabeth, you have no idea. But I can't know what they do or say to you." My voice was barely audible. "It makes me want to kill them, and I have never wanted to kill anyone before. When I think of them saying things to you, making you cry, and doing God only knows what else. I just can't know." I caught the tiny nod that told me she understood.

"You did good," I added quickly.

Dinner was over, and the nurse took the trays from in front of us, not bothering to ask if we were done.

"One day," I said, with clenched fists, "I am going to look at you over dinner, and we're going to be free to talk. And *we'll* decide when it's over." I glared at the back of the nurse's head.

~ ~ ~

I LAY IN bed and tried to think about Elizabeth. I preferred it to the other thing that had been bothering me lately. I saw her in my mind, but recently, the last person I expected to cloud my thoughts of her was me.

I didn't like how I felt most of the time. I was always on edge and paranoid. I didn't like the things I thought or the way I felt. I was never, well, rarely, if I were to be honest, a violent person, but later, I caught myself thinking thoughts that made me shudder when I was alone and calm. I rolled to my side and told myself that this place was simply starting to get to me. It had been close to six months, I think, and that's a long time for a sane person to try to keep their sanity among the insane. The line between normal and abnormal behavior had begun to blur.

I closed my eyes and told myself that tomorrow I would wake up acting and feeling the way I had before Elizabeth. Before her, I was biding my time. Learning their game and playing it well, hiding my visions from the staff. I was generally a harmless smartass who was mildly entertaining. I would try to get back to that. Calm, casual, and quick witted, biding my time. I grunted in frustration at myself. *You know that's not possible now, idiot.*

I rolled onto my back, but I couldn't get comfortable. I tried to focus on her again. I tried to find her eyes, but they faded as my mind wandered. I wondered when exactly I had fallen in love with her. I couldn't put a day, hour, or moment on it. I knew within days of her arrival I would love her more than anything. I had seen it. So I sought her out, started loving her before I even knew her because I knew I would.

Still, I was confused. *No. Don't start questioning it. You know how you feel. Did I even have a choice?* I wondered. *No, I was destined to love her.* Now, it felt as if everything had spiraled out of control in a place where I had none to begin with. I was so utterly, violently protective of her, of us, that I could hardly enjoy it anymore. She—we, were the only tiny bit of happiness there was in this hellhole, and they had me so worried about losing it, I couldn't even enjoy it!

I put my arm over my eyes to block out the light coming through the small window in my door. I tried to get some sleep. Lack of it hadn't helped my less than sunny disposition.

~ ~ ~

BEFORE THE HOSPITAL had hired a full staff again, David had one more surprise for us. He came for me late the next evening, stepping softly and whispering. As usual, I worried he was trying too hard to help us, risking losing his job, exposing us or both. But also, as usual, I couldn't resist a few precious moments alone with her. I walked into the commons, which was dark and tidied for the night. Slightly confused, I turned to see David holding out a heavy winter coat. I took it and he pointed to the left. I saw that the metal door to the courtyard was propped open a crack. I smiled wide and raised my eyebrows.

"Really?" I asked in disbelief, glancing back at the door. Talk about the illusion of freedom.

"I can only give you twenty minutes," he whispered apologetically.

"I'll take it," I said with a smile and slipped on the coat. I didn't bother to button it as I nearly jogged to the door. She waited in the shadows, leaning against the wall in a coat far too big for her. *Loretta's,* I thought. I could see my breath in smoky plumes in front of me as I walked. The full moon lit the courtyard just enough to see her. I walked a little faster until I reached her, and with the last step, my lips crashed into hers. I gathered her up, baggy coat and all, and kissed her like the starving man I was. I only broke the kiss once to tear apart the opening of the black coat, slip my arms in and around to pull her close to me. I'd be damned if even that would stand between us. Her hands found their way into my coat, and a hard shiver went through me as they slipped under my shirt. Her hands were warm, almost hot on my cold skin as she felt every muscle from the tops of my shoulders to the curve of my lower back. I gasped, pulling the breath from her lungs into mine as her hands slid to the front, covering every inch of my chest. I don't know how long we stood there, pressed against the cold, brick wall. I lost consciousness of everything around me—time, space, and temperature. It was freezing cold and I didn't even care. Where I ended and she began blurred. At some point, I pulled away reluctantly with numb, swollen lips. I laughed and so did she.

"It's nice to see you, too." She laughed.

I looked to each side, holding her by the waist and then dropped my forehead to hers. I had to find a way to cram everything into the few minutes we had left. There were things I wanted to tell her, plans we needed to make. Our time here at the asylum was coming to an end, and I needed to know she would wait for me if she were the one who left first. She wiped my mind clean with another kiss, pulling me to her. Slower, we took the time to enjoy it. My hands neared dangerous places, and I ground the palms of them against her hipbones, pressing her into the wall. Away, but not too far away. I would suffer alone in my room for this later, but I didn't care. Her hands hovered over my stomach and then dipped below the invisible line. I broke from her abruptly and grabbed her wrist.

"Don't do that." I smiled, but my voice begged. Her face changed in the dim light. "If you go there, there's no going back," I explained.

"Does it still work? You know, after what they did to you," she asked boldly.

"Well, it works for one, so I suppose it will work just fine for two." I laughed, but she missed the joke entirely and moved on to her next question.

"But you know it works from girls before?"

I squirmed under her stare. She wanted to know about the women before her. Before I came here. "I have these precious few minutes with you. I don't want to talk about them."

"But I'm curious. I can't picture you outside of here. What was your life like?"

I took her hand, and we walked slowly as we began a loop around the perimeter of the courtyard.

"There weren't a whole lot of girls who wanted to date the local psychic. But a few were brave enough or curious enough. And they were all weird."

"What were they like?" she asked, hugging my arms with both of hers.

"There was Cassandra. She was with the circus." I saw her eyebrows shoot up and I smiled. "I told you they were weird. Anyway, this was before we lived here. We lived in upstate New York. I was looking at the animals behind the tent. I felt sorry for them. They looked so sad, caged up, and lonely. She was one of the acrobats and we hit it off. I wasn't anything new or scary to her. She lived her entire life with freaks. She was my first," I confided.

"Girlfriend?" she asked.

"First everything." Her face didn't change as she walked slowly beside me. "Then there was the one that had shaking fits. *That* was interesting." She looked up at me in question. "Going swimming was tricky," I joked. "She would stop and stare, but she wouldn't see things like I do, she would just shake all over. She was always very tired after."

"Was she crazy?"

"No, it was just something in her brain, they said. She couldn't help it."

"Who else?"

Actually, there were a string of short relationships with girls who didn't know about me and would take off as soon as they found out, and some oddballs who didn't mind my freakish visions. In return, I would look away from the flaws that kept them from dating anyone considered normal. But I had no time for all that.

"There were a few of them after graduation and before here. But I don't want to talk about them." I insisted this time and she dropped it. "Besides, I don't remember half of their names, and more importantly, it was *nothing* like this."

She seemed to like that and snuggled closer, putting her head on my shoulder as we walked.

"What about you?"

"What about me?"

"Did you have someone special before here?"

"Not really. The closest thing to a beau I had was the son of one of my daddy's customers."

"And?" I nudged her thick coat.

"It's stupid." She laughed nervously.

"No, it's not. I want to hear. I told you about mine."

She sighed and I thought about the ticking clock. "Like I said, he was the son of one of Daddy's customers who came from halfway around the world to hand pick leather for his furniture business. There was always such a fluster before they came. My mother would clean the house, top to bottom, and cook for days on end. I never understood that because they never came in the house nor stayed to eat. Anyway, Pierre was a year older than I was. While our fathers would conduct their business, we would go off and have fun."

"What was having fun?" I teased.

"No, not that," she said, flustered. "Close," she added with a laugh. "But no. At first, we'd just sit by the lake and talk, play games. His father took all day to pick his leather, so sometimes we would go on a picnic."

"So was he a beau?"

"Well, no. Not really. Sort of."

"I'm really confused." I laughed.

"Well, we only saw each other four times a year, but we had a lot of fun when we were together." She smiled.

"And you never?"

"No," she said, laughing. "Though he loved to talk about it. He was more than happy to tell me everything I'd ever need to know." Her face scrunched up in distaste.

"And a few things I could have done without."

"I don't think I want to know," I said, smiling and relaxed.

"You don't." Her eyebrows rose in agreement. "But just like you said," she stopped and hugged me suddenly, "it was nothing like this."

David whistled lightly from the door. He couldn't see us, but I was pretty sure he wasn't worried. I looked back at her with a heavy sigh.

"One more." I kissed her in the shadows of the trees, quick but thorough before we walked, hand-in-hand, back to our cage.

~ ~ ~

SHE CAME TO lunch the next day looking exhausted again. I didn't need to ask. I already knew. She looked up and smiled, tired and weak. "I did good," she said.

Later that day, the doctor told me something I hadn't seen coming in any form. He said I was doing better, and they were going to begin the process of thinking about, maybe, letting me out. Eventually. I smiled, remembering the vision of us leaving here together. I knew it might not be physically together, walking out of the iron gates, holding hands. It may be me first and then her, or her first and then me, but either way, I knew it would happen, and I knew we would be together out there. It looked like it was all falling into place, and it gave me some hope and helped me get through the next few days.

I saw little of Elizabeth for three days. Like a junkie coming off morphine, I twitched nervously with a constant anxious feeling. I didn't want to eat, and I had little interest in anything. I couldn't concentrate, even on the visions that came. They had grown stranger, involving faces I didn't recognize, places I had never been. I didn't understand them, and I didn't have the mental focus to try. *It can't be like this all the time,* I thought to myself, running my hand through my tangled hair. *If love were like this all the time, for everyone, then society would collapse in on itself. It was completely focused, yet as unproductive as possible. No, it can't be. It's this place. It's the lack of control. The inability to protect her. To enjoy her. It'll be better when we get out there. It has to be,* I assured myself.

~ ~ ~

THEY STARTED HER on a new medicine. The other one had slipped out only twice in several dozen times they had pushed her to her limit, and they hoped that with this new medicine, they could keep it from happening at all, and she could leave. I didn't like it. It made her sluggish and foggy. She wasn't my Elizabeth. Her eyes were dull and she moved in slow motion.

One day, she sat, heavy-limbed and clumsy, next to Ronnie and across the table from me. She had forgotten that I had told her to sit with her roommate and I would sit with Ronnie. I was dosing out our time together, trying to keep the staff oblivious. Ronnie glanced over at her nervously, mumbling as he ate. She didn't even notice him. We didn't say much through the meal. I decided when we got out, I would toss whatever mind-numbing pills they had her on into the lake I had seen us walking by. She was just fine before. She was gaining more control, keeping the other one deep down. I knew, with the peaceful life I would give her, it wouldn't ever need to come out again. It wouldn't need to because I would be strong for her when she couldn't be. She smiled at me as she stood, swaying lopsided and groggy. She rolled forward, and I could imagine the room spinning around her. She reached open palmed and blinded for anything to grasp, and her hand came down on the corner of Ronnie's tray. Everything happened in slow motion and still flashed too quickly for me to stop it. Ronnie's tray fell, dumping the contents of badly over-and-undercooked food into his lap. He stood, thrust his chair out from behind him, and screamed, loud and angry. He lunged at her, his long bony fingers spread wide and aimed for her neck. He took a hold of it and fell, tumbling back over the chair, screaming and squeezing her neck in a vise. Her head bounced off the hard floor repeatedly as her face turned blue.

I seemed to be watching from outside my body. I saw myself in one fluid movement toss the wooden table out of my way. It flipped and skidded, providing a direct path to her. I heard the nurse blow the whistle in long earsplitting bursts, but no one came. I grabbed Ronnie by his hair and shirt and ripped him off her. After throwing him to the floor, I stopped for a split second to glance back at her. She was lying on her side, gasping and choking. I could see the patch of blood seeping through her dark hair, the back of her head split open from the impact of hitting the floor. I dropped onto him and swung with all my strength, hitting his face blindly. Then I choked him. He had choked nearly everyone in this building, and the bastard had it coming. I heard her coughing and crying behind me, still trying to catch her breath, and I couldn't squeeze the bastard's neck hard enough.

I felt two sets of hands pulling on each arm. Another wrapped around my neck, choking me as they tried to pull me away. Suddenly, everyone let go, and I fell forward on Ronnie with the release of counter pressure. David grabbed each wrist and wrenched my hands from Ronnie's neck. He was yelling at me, but I didn't hear what he said. He pulled me several feet away and dropped me on the floor like change. I went sprawling, hitting the side of my head. I looked around frantically for Elizabeth, but I couldn't find her. Something shiny caught my eye, and I saw the nurse coming at me with a needle. I scrambled backward like a crab, trying to get away. My back hit the wall and there was nowhere to go. I looked to David for help. He bent over Ronnie, his back deliberately turned to me. It took six of them to hold me down as the nurse shoved the plunger down, shooting burning milky liquid into my thigh. I vaguely remember being confused when they were preparing me for the shock. I passed out with the first blast of current.

Sometime later, I opened my eyes and saw the blurry, white door of the confinement room standing on its side. I blinked hard several times, the side of my head throbbing from the concrete floor. I sat up slowly. The first thing I did was lean my head back on the wall and close my eyes, taking my inventory. It was all there. Including a few new images of her that I didn't want. Her mouth moved like a fish out of water, and her flooding eyes bulged as he choked her. Blood dripped down onto the floor from the gash on her head. I remembered that's why I was here, and I could only hope I hadn't killed him. I'd never get out of here if I had. *Though he would deserve it for touching her,* I thought. I shuddered to think, had David not been there, how easily I could have killed him.

They left me there the rest of the day. The room was so small I couldn't take three full paces across it. There was nothing. Just a white cube with a drain in the center of a concrete floor, and a bright light overhead too high to reach. The sound of my breathing echoed and it irritated me. I passed the time thinking about her, pulling out her words with the images.

'I've never been so happy.'

'I'm better because of you.'

'As long as I have you, I can stay strong.'

That one was my favorite. I told her she never had to go back to her home if she didn't want to. We could start a new life somewhere, and she would never have to see another cow if that's what she wanted. In hushed whispers mingled with our own sort of sign language, we had talked about what our life would be like out there, one day. I groaned and grabbed two handfuls of my hair when I realized I had most likely severely postponed that with my little outburst. Pushing the fear aside, I went back into my head to be near her.

David came to get me a few hours later. The door swung open wide and he loomed in the doorway, staring at me, not happy.

"I can't believe you did that," he said. He was obviously alone to speak to me so freely.

"Yeah, well, I suppose you'd just wait patiently for the nurse's needle if it were Loretta he was choking the shit out of," I said as I walked past him. My legs were sore and my head still hurt.

I stopped and looked at him. "Well, would you?"

He shook his head, and we walked slowly down the long hall back to the men's wing.

"You have to watch your step, Simon. There is, well, there *was* talk of you getting out of here. I don't know how this is going to affect that." He shot me a stern look.

"What was I supposed to do, David?" I stopped and stared at him. He pursed his lips, unable to answer and started walking again. "What time is it anyway?" I asked. I hadn't seen a window, and it was impossible to tell without the sunlight.

"Seven-thirty in the evening."

Too late for dinner, I thought.

"I need to see her." I hoped that his feeling of obligation for saving his life hadn't run its course.

"Maybe later." He turned and looked both ways down the hall before continuing. "I'm working until midnight. Maybe when the other one goes to break, I can give you a few minutes," he said reluctantly. "Lord knows she wants to see you. She's been a mess since it happened. The other one has come out twice."

"What happens when the other one comes out? She doesn't remember, and I've never seen it." He shook his head. "David, please, I'm just curious. It's not going to change how I feel."

He looked almost ashamed. "It's not that, I've just..." He shifted his weight and avoided my eyes. "I've never quite seen anything like it," he whispered. "The other one, it keeps tabs on what's going on. Like it's watching from the back of her mind. I've never been afraid of a split person before, but I've been afraid of this one."

"It's all her so, of course, it knows. It's just stronger. It's like this. When it comes out, she's putting on an extra layer of muscles for difficult jobs. The other one handles the things she thinks she can't. It can handle remembering the hard stuff, so it does, and Elizabeth doesn't have to."

I thought about picking up my honorary psychology degree on my way out of this place.

"It's more than that," David insisted. "The other one sees and remembers everything, even when it's not in control. Elizabeth doesn't do that. She doesn't remember anything when the other one is in control."

"Well, she said she's getting better at controlling it. She told me they push her, and she keeps it from coming out."

"When did she tell you that?" David asked suspiciously. We had gotten to my door and he unlocked it. We were alone in the hallway.

"Just last week. She said they push her in therapy to try to get her to show that she's in control. She does really well," I said.

"No, Simon. It's not quite like that." He looked at me, long and ominous.

"Well, how is it then? Because Elizabeth would never lie to me. She has no need to."

He sighed in hesitation. "She's worse, Simon. A lot worse."

~ ~ ~

LATER, I WAITED on my bed, hands behind my head. It was a quiet night, and I could hear the ticking of the black and white clock in the hallway. David had left my door closed but unlocked to avoid unlatching the loud bolt in case he could sneak Elizabeth down the hall to me. I strained to hear anything, anything at all. It was as if the whole building were abandoned, it was so quiet. I thought a lot about what David had said. He had no reason to lie to me. But neither did Elizabeth. *Maybe she doesn't know she's getting worse,* I thought in her defense. How could she, if she couldn't remember the times that the other one came out? A shiver ran through me, and I was more curious than ever to see what it looked like when the other took control. *Would it know me and love me the way she does? After all, it's all still her in there,* I thought.

I heard light footsteps and a soft murmur that I recognized immediately as hers. I swung my legs over the side of the bed and listened again, just to be sure. Yes, it was she. I closed my eyes in relief.

David pushed the door open, and she stepped in around him.

"Five minutes," he whispered.

I grabbed her in a tight hug. "Are you all right?" I asked into her hair. She nodded. I pulled back to see for myself. She looked well enough, and I held her head in between my hands.

"I'll kill anyone who tries to hurt you," I whispered. "Anyone." I pulled her back and held her tight against me. We had very little time and I needed to know. "How have you been doing in therapy?" I asked after a moment.

"I'm doing good, Simon. The other one hasn't come out. Even after what happened with Ronnie."

"When was the last time?" I asked, moving a few inches away, watching her face.

"It's been weeks," she said with a big smile. "And it's all because of you." She reached up to hug me, but I grabbed her arms, holding them away from me.

"That's not what David said," I said softly.

"What do you mean?"

"I mean, that you don't have to lie to me, Elizabeth. If the other one is coming out more, it's not going to change how I feel about you. About us."

"You don't believe me?" she breathed.

"It's not that I don't believe you, I just think..." I stopped, remembering all of the lies I had told her, under the disguise of being for her own benefit. All the little lies that I let slip, for the sole purpose of making her feel better, even if only for a moment.

"I can't blame you," I said.

"No, you can't because I didn't do anything," she said, raising her voice a little too high, recoiling. "I can't believe you believe him and not me!"

"Elizabeth, shh!" I turned to look at the door. "Lower your voice!" I hissed.

"Why wouldn't you believe me?" she asked.

The light was dim, but I could tell her eyes were narrow with disbelief.

"I do," I said finally. "I do." I held my hand out to her. She stared at it for the long count of ten before taking it. "I believe you," I reassured, and she walked back into my arms. I couldn't be mad at her for doing the same thing I had.

She wanted to make me feel better like I had made her feel better. And maybe a small bit of that was still true. She never changed around me. I felt her breath on my neck, and it sent a shiver through my entire body.

"Are you cold?" She giggled.

"No." I smiled and ran my hand slowly from her neck to the low small of her back. "Not in the least."

David gave a signal from the door. I sighed and held her closer.

"It doesn't matter," I said, with my face buried in her hair.

"What doesn't?"

"Any of it," I said just before kissing her goodnight.

~ ~ ~

THE DOCTOR WANTED to see me first thing the next morning. My mind raced, trying to think of an explanation for my outburst that wouldn't involve Elizabeth. Something that sounded crazy enough to warrant the action, but not crazy enough to keep me here. I had seen, right after she left my room the night before, the lake and the small cabin. It was cold and we were sneaking through the woods. After hiking for a long while, we saw a white house in the distance. We waited, for what, I don't know, and then broke into the house, gathering food and blankets. I had walked into the living room and noticed a newspaper lying on the arm of the couch. The date was January, nineteen thirty, but I couldn't see which day. We had less than six weeks. It made less and less sense as we both were becoming less stable. I had to rely on faith in my visions. Each one had been right, except about David, and I went out of my way to change that.

Then I thought with an icy shudder of my own death. I had seen it very clearly within days of seeing Elizabeth. Maybe I might be able to change that, too. At least, I hoped. I didn't like to think about it. If I had changed David's outcome and saved his life, then maybe I could save my own. I argued with myself that I might be bringing it on with my actions. My mind was spinning, and I didn't know any longer if I was changing my own fate or pushing myself closer to it. I wasted the walk to the doctor's office with my hands shoved in my pockets, these thoughts filling my mind. I walked in completely unprepared.

"I hear you had quite the outburst, Simon. Completely out of character for you." He sat back in his chair, staring at me. "What do you have to say for yourself?"

"I don't know, Doc," I lied. I rubbed my face hard and then looked out the window. I knew I couldn't pull off unreadable today.

"It wouldn't have anything to do with Elizabeth,

would it?"

"No," I said calm and even, staring out the window.

"Well, how do you explain the fact that you have gotten worse since she arrived? You're having more visions, more outbursts. It's all very confusing."

It wasn't for him, though. I knew he already had it worked out in his own head. Irritated by the look of him, I looked away.

"You said you were beginning the process of releasing me. Now you're saying I've steadily gotten worse. Which is it, Doc?"

"Letting you go didn't have anything to do with you getting better, Simon."

"So you were lying to me." I shook my head in disbelief. "And you wonder why I don't trust anyone here." I instantly wished I could take it back. I had no room to be defiant.

"It had more to do with the fact that the state is rather bankrupt, and we were asked to release some of the more stable patients to reduce the financial burden. You aren't..." He paused and started over. "You weren't considered a threat to society, so you were first on the list to go."

He rose from his chair and slowly walked around his desk, sitting on the corner of it, close to me. "I have to admit, Simon, I was disappointed. I was hoping we would be able to cure you. I was hoping I could write a paper on your condition if it could be cured. So it might help others."

"Sorry to let you down, Doc," I said. I was a damned research paper to him—that was all. He didn't see a human being. He saw a banquet dinner where he would receive an award for prizewinning research and a thesis. I wanted to kill him then, almost as much as I had wanted to kill Ronnie.

"So help yourself out, Simon. Explain yourself to me so we can try to move forward with your release. Help me understand why you did what you did."

I took a deep breath and blew it out slowly. *Here goes nothing.*

"I just snapped." His eyebrows rose. "I've watched him choke every single person here, and I just couldn't take it again. I'm sick of it. You said yourself to your little student that I'm quite sane. That's why the others don't care. But I do and I'm sick of it." I thought quickly and used his words to my advantage. "I feel sorry for them," I said, adding a sane human element to my explanation. "And when you told that student that I was the sanest of the group, I started looking at them differently. Like I had to protect them, look out for them." He nodded at me slowly with narrowed eyes. It bothered me, not knowing if he believed me or not. "So that's it." I shrugged.

"You feel it's your job to look out for the weaker ones."

"Yes." The weaker one, if I were being honest. Just her. To hell with the rest of them.

"That's very noble of you, Simon." I shrugged and looked away again. "So that explains your behavior the other day. However, I am still trying to make sense of the rest of it. Your increase in visions seems to be directly correlated with Elizabeth's other personality surfacing."

"I haven't noticed."

"Well, I have. Take a look at this." He handed me a piece of paper. It looked like childish writing in crayon, but it was readable. My blood ran cold. It was a timeline showing that every one of my visions happened very close to or at the same time as Elizabeth losing control. Little blue spikes were my visions, the ones that were caught anyway, and the red ones were for her, the times when the other one took over. There were many more red lines than blue. I looked closely at the dates, and those even matched up with visions I hadn't been caught having.

"Who did this?" I asked.

"I was hoping you would know," he said. "I found it on my desk this morning. I have read both your charts and it's all correct. It matches up." He pointed to the lines with an old crooked finger. "They are nearly mirror images of each other. It is rather—" He rubbed his chin. "Interesting."

God, I hated that word. I tossed the paper onto his desk.

"It makes no sense to me," I said, folding my hands to hide the tremors. "I don't see the connection."

I danced around through the rest of the appointment until he finally let me go.

I passed David in the hall on my way back to my room. He was half-pulling Ronnie along. *At least he's alive,* I thought, noticing the swollen bruises all over his face.

David stopped and Ronnie shrunk away from me.

"I need to see her," I said urgently.

"Is everything okay?" he whispered.

"No." I glared at Ronnie. I knew now that I would leave first, and she would be left here, at least for a little while. I took a step toward Ronnie. "You're not even going to look at her, are you, Ronnie?" I asked through my teeth. He shook his head with his eyes at my feet.

"I'll see what I can do," David said and pulled Ronnie along to his appointment.

Three long days passed before David could bring me to her room. The women's wing was short staffed, and we had to wait until near midnight. She knew something was wrong, but it was impossible to talk to her about it during the day. We were watched every second now. Loretta showed me to her room and waited outside.

"What's wrong?" She jumped up to hug me.

"Everything," I said. "I think they know." I swallowed hard, not wanting to tell her what I suspected. "Sit," I said, pulling away. "We don't have a lot of time." I sat beside her on the bed, which was equally as uncomfortable as mine was. In fact, the room was identical, except they had let her have a hairbrush. "I think I know what's going on," I said. She waited with owlish eyes. "I think it's the other one." She continued to stare at me. "Look, the doctor showed me something the other day. A chart that someone drew. Someone who has been watching us very closely. It showed every time I had a vision, and every time the other one showed itself."

I could see she was getting upset, so I held her hand.

"Think about it, Elizabeth," I whispered. "Who else would know every time I had a vision? I only ever told you about the ones that I didn't get caught for."

"I don't understand," she said slowly.

"I've had three days to think this over. I think the other one is watching. David thinks it takes notes of everything you say and do, everything that goes on around you. It knows it can't come out when we're together because you're strong enough to keep it down. I think that makes it angry, and it's trying to keep us apart. I just don't know how you got the paper on his desk. Not you," I backtracked quickly. "The other one. That's the only thing I can't figure out."

"This doesn't make any sense," she said, on the verge of tears.

"It makes perfect sense. The other one is stronger. It wants to be in control. The only way it can be is if you get rid of me."

"No. No, I would never do that, Simon. You have to believe that." She grabbed my shirt, shaking her head.

"I don't think *you* did," I said. I glanced at the door, as our time was almost up. I grabbed both of her hands in mine and kissed them quickly. "I need you to fight harder, harder than you've ever fought before, to keep this other one down. I'm going to be getting out soon." She looked panicked. "It'll be fine, you'll be right behind me. I promise. I've seen it, but—" Loretta gave a soft knock on the door. "Just be strong. Fight hard, all right? And remember," I said as I stood and hugged her, "this is *your* mind, Elizabeth, and you are in control of everything and everyone in it." She nodded silently against my shoulder. I gave her a quick kiss and hurried back to my room.

That night I dreamed vividly. It was Christmas. I saw muddy fingers molding a small heart made of clay. Tiny cracks covered the surface of it from sun drying. I saw the heart in the palm of her hand and then looked up to see her face, smiling and bright.

Two days later, the nuns came again to do art projects with us. They worked with women and men separately, and I sat in the far corner of the room and watched the other guys make a mess. One of the nuns called to me, inviting me over, but I shook my head and looked out the window.

"No, Ronnie, don't eat the clay," one of the nuns called out. My head jerked toward the group, and I squinted to see everything the nuns had spread out over the table. On the end of one table was a chunk of molding clay. It was the same color as the clay heart in my dream. The nuns seemed to be pleased when I walked over and sat down. I ripped off a piece of the sticky clay and played with it mindlessly. When no one was looking, I took another piece and slipped it into my pocket.

Once back in my room, I molded it in the dark into the heart I had seen in my mind.

"Psst." David's eyes adjusted to the darkness of the room, and he saw me sit up and reach for something under my bed.

"Can you put this on the windowsill for me?" I whispered. It was far too high for me to reach. He stepped in, and I placed the heart carefully in his hand. "Be careful, it's not dry yet," I whispered.

He stared at it for a moment with an indescribable expression, and I thought I saw his eyes mist just a little.

"What?" I ask defensively, worried he thought it was stupid.

He shook his head, cleared his throat, and reached up high to place it on the windowsill to dry in the sun, undetected. He left without explaining his odd behavior.

~ ~ ~

ON CHRISTMAS EVE, David and Loretta planned something spectacular for us. Well, spectacular from the perspective of a caged animal. Not just for Elizabeth and me, but for all of us.

We had been shooed out of the commons area after dinner, sent to our rooms without explanation. Half the staff had a buzz of excitement about them, and the other half looked nervous. I was grateful, later, when I woke up from a vision undetected. If I had been sitting in the commons for radio time, I would be strapped to a table right now with a bit shoved in my mouth. It was another one I didn't understand. So many of them didn't make sense anymore. I saw a man, hopeless and broken, sitting in a white bathtub about to end his life. The room smelled musty and sour. I recognized the jet black hair and wondered if it was the same man who I had seen on his knees several weeks ago. Another man was sitting on the floor near the sink. Though I tried, I couldn't hear what they were saying. I woke up from it, and the heavy sadness that filled the bathroom hadn't disappeared with the sight.

The hallways echoed easily and I heard bustling and unfamiliar voices. I crammed my face into the small window in my door but couldn't see anything. A half-hour later, I heard doors unlock one after another down the hall.

Finally, mine was unlocked and David came in. He reached up high to the windowsill for the heart. He handed it to me. "Tonight might be a good time to give this to her," he said.

I wanted to wait for Christmas morning, but the gleam in his eye made me trust him, and I slipped it into my pocket. We filed into the commons area, and there were chairs arranged in half of the room. Like seats in a playhouse with an empty space in front of them. Three tall ugly lamps were spaced three feet apart on the floor, and on the other side stood a dozen people, normal people from the outside, looking very scared and nervous. They were dressed up in Victorian era outfits, huddled together in the corner.

"We don't bite," I said as I passed them. I glanced over the crowd of nut jobs and looked back. "Well, *most* of us don't," I said with a smirk.

The women were already there, and I noticed Elizabeth had sat in the last row, an empty seat beside her. I looked to David in question. He nodded with a smile.

I made my way over and slipped into the chair. She smiled sideways at me, and I leaned slightly so our shoulders could touch. She was dressed in hospital pajamas with a small blanket over her lap.

"Cold?" I whispered out of the corner of my mouth.

"No," she said, smiling to her lap again.

David turned on the ugly lamps instead of the overhead lights. Three orderlies with small mirrors sat behind the lamps in an attempt to make a spotlight effect for the timid group of what I now assumed were carolers. It was a poor job of it, but it redirected some light away from us, and I felt more alone in the dark.

She lifted the blanket without taking her eyes off the carolers, who were starting to arrange themselves in front. In one smooth movement, she flipped one edge of the blanket to cover my leg, leaving her hand on my thigh. I looked around. This was really daring and I was already nervous. The carolers started singing, and all of the sad souls in the room were entranced. The troublemakers, sedated for the event, sat drooling and half-oblivious to what was going on. I felt sorry for them that they would miss this, one way or another. With everyone's attention on the carolers, I slipped my hand under the blanket and held hers. I waited a fearful minute, and when I realized no one had seen, I relaxed and squeezed her hand. Their voices really were beautiful, the Christmas carols upbeat and happy. I tried to pretend we were anywhere else and leaned over to include Elizabeth in my escape.

"We have just tucked the kids into bed, left them with the nanny and are going for a horse drawn carriage ride," I whispered. "You're dressed in blue velvet and silk, and I'm wearing a custom made tuxedo."

I saw the fabric come up out of the hard wooden

chair, up from under and behind, and wrap itself around her to form a beautiful dress. I looked at her neck and a string of pearls appeared. Her hair lifted up from her shoulders and piled elegantly on her head. "This is a famous opera house, and we're sitting in one of those alcoves, high up on the wall. It's beautiful here. The walls are tall and grand, the woodwork is breathtaking." I leaned my head close to hers and watched as her eyes lost the dingy room, and she smiled. I imagined her seeing our chairs rise up above everyone else.

The floor where the carolers sung dropped far below us as a heavy, red velvet curtain pulled back on either side of the stage. The beautiful plaster etchings carved themselves as the walls of the opera house rose up around us, and we watched the show in elegance.

"It's beautiful," was all she said, and I knew she was there with me. The feeling came over me again, the feeling of how this perfect time with her was ending, and I glanced at the clock. Forty minutes had passed, so I decided I had better give it to her now, or I might miss the chance. I pulled out the heart from my pocket and slipped it between our hands under the blanket. She felt it with confusion on her face and then looked up at me in astonishment. Peeking under the blanket, her mouth dropped open when she saw the heart in the palm of her hand. A huge tear welled up and spilled over. I was hoping she would like it, but I had no idea it would have this much effect on her. She looked up at me, wordless, although it wasn't quite the expression I saw in my dream. She turned away slightly and rustled for something under the blanket. When she turned back around, she held out her hand. In it lay another identical heart. I gasped quietly, looked up at her, and saw my image of her, smiling. Shining. I took it from her and smiled.

I had seen the heart she was making for me. I realized we were connected on a level ordinary people wouldn't ever be able to understand. I tried to clear my throat silently, and my eyes stung from the lump in my throat.

She was still smiling, holding the heart I had made when I looked up.

"I love you." I was disappointed my voice was so hoarse. I wanted it to be smooth and romantic. I watched her smile and her eyes lit up.

"I love you, too," she whispered.

I should have remembered we weren't really in our opera house. How what we saw around us really didn't exist and we were far from alone. I kissed her without remembering all that, and when I lifted my head, I saw three shocked nurses and two orderlies staring at us. Dread washed over me so deep it made me sick to my stomach, and I immediately apologized to her under my breath.

The game was over.

~ ~ ~

I WAITED TWO days to see the doctor. They were two of the most nerve-wracking, stomach-twisting days of my life. *How the hell are you going to explain this one?* I thought. I flipped back and forth from fear to anger. Fear because they had power over my entire life and anger for the same reason. I shouldn't have to hide how I feel. They should stay out of my business. Elizabeth may be getting worse when away from me, but near me, she was perfect, and they would not recognize that.

David walked me to the office. We didn't speak. His

face was sad, though, and I really needed him to reassure me. To tell me everything would be okay and help me see a way out of this. But I didn't know how to ask, and even if I had, I doubted he would have any words of comfort for me. For the last two months, I had worried to the point of sickness someone would ruin this, and that person had turned out to be me. I shook my head in self-disgust. I had really blown it. Blown it wide open.

I sat across from the doctor. He didn't look up at me for several minutes, just scribbled on that damn notepad of his. Finally, he raised his head and he looked mad. Personally offended mad.

"Why didn't you tell me you and Elizabeth were so close, Simon?"

"We're not." I decided to give lying one last shot. "I'm not sure what happened the other night, it just happened."

"Really?" he said, leaning back and narrowing his eyes at me.

"Really. It gets lonely around here. It could have been anyone."

"I think you're lying, Simon. I think you and Elizabeth have been having a relationship under our noses all this time." I stared at him blankly. "You know that's against the rules, Simon."

"Why? Why is it against the rules if we make each other happy, and we're better when we're together?" I demanded. It was out and there was no hiding it. I could at least ask why I had been forced to hide it in the first place.

"It distracts you from your therapy, Simon, and Elizabeth from hers." He glanced down at the childish crayon chart in front of him. "It really does all make sense now. As your relationship has grown, you both have begun to deteriorate. You're not good for each other, Simon."

"That's not true," I said through my teeth. I lurched forward and stopped myself at the edge of his desk. "She's better around me, and I never have visions around her." I realized my voice was almost pleading, and it made me sick to sound so weak in front of someone who loved the power he held.

"But the moment you're apart, it's worse than it was before. Every time. You can't live your entire life by her side, Simon, keeping the other one down."

"Yes, I can."

He laughed and it enraged me. My fists were clenched and my heart pounded in my ears. "Don't laugh at me," I growled at him.

"You are not thinking realistically, Simon. I tried to warn you to stay away from her. Do you realize that if you had not mixed yourself up with that pitiful girl that you would most likely be free by now? We would have let you go."

"You're lying."

"No, it's true. She's holding back your progress, Simon." He fished through his papers and pulled a file from the stack. He opened it and scanned, reading and then began the blasted scribbling again. He talked to me as he wrote. "I'm afraid I am going to have to have you transferred, Simon."

"No!" I yelled, my eyes darting from the file to him and back.

"You'll never progress, and neither will she if you are in the same facility. I'm transferring you to a men's asylum out of state." He said it as casually as if he were telling me what was for dinner.

"No, you can't," I said, shaking with fear and anger.

"I'll stay away from her. I'll act like I don't know her. I'll never sit by her at meals again, just please." I realized I was very close to tears. "Don't transfer me. I'll do better, I swear," I begged like a child and tossed aside pride for her. For us.

"I'm sorry, Simon. I have no choice." He slammed the file shut and stood, signaling the meeting was over. "I hope the next hospital is able to help you," he said flatly.

I stared at him in disbelief and then rose slowly. David was in the doorway, staring at the floor. I think he had been there the whole time. *That's why they sent him to walk me here. He's the only one who could have stopped me from killing the doctor*, I thought. I usually had privilege to walk to and from the appointments alone.

He avoided my eyes as I stood and kept his head down. I walked slowly beside him, my mind racing, trying to find a way out of this mess. I stopped and turned around. *I should go back in there and try again. Beg more. Promise him anything and everything.* I turned back toward my room with a ragged sigh and sniffled. I coughed, trying to hide imminent tears. I felt hard, twisting pain in my chest. My heart was being ripped out as I realized everything I had seen of our life outside this place had been a lie.

I sat doubled over on the side of my bed, holding my head. Everything was falling apart, and I was powerless to stop it. I had changed fate through my actions, and that inadvertently was taking me further away from what I wanted most. My head felt like it was about to explode, and I screamed a muffled growl of frustration. I rarely cried, but I did then, choking back hard sobs that I kept as quiet as I could. David told the others I had a headache and to leave me alone.

I didn't look at her the next day at breakfast. I sat across from Sobbing Susan, crying all through breakfast as she usually did. My eyes were swollen with dark circles. I only pretended to eat. I could feel her looking at me, and it killed me to keep my head down. But it was easier like this. I would ask David to try to arrange one last meeting in the courtyard. I would say goodbye, for now, and we would set up a meeting place, somewhere out there. After I got out of wherever I was going, and she got out of here.

I turned my head away so I wouldn't be tempted to look at her, and watched the bare, icy branches sway in the winter wind. That's when I got the idea.

~ ~ ~

DAVID SAT ON the side of my bed, shaking his head. "You can't do that, Simon," he said. "There's no way."

"There has to be a way," I argued. I sat at the head of my bed with my back against the cold, gray wall. "There has to be," I whispered and leaned forward, trying to reason with him. "What if it was you and Loretta? What if everyone found out and you both lost your jobs and your home and had to move, start somewhere new in order to keep her?"

"I have, Simon. Three times. We've been here the longest because we've been careful." He shook his head with regret. "She can't even take my name," he said quietly.

"Well, what if they found out and said you couldn't be together anymore. What if they tried to—" I paused trying to look for a parallel. "What if they tried to annul your marriage?"

He turned his head to look at me then. "We were

married by a preacher, not by the law."

"What did you do, David? When they tried to take her from you?" He put his head back and stared at the ceiling, and I knew I had him.

"We left," he said. "Disappeared."

"And we don't have a choice any more than you did."

He shook his head in dread, and I locked eyes with him, imploring. "You're the only one who can help us."

"I don't know how we'd pull it off, Simon."

"We just have to, and quickly. The transfer will be delayed because of the holidays, but we still don't have much time."

He nodded, deep in thought. "Give me twenty-four hours," he said finally.

"Thank you," I exhaled with relief.

He walked to the door and then stopped, speaking softly without turning around. "If you're right, if it's the other one telling the doc about you two, I wouldn't breathe a word of this to Elizabeth," he said.

"I'm way ahead of you. She won't know a thing until it's time to go." I couldn't help but smile. He nodded and left, locking the door behind him.

I lay back on my bed and thought my plan through. We would sneak out with David's help in the middle of the night. By the time they realized we were gone, we'd have a five or six hour jump on them. We could hide in the woods until it was safe to go on to her family's cabin on the lake. We'd rest there a while and then take the back roads to cross over into Canada. We'd start a new life there or make our way west, dip back down into the Midwest somewhere. I could hardly sleep from the excitement.

The next night, David came to my room again. Sweating profusely, he looked nervous.

"Are you sick?" I asked as he mopped his head with a handkerchief.

"In the head? Or the body? In the head, yes. Very much so. I can't believe what I just did," he said, slightly out of breath. He shook his head and then glared at me. "After all this, you better name your first child after me."

"Consider it done." I laughed.

"All right. I broke into the doctor's office and read your file."

"You what?"

He pointed to his forehead. "I'm not sweating because it's hot in here. Anyway, the transfer is set for January second."

"Okay, how soon can we get out of here?" I asked impatiently.

"I'm still working on that. I needed to know how much time we had first," he said. We were both quiet for a moment, thinking. I imagined mice trying to escape a maze, frantically looking for the way out. Every thought I had seemed to dead end, so I would backtrack to the beginning of the maze and start over.

"New Year's Eve," David whispered, his eyes lighting up with the idea. "We'll be short-staffed. That's the best time," he decided aloud.

"That's great." I grinned. Two days. Just two more days.

"Can you get to our regular clothes in storage? It'll be freezing out there," I said.

"I'll take care of all that. All you need to do is be ready to go when I come for you. Remember, night after next, just before midnight." The excitement was contagious and he smiled at me. "This is crazy. You do know that, right?"

"Yeah, well, this place can make you nuts." I smiled

and relaxed my back against the wall.

I had to bite my tongue with every other sentence I managed to whisper to Elizabeth. She still thought I was going to be transferred, and she was sad, on the verge of tears all the time. It killed me to leave her in limbo like that, not to be able to reassure her.

"Do you think we'll have any time together before you leave?" she asked over dinner.

"Maybe."

"What am I going to do when you leave?" she asked with tears in her eyes.

I had to hold my mouth shut to keep from telling her everything. Telling her this was the last night that we would have to worry and whisper. That we were about to run away, in just over twenty-four hours. Our new life awaited us.

"It'll be all right," I said, stripping any emotion from my face, but bouncing my leg under the table.

"So that's it? You're getting transferred, and I'm stuck here, and you're okay with that?"

"No, of course not," I said, keeping my head low. I lifted it up to look around nervously before looking at her. "I told you what I saw. We *will* be together out there. I just don't know exactly when." Another little lie, not to make her feel better this time, but to protect the plan. To keep the other one from knowing. I prayed she wouldn't throw a fit, let the other one out, or do anything that would require sedation or confinement.

"Please, Elizabeth, just stay calm and be patient. I promise it will all work out."

She dropped her eyes hopelessly. "I just don't see how."

"Trust me," I whispered.

The last day was agony. At every meal and combined

activity, she walked in the room and searched for me anxiously. When she found me, her face would relax a little, but the worry remained. The hands on the clock ticked by with a slowness that I thought would drive me insane. It felt like the day that wouldn't end. I had the idea to take a nap in order to make time go faster and rest up, as we would be running all night. Nervous energy made that impossible.

"It's all gonna work out, you know." I looked at her over dinner. She caught something in my eyes and smiled. All the worry and fear disappeared from her face for just a moment.

Bedtime wouldn't come quick enough and the waiting after, as they locked all the doors, settled all the screamers, and turned off the lights, was maddening. I couldn't sleep. I could only lay with my eyes closed, willing slow and even breathing. I heard the lock on my door turn and my eyes popped open.

It was time.

David stepped inside quietly. I was already on my feet. He huddled close to me, whispering his instructions.

"All right, here's how this is going to work," he breathed, barely loud enough for me to hear. "There are two gates in the fence surrounding the courtyard. A skinny one to the south and a wider one to the north. Both are unlocked. I left the chain looped around so they'll look normal when security does the rounds. The larger one is nearly overgrown with bushes. Might be hard to find so I made maps." He shoved two folded papers in my hand. "There are two different routes you can take away from the hospital. A guard walks the perimeter all night, but I don't know what side he'll be on when you get out there. Wait and listen. If he's near one, double back and go out the other."

"David, I—"

"I'm not done. Exactly sixty feet straight out from each gate, I've buried a bag. I covered the hole with dead brush. There're some clothes, coats, a few dollars and food to get you through tomorrow."

My hands trembled as I held the maps, speechless. I only ever expected him to open the door and leave the rest to us.

"Thank you, David," was all I managed to whisper.

"Take care of yourself, Simon. And your girl." He grabbed my shoulder and squeezed it hard.

"I will," I whispered as my throat closed. He had been my only friend for a long time, and I realized then how much I would miss him.

"Let's go," he nodded.

He poked his head out and looked both ways down the hall. He waved at me and I followed close behind him. We ran quietly to the commons room. He took forever opening the heavy metal door, slowly, silently. We slipped in and stood stock-still for a moment, letting our eyes adjust to the darkness and listening for any sign that we'd been found out.

"Over here," Loretta whispered from the darkened corner of the room, and I nearly jumped out of my skin. David reached into his pocket and shoved a stubby candle and a book of matches into my hand.

"So you can see the map," he whispered as Elizabeth stepped out from behind Loretta.

"What's going on?" she asked.

"Shh!!" we hissed in unison and then all looked at the door.

Only silence from the other side. I took quick steps and grabbed her hands. "We're leaving. Tonight," I said.

"What? How?" she squeaked.

I glanced back at David, who stood with his arm around his wife, their secret safe in the shadows of darkness.

"Really?" she asked. I could almost see the excitement on her face, and I could feel her heart begin to race.

"Really. I told you it would work out," I said. She threw her arms around my neck and squeezed hard. "I'll take care of you now," I promised. We jerked apart at the sound of a voice in the hall.

"Go!" David said as he automatically pulled his arm from Loretta. We walked quickly to the door, propped open a crack.

I pushed it open, and a frigid gust of air blew past us. I turned briefly, took one last glance at David, and then looked at Elizabeth.

"Are you ready?" I asked. I could already see the answer in her eyes. She smiled, squeezed my hand, and we ran.

VISIONS

THE MOON WAS nearly full and cast just enough light to see the ground in front of us. We ran north toward the larger gate and dropped down to crouch under the low boughs of the trees. Crawling under the branches along the fence line, I felt for the gate. I looked back often to check on Elizabeth. She looked scared but crawled on her hands and knees, breathing as though she were running a marathon in order to keep up with me.

My hands found the metal pole on one side of the gate, and I held a hand back to Elizabeth, signaling her to stop. We kept still for several minutes, our hands, and knees burning with cold from the frozen ground underneath them. It was so dark under the branches we could barely see our hands in front of our faces. Elizabeth started to shiver, and I pulled her against to me and put my arm around her. We were in thin cotton hospital clothes wedged between the tree trunk and the fence. I could see the padlock above us, open, hanging from the chain on our side. From the outside, the gate would appear chained and locked. We waited another minute, and I was glad we did. I heard the light whistle of the security guard as he walked the perimeter in the distance. It grew closer and my mind raced, stay or run, stay or run.

We could turn and run along the tree line to the opposite gate or hide and wait. Elizabeth's teeth started chattering, and she pursed her lips but couldn't stop it. It wasn't loud, but it was the only sound as everything lay in frozen silence around us. Even our breathing seemed too loud.

He was getting closer now. I could hear his breathing, which meant he could hear ours if he stopped whistling. *If we run, he'll hear it,* I thought. As quietly as I could, I crawled around the tree trunk, pulling Elizabeth behind me, and leaned against it. It was the only thing between the fence, the guard, and us. I prayed it was wide enough to hide us. Elizabeth curled up in a shivering ball with her back against me, and I put my hand over her mouth to quiet the chattering. I pulled my shirt over my mouth to hide the white plumes of breath and closed my eyes. I heard his footsteps slow and then stop just on the other side of us. He was only feet away. I squeezed my eyes shut and held my breath. *Please God, Please God.* He started walking again, slowly, whistling. It seemed like forever until he was out of earshot.

She was shaking hard now. I rubbed her arms and face briskly. "We're almost out," I whispered. "Th-There's a coat for you j-j-just on the other s-side." She nodded, too cold to speak. I peeked around the corner and then crawled under the branches to the gate. My hands shook from fear and cold. I unwrapped the chain from the pole as carefully as I could. Slowly, I lifted the latch and pushed the gate open a bit. It made a high-pitched squeal and I froze. I waited with my shoulders hunched up to my ears until I was sure the guard hadn't heard it. It took minutes to open the gate. I had to move it slowly so the rusty metal wouldn't make any more noise. Elizabeth shivered violently behind me. When it was opened just enough to squeeze through, I pulled her up off the ground and pushed her through first. I had to take care not to bump the gate as I squeezed my body through sideways.

We couldn't enjoy the first breath of freedom because we were so cold and scared. She stumbled next to me as I counted out sixty feet in front of us. I could only think of one thing—getting warmer clothes on Elizabeth. I briefly worried, with me or not, if she were this cold and scared, the stronger one might take over. I figured I would see it one day and have to deal with it, but in the middle of escaping an asylum in the dead of winter was not the place I wanted that first meeting to happen.

"You're doing great, honey. Keep walking. We're almost there. You're doing so good, Elizabeth," I whispered. She nodded, but her teeth chattered too hard to answer me. I nearly walked past the small pile of branches and leaves covered with a light dusting of snow. If there had been a heavier snowfall, I would have missed it completely, and we would have wandered forever.

I let go of Elizabeth and dropped to my knees, throwing aside the brush and dug with my hands in the frozen ground. It wasn't packed hard, but the clumps of frigid earth made my hands ache. Finally, I felt something like fabric and pulled out a bag. It made noise as it popped out, but I couldn't waste time slowly pulling it out. I could see just well enough in the moonlight, and I tossed her a shirt and pants. She slipped them on but couldn't button either with fingers numb from the cold. I pushed her shaking hands away and worked the buttons as quickly as I could. I pulled a knit hat from the bag, put it on her, and then slipped a second shirt and a coat on myself. It must have been David's because I swam in it. Once we had put on every stitch of clothing David had packed for us, I threw the nearly empty bag on my back and grabbed her hand.

"We have to go," I whispered. I could hear the faint whistle of the guard. He was on his way back around the full circle.

We ran clumsily into the thin woods. I would look at the map once we were safely out of sight. I willed my frozen legs to run faster, but they wouldn't cooperate. I let go of Elizabeth's hand to adjust the bag and heard a thump behind me. I turned to see her sprawled out on the ground. I jogged back and pulled her up.

"*Are you okay?*" I whispered. She nodded, held her knee with both hands, her face scrunched up in pain, trying to silence a cry. I dropped the bag and pushed the leg of her pants up. I could hardly see, but I could feel the warm, wet blood running down her leg.

"Shit." I reached under my shirt and ripped off a strip of the thin hospital shirt. "You're bleeding all over the place," I whispered as I wrapped the strip around her knee. The white material quickly turned dark as the blood seeped through. "We have to keep going," I said, pulling her up. She limped a few steps, and I put my arm around her. "Use me as a crutch," I said and almost laughed at the irony.

Her injury slowed us down considerably, and I grew more nervous, glancing back, worried we wouldn't get far enough ahead of them. We had to move faster.

I stopped, adjusted the bag, and then reached behind

her back and knees to pick her up. She gasped in surprise.

"I'm sorry, we have to make better time," I said and kissed her quickly. She hung onto my neck tightly and put her head down on my chest. I knew she was exhausted already.

She wasn't heavy, but I was huffing and puffing after twenty minutes.

"Sorry," she whispered.

"It's not you." Her warm breath on my neck gave me a surge of energy, and I smiled down at her. "I'm a little out of shape. Months of doing nothing," I said quietly with a shrug and then turned, swinging her around, and we could barely see the sprawling hospital in the distance. There was no other sound, except the crunch of the frozen ground under my feet, and I relaxed a little. I hadn't realized we had climbed slightly in elevation, and we looked down upon the hospital and grounds surrounding it. Everything had an eerie blue tint of moonlight and ice. If it had been any other place, it would have been beautiful. I turned away and walked steadily for another hour.

~ ~ ~

I SET HER down on a rock surrounded by trees. I shook my arms out and then knelt on one knee to look at hers. The white cloth was soaked through, but I saw it wasn't actively bleeding anymore when I took off the bandage. I lit a match to get a closer look and saw a long jagged tear that gaped slightly. It needed to be stitched, but that wasn't an option right now. I ripped off another clean strip of cotton from my shirt and rewrapped it. I was sweating from exertion, but she had shivered steadily since we left. I thought about starting a small fire just long enough to warm up before we pressed on. I sighed heavily, trying to decide.

"What are you doing?" she asked as I crawled around, feeling for small sticks and dry leaves.

"I'm going to start a fire," I told her. "You have to get warm. We won't stay long." It took three matches to get the chilled branches to light, and soon, we had a pitifully small fire to warm our hands. She looked tired with bloodshot eyes and bedraggled locks of hair poking out from the edges of the knit cap. In the dim light of the fire, she was the most beautiful thing I had ever seen.

"We did it," she said with a shivering smile. I was hesitant to celebrate just yet. I probably wouldn't relax until we had crossed over into Canada. I just smiled and nodded, keeping my eyes on the fire. We sat cross-legged on each side of it, trying to pull out every ounce of heat.

"Are you hungry?" I asked, already reaching for the bag on the ground next to me.

"No."

I was starving after our hike, but I closed the bag. I would save it for her, just in case. It was just beginning to dawn on me after the food and money were gone David had provided, I had no idea where more of either would come from. A new pressing burden added to the anxiety of putting distance between the hospital and us. Elizabeth looked like she was ready to nod off, and I held out a hand to her. She scooted around the fire until she was close to me.

"Rest for a few minutes," I told her and guided her head down onto my thigh, facing the fire. She curled up on the cold ground and closed her eyes, and I heard the soft, even breathing of deep sleep within minutes. I would let her sleep for fifteen or twenty minutes, I decided, then we would have to move again. I was wide-awake listening to every sound coming from the woods around us. Each one made me jump and strain my eyes to see what was coming. It was only small animals attracted by the fire.

I pulled up my other knee, rested my arm over it and my head on that, keeping one arm around Elizabeth. I closed my eyes for a moment and tried to figure out our next step. I had to put out the fire and then hide it. I needed to get a look at the map to figure out where we were and the fastest way to the lake, where we could eat and get a good night's sleep. I assumed they would check there first, once they discovered us gone. They would search both of our houses, so I had to give them time to do that. I would have to find shelter nearby until they had. After that, they would look south—that much I knew. They would never think to look north after what I left for them.

The evening we left, I had killed a good two hours writing on scraps of paper, detailing visions I had had, like diary entries. I wrote about Elizabeth and me in Mexico. I described things I had seen on pictures and postcards, and then wrote out what they would see as a plan of how to get there, zigzagging across the country. I wedged it in between the coils of the springs under the bed frame. I knew they would turn the room upside down and find it. It would keep them busy for a few weeks, plenty of time for us to get up north.

I smiled at myself, knowing we would just have to wait out the first few days before we could breathe easy. It would be so wonderful to relax, not to have our every movement watched. Not to whisper and have that surge of tingling fear countless times a day. To decide for myself when dinner was over.

I flinched my head up with a jerk, looking around me. I had no idea how long I had slept on my arm, and I was mad at myself for letting it happen. It could have only been a few minutes or it could have been hours. I wished I had asked David for a watch. I had no idea how long it would be before sunrise. I shook Elizabeth's shoulder gently, and she stirred, rubbing her eyes and stretching.

"How long was I asleep?" she asked with a yawn as she sat up.

"I don't know." I frowned as I scooped up handfuls of cold earth to dump on the fire. I stomped it down and then strained my eyes for something to cover it all with and eventually, found a few fallen branches and tossed them on top, hoping it looked like they had randomly fallen that way. She was already on her feet, trying to walk on the busted knee. "Are you going to be able to manage?" I asked as I tossed the bag over my shoulder.

"I think so," she said, taking a few experimental steps. "It hurts, but I can walk," she said.

"If it hurts badly, let me know. I'll carry you." I dug around in my pocket for the map. The second one fell onto the ground, and I picked it up and handed it to Elizabeth. "Here, hold onto this." She tucked it into her coat pocket as I lit a match to study my copy. I folded my map a moment later, shoved it in my pocket, and took her hand. "I think I know where we are. We need to head east now. Toward the ocean."

We walked for what I thought was about four hours before I noticed the first light of dawn. We couldn't hear the telltale signs of the ocean yet, but I could hear the stirrings of the small town ahead of us. We walked around the western edge of the town, as it grew lighter. Turning our heads to the side to avoid recognition as a car sputtered past, I saw a white house in the distance. It was similar to the one I had seen in a vision but not exactly. The resemblance was close enough, and my legs tired enough, so we turned up the long dirt road toward it.

We quickly moved out of sight of the main house when we heard signs of life coming from inside. Running from one small outbuilding to another until we reached the barn, we kept from being seen. It was almost fully light, and we waited around the corner, pressed against the red boards of the barn as an old man walked out with two full pails of fresh milk. An older woman called him to breakfast from the porch. We slipped into the back hatch of the barn a few moments later. I saw a milk cow resting in its pen and wrapped my arm around Elizabeth's head, pulling it into my chest to blind her like a horse before she could see it. I spotted the hayloft high in the rear of the barn. I looked for the ladder as I walked, nearly stumbling over a goat that came to investigate us. I found a wooden ladder and put Elizabeth in front of me. It hurt to bend her knee as climbing put pressure on it, and she winced with every other step. I kept one hand on the ladder, and another on her back, as we wormed our way to the top.

It was warmer here, and I led her to the back of the loft. We collapsed onto a fluffy pile of hay and blew out an exhausted breath. I lay silent for a moment and then pushed up on one elbow, facing her.

"We can sleep now," I said quietly, pushing the stray hairs out of her face and tucking them back under the hat. "Are you hungry?" She shook her head with closed eyes.

"Are you?" she asked back.

"No," I lied. "Just tired."

She raised a limp hand and rested it on my cheek.

"Then sleep," she mumbled. I put an arm under her shoulders, and she rolled toward me, stretching an arm over my waist, her head under my chin. I only had the energy to kiss her head, and we were asleep within minutes.

~ ~ ~

MY EYES POPPED open when the latch was thrown with a loud thump and the barn door swung open. The hinges groaned and light flooded in, illuminating the depths of the loft. I heard the farmer mumbling to himself, scuffing his feet and the tinny clink of a milk pail. The cow let out a low noisy grunt, and my hand was over Elizabeth's mouth just as her eyes flew open, wide and lost. She twisted her head up, looked at me, and then relaxed under my hand. I pointed toward the edge of the loft and then put my finger to my lips. She nodded and I slowly removed my hand. We lay still, listening intently as he puttered around the barn with his evening chores. The hay tickled my nose, and I pinched my nostrils, holding off a sneeze. I hoped he would hurry.

"Evenin', Hubert," a voice echoed from below. The cow made more noise and a pig squealed loudly. I heard what sounded like a stool being kicked back, then more shuffling.

"Sheriff. What brings you out our way?" I heard the light slap of two hands meeting in a shake.

"Well, I just got word that there's been a couple people escaped from the hospital, up the way."

"You don't say. You mean the asylum?" he asked with morbid curiosity.

"I'm afraid so. Just brought by a couple drawings of 'em, in case you've seen them. Man and a woman."

My heart pounded in my ears, and I had to force slow, quiet breaths through the panic. I could feel Elizabeth tense under my arm and pulled her tighter.

"Nope, can't say that I've seen 'em. But I'll be sure to let you know if I do."

"Appreciate that, Hubert."

"Can you stay for coffee, Vincent?" An older woman's voice now, I pictured her gray-haired, plump and smiling in an apron.

"No, 'fraid not. I'm going house to house through the county, lookin' for these two."

"Are they dangerous?" the woman again.

"Well, I don't know. The hospital said they weren't there for bein' the violent type, but they were in there for *some* reason so I wouldn't take any chances."

"Well, thanks for stopping by. We'll keep a lookout." I heard one set of footsteps leave. It was quiet for a few moments and then I heard the older woman again.

"Well, that's scary, isn't it, Hubert?"

"Sure is. We'll lock up the house tonight and keep the shotguns close by. It'll be all right." I heard fabric rustling, maybe they had hugged. I heard him reposition the stool and then grunt, his knees making little popping noises. The rhythmic sound of thin streams of milk hitting the side of the tin pail had gone on for several minutes before the woman spoke again.

"I got another letter from Caleb," she said quietly. The milking stopped briefly, and he grunted an unintelligible reply. "Do you want to read it?" she asked timidly.

"Can't. Got chores to do, Ethel."

"Hubert, you have to get past this. He's your son. He made a mistake, that's all. He was young and stupid and—"

"And he sold my daddy's farm without even speaking to me about it. That land was in my family for a hundred years."

"I know, Hubert," she sighed, "but it's just land. He's your only son."

"And then he runs off with that wild woman, livin' the high life in New York, her running around scandalous all over God's earth and him just letting her. Did you know she's been to *jail*, Ethel?"

"Yes, Hubert, I know. But she loves Caleb. And he's happy with her, scandalous as she might be."

"And he never wrote so much before. Just sent money and that truck, pictures from fancy places. But now, well, now, he's got nothing, and they're writing all the time."

I felt like an intruder now, not just physically, listening in on this couple's private quarrel over family.

"You don't want to read it?" she asked again, disappointed this time.

"Leave it on the table. I'll try to get to it later." He grunted.

I heard soft footsteps leave and then a heavy sigh from below.

It took him another hour to finish his chores and button up the barn for the night.

My back was aching from staying in one position for so long, and I thought my bladder would burst at any moment. I crawled to the edge and peeked down to make sure it was empty, then crawled back to Elizabeth.

"You should eat something before we get going again." I dug around in the bag and found a small box filled with sandwiches. "I have to run outside for a minute," I said as I held out a sandwich to her.

"Why?" her eyes darted around, and I knew she

didn't want to be left alone.

"Nature calls," I said with a grin and crawled my way to the ladder.

"Hurry," she whispered as my head disappeared beneath the edge of the loft.

Outside, the air was cold, and I stood behind the barn, looking up at all the stars shining brightly in the blue-gray sky of late evening. I tried to remember exactly where we were on the map and to decide what direction to go when we left here. I found the North Star, and by picturing the map in my mind, decided which way to go. David's map stopped at her family's house so we would be on our own from there. I assumed after we put a big enough stretch of road behind us, we would be safe to stop and ask directions.

I tiptoed around the corner and slipped through the small side door of the barn. I found Elizabeth holding her knees to her chest with one arm, eating her sandwich. She looked relieved when my head popped up over the edge of the loft.

"I wish we could stay one more night," she said as I crawled over to her. "It's warm here."

"I know." I wasn't looking forward to putting her through another freezing night on the run, but this whole town would have word of us by the next morning. "We have to keep going. I'm sorry," I said.

I didn't expect her to crawl to the edge and peek down. She couldn't see much, but what she could see didn't frighten her.

"This barn isn't scary like ours," she said. "It smells how a barn should smell."

"Stinky?" I laughed with a mouthful of sandwich.

"Sort of." She grinned back at me. "It should have that musty smell from the animals, like wet dog, the slightly sweet smell of their feed, the sour smell of their mess, and a deep earthy smell, all combined together."

"Yours didn't smell like this?" I asked.

Her face fell quickly. "No."

"What did—" I stopped myself from asking. I assumed it wasn't something she wanted to relive. "If you're still hungry at all, you should eat now. We'll leave when it's fully dark," I said instead.

"I'm fine." She crawled back and sat close beside me.

"Do you want to have a barn, you know, when we have our own place?" I asked as I picked out a few pieces of hay sticking out of her hair and tossed them away.

"Yes. And it will smell sweet and musky like this one," she said with a smile.

"It'll smell however you want it to," I said. I kissed her and took my time about it. It was the first time we weren't rushed or scared of being caught, and that made it all the sweeter. I tangled my hands in her hair and traced her lips with my tongue. Then she bit my lower lip playfully and pulled me down into the hay.

Several moments later, our coats opened as we tried to get as much of each other as we could, she broke the kiss. Holding my head with both hands, she didn't let me more than an inch away from her.

"Let's stay one more night," she whispered. I had thought about it, even told myself we would, while my hands found their way under layers of clothing, gripped her waist, and then ran down over her hip and back up over the smooth skin of her stomach. My fingers felt her ribs expand with every hard breath and then above her ribs...

"We can't," I breathed. I put my forehead to hers and ground my teeth in frustration. She kissed me twice quickly, trailing one hand lightly over my back. "Please.

Elizabeth, you're killing me," I whispered with a smile. I pulled myself up to a sitting position and ran my hands through my hair, trying to tame it. Almost every trace of light was gone from the cracks in the wallboards of the barn. I looked back at her, still lying in the hay, hands folded over her stomach.

"We have to go," I said, none too happy about the fact. She sighed and sat up, pulled her shirt down and brushed bits of hay off the arms of her coat before buttoning it up. "We can relax soon, I promise." I gathered our bag and buttoned up my own coat.

I went down the ladder first and waited for her at the bottom. We snuck out the side door and tiptoed to the back where the people in the house wouldn't see us. I looked up and found the North Star again, and we started walking through the frozen field.

"How's your knee?" I asked.

"Sore. It's all right."

"I'll look at it again when the sun comes up." I should have thought to change the bandage one more time before we set out, but I was highly distracted. I tried not to torture myself by reliving it, but with little else to do, I couldn't help it. She caught me grinning and squeezed my hand.

"What are you smiling about?" she asked. I glanced at her, eyes slightly narrowed and devilish. I assumed she blushed though I couldn't see it in the dark. She looked away and let out an awkward giggle.

I couldn't walk fast enough to get to the cabin.

The moon was high and gleaming white when we stopped to eat. We stayed just west of the town and dipped back into the woods to make a small fire. She sat close, holding her hands over it. I found a rock with a flat top, put it in the middle of the flame, and placed a can of beans David had packed on top of it.

"Shouldn't take that long," I said as I fed the small flames around the rock. She watched the flames dance around the can, catch onto the paper label, and then go up in a quick flash. I could see her face clearly in the few seconds of bright light, and she looked deep in thought. "You did really well back there." She smiled without looking up. "In the barn," I clarified and the red in her cheeks wasn't from the firelight. "With the cow," I further clarified.

"Ah. That," she said and the teasing smile disappeared. "It wasn't so bad. Those animals were happy. They were taken care of, you know. What's Canada like?" she asked suddenly.

"I don't know. I've never been there."

"I wonder if it'll be like a whole other world." She tucked her now warm hands into the sleeves of her coat.

"Well, it can't be that different, I wouldn't think." We were quiet, listening to the small sizzling noises coming from the fire. It was cold, and the world was quiet around us as if we were the only ones in it. I wished for a moment that it were true. I used the sleeve of my coat to lift the can out of the fire and put my can in.

"David even remembered spoons," I said, smiling and holding one out to her. After we had eaten, I pushed one leg of her pants up to look at her knee. It was red and starting to swell. I tried to rub the grimace off my face.

"What?" she asked, looking from her knee to me and back.

"I think it's getting infected," I said. "We'll get you to a doctor as soon as we're in Canada." I sighed, frustrated and stood up. "Let's go," I said and pulled her up.

Halfway through the night with warm food in our stomachs, we set out again. I did my best to hide evidence of the fire and stuffed the empty cans into a hollow log. The memories that caused my heart to beat fast and thread, and the fluttering sensation deep in my stomach were harder to enjoy with the new worry of a possible infection. Adding that to being on the run with little food, little money, and no concrete destination, my nerves were raw by dawn. We reached the edge of her family's property with the first light.

"The cabin is that way." She pointed to the right. Staying west of the town eight miles behind us, we had run smack into the middle of her father's sprawling property.

"This must be a hundred acres," I said. We had reverted to whispering.

"Two hundred and fifty," she said and set out ahead of me, leading the way. We cut through the trees down a steep hill, and I could see the glimmer of water in the distance. We walked for a half-hour, and then I stopped dead in my tracks, holding out my arm. She came to an abrupt stop behind me, grabbing my shirt to keep her balance.

"I heard something," I whispered back to her. We crept, ducking along the short shrubbery near the lake for about thirty feet and stopped when we saw the corner of the cabin. She gasped, and I put my finger to my lips with a scowl.

We dropped down flat on a small hill of dirt at the lake's edge that hid us from sight. I poked my head up above the edge to see what was happening. There were several people at the cabin. The sheriff stood on the porch, holding his hat, talking to a short woman with dark brown hair sprinkled with white. I could see, even from that distance, the resemblance and knew it was Elizabeth's mother. Two orderlies walked out of the cabin.

"Well, they're not here." Vincent's voice echoed down the terrain. "And there's no sign they've been. Place hasn't been touched in months by the look of it."

"We only come here in the summer," her mother explained.

The doctor stepped into view, and my heart pounded so hard I could hear the blood coursing through my ears. Elizabeth put her head down, covered her ears, and closed her eyes tightly.

"Well, thank you for your cooperation, ma'am," he said. "If you see or hear anything, please don't hesitate to let us know."

She nodded, crossing her arms tightly over her chest with a worried frown. The doctor turned his attention to the sheriff. "I think it's safe to expand our search to the south."

"I'll alert every agency between here and Mexico."

"I do believe now that's where they would be headed," he said. The doctor nodded thoughtfully.

I closed my eyes and put my head down. I listened to the sound of footsteps on the wooden porch of the cabin, car doors slamming, sputtering engines roaring to life, and then silence.

We had lain hidden by the brush for two hours. We shivered from cold and fear. We nodded off at some point. I had closed my eyes, just for a moment, and then opened them suddenly. A duck made loud splashing noises near us in the water, and Elizabeth lay half on me, sleeping.

I knew it was midday as the sun was directly above us, and my stomach growled loudly. I nudged her and she woke, breathing in deeply through her nose. She rolled off me, rubbing her eyes, and I flipped to my stomach, poking up my head slowly. The cabin sat in the distance, quiet and alone. I slid back down next to Elizabeth.

"I think it's safe now." She nodded as I gathered the bag, which I had dropped ten feet away in a panic to get to the ground. "Are you sure the cabin can't be seen from your parents' house?" I asked again, adjusting the pack on my back.

"Positive. The house is quite a bit down the way. It's a twenty minute walk at least."

"Okay." I was still apprehensive. We walked hand in hand toward the cabin. She seemed very relaxed, but I was on edge, looking all around, jumping at every noise. I was grateful when she pushed the door open, and we slipped inside, closing the door quietly behind us.

"Here it is," she said and walked over to the hearth of the fireplace. It was small, only two rooms. The fireplace was deep and wide. I imagined it would heat the place up nicely if we dared risk the smoke of a fire. In the corner was a table and small cabinets, the most primitive of kitchens, and a sofa with end tables faced the front window next to the door. I walked past her through the only other door and saw it was a bedroom with one bed, an antique dresser, and a wash table with a pitcher and basin. I walked back out, and she was picking small kindling out of a box near the hearth.

"It's cold in here," she said without looking up.

"Should we risk a fire in the daytime?" I asked. She stopped and thought about it, then dropped the kindling back in the box. I was extremely tired, but still far too on edge to sleep.

I sat on the couch, and the coat bunched up around my neck. The view out the front window was beautiful. It encompassed the entire lake and the gentle rolling hills beyond it. The thin woods we had emerged from were on the left and flat bare land was on the right as far as the eye could see. I watched as birds swooped in and made graceful landings on the water, and the tall dead lake grass moved with the breeze. I felt like we could finally relax. A little. My eyes burned from lack of sleep and my joints ached. Elizabeth curled up next to me and quickly fell asleep on my shoulder. I moved my arm, putting it around her, and then put my head back and dozed. I woke up several hours later to the dim orange-red glow of sunset. After moving Elizabeth without waking her, I stood, stretched, and yawned.

A gust of wind rattled the small cabin, and I looked out the window, up to the churning and dark clouds.

Tall, ominous thunderheads pushed the sunset deeper into the horizon. A storm was good. We could have a fire undetected, and they would hold off the search if it were powerful enough. I slipped outside quietly. It was cold, and I could feel the electricity in the air of an impending storm. Firewood set stacked all along one side of the cabin, and I took an armload back inside. Elizabeth slept as I started a fire as quietly as I could. A few moments after, she sat up suddenly with a gasp.

"Simon!"

"Right here," I said, dropping the log and going to her. "I'm right here."

"I had a nightmare." She clung onto me, terrified.

"There's nothing to be afraid of. We're safe now," I said. A half lie—we were safe enough, for now. "I'm starting a fire, and I'll warm us up something to eat, okay?" She nodded, rubbing her face with a deep sigh. She disappeared into the bedroom and returned a moment later with the washing pitcher.

She filled it from a small red hand pump just off the side of the porch, poured it into a black pot, and hung it in the fireplace to heat.

"We need to wash," she said and sat down, trying to comb out her hair with her fingers. Bits of mud and straw fell out as she pulled apart each thick lock. "I need a brush," she said to herself.

"I need a razor." I laughed, rubbing my cheek, dark with two days' growth.

"Look under the cabinet where the wash basin sits," she said. "I think there's one there, with soap and cloths."

"It'll feel good to be clean again," I said and found a small basket with everything she mentioned tucked in the back of the tall narrow cabinet. She picked apart tangles as I dug in the bag and pulled out cans of soup and stale sandwiches. When the kettle of water was steaming, she poured it into the pitcher and gave me a peck on the cheek.

"I'm going to wash before dinner." She lit a candle and carried it with her free hand into the dark bedroom, closing the door behind her. A flash of lightning lit the room, and then deep thunder sent a vibration throughout the cabin. In seconds, the rain came down in sheets.

She emerged just as I had finished warming up our food. Long wet tendrils hung over her shoulders, and her shirt wicked away the water, leaving damp patches all over. She took one look at me, pointed, and started laughing.

I had taken off most of the layers of clothes as the cabin warmed up, and the wool shirt I had put on in the dark during our escape was obviously meant for Elizabeth. I grinned down at the pink material covered in a rose pattern.

"Hey, it was dark," I said, looking up at her. She wore David's gray wool shirt, which came to her knees, and nothing else.

"My pants and dress are drying," she explained. I swallowed hard and nodded, realizing for the first time how alone and free we were.

"Dinner's almost ready," I said, with a nervous throat clearing, avoiding her eyes.

She sat down at the small table, watching my every move. "Thank you, I'm starving."

I put the soup and barely edible sandwich in front of her and then sat down across the table.

"So I thought we would stay here tonight and then head out after dark tomorrow," I said and took a bite.

"So soon?" She looked disappointed.

"I don't think it's wise to stay too long."

"I just thought we could stay three or four days. You know, really get rested."

I shook my head. "I really want to get across the border as soon as we can. Then we can really relax."

She nodded and bent her head over her plate.

"Hey," I said.

She raised her eyes to peek at me and then lifted her whole head with a smile. "That's right. We don't have to hide anymore."

"And," I smiled wider, "I'll decide when I'm done with my dinner." She returned the smile, and we ate for several moments in silence. I broke the silence with a laugh.

"All this time, we've had to whisper and peek, and now we're free to talk, but we can't think of anything to say."

She giggled and shrugged her shoulders. "Nice weather we're having?" She nodded at the front window, now pelted with rain.

"Very funny," I said. "I told you how I ended up at the hospital. But how did you end up there?" She looked down uncomfortably. "I'm just curious, it won't change anything," I said and reached across the table for her hand.

"Well, Daddy didn't want me to go. He was really angry with my mother for suggesting it. But she was really scared of how bad I was getting." She hesitated and glanced up at me nervously.

"Go on," I said, giving her hand an encouraging squeeze.

"Well, the other one would argue with her a lot. It doesn't like her. She said she was afraid of it. But Daddy understood. He had medicine that helped keep his—" She looked at me again and took a deep breath. "It kept *his* other one away."

I didn't mean to react, but my spoon stopped midair, and my mouth hung open for a second.

"You mean," I swallowed and tried to keep my voice even. "Your father has another also?" She cast her eyes down, ashamed, and nodded. "No, Elizabeth, it's okay. I heard the doctor say it runs in families sometimes. Really, it's all right." I tried to sound reassuring. I loved Elizabeth, and it didn't matter what demons she fought within her. But the thought of a split person, other than her, scared the hell out of me.

She stopped talking, eating and stared at the table. I looked for some way to continue. "The medicine he takes, why can't you take that, too? If it helps him, maybe it will help you, too."

"That's what my daddy wanted to do. But my mother wouldn't let him. She said there was a better way to help me than for me to be stuck having to take that medicine every day. So she brought me to the hospital. I thought we were going on a picnic. When we pulled up to the gate, I realized where we were and tried to get out, but she held onto me, and they said the other one came out and fought."

"We all tried to fight when we first got there. That's not just you."

"Well, I knew the other one was out then because I don't remember the first few days there."

I thought back to that first day I saw her being dragged in, flailing and screaming.

"Do you remember seeing me? In the hallway? You passed by me when they brought you in."

Her brow furrowed in thought and then her face lit up. "I do! I remember seeing you, just for a split-second, leaning against the wall, and I said something to you, but then I blacked out again."

"You said, 'help me,'" I told her quietly.

"I did?"

I nodded and finished my sandwich. She was deep in thought for the rest of dinner, and I hoped I hadn't put a damper on our first carefree dinner alone.

"Well, I'm done," I said and pushed my plate a few inches away.

"No, wait." I pulled it back, took another spoonful of soup, and then sat back. "Now I'm done... No, wait." I took two more bites and Elizabeth laughed.

"What are you doing?" she asked.

"I'm deciding for myself when dinner is done." I grinned wide. "And I'm changing my mind about it as many times as I'd like." I pushed my bowl away and pulled it back two or three times, and so did she, giggling with me, reveling in the ability to control the smallest aspects of our life. I sat back and smiled at her. "Well, now that I'm really done, I'm going to go wash," I said.

"I'll clean this up," Elizabeth offered, waving her hand at the two bowls.

I refilled the pitcher with hot water from the fireplace and closed the door to the small bedroom.

After lighting five candles huddled on a plate below the mirror, I could make out a round, wet patch on the wood floor in front of the washbasin where Elizabeth had bathed. A shock ran through me as I undressed, from the thought and the cold. I heard the clinking and swishing of water as she washed our dishes and I smiled. We were only playing house right now, but soon, it would be for real. We would settle down in some small nowhere town and make a real home. Someday adopt children. I smiled wider when I remembered that our first child would have to be named David. I wondered about him for a few minutes and hoped he was unsuspected in helping us escape. He didn't need the trouble of that. I consoled myself with the sad fact that he and Loretta did know how to disappear and start a new life if they had to. My skin felt tight from the scrubbing, and I stood at the small mirror with a towel around my waist to shave. I was finishing the last few lengths under my chin when the door opened slowly. I watched her from the mirror as she took a step inside and then hesitated. Her face was serious, almost troubled. She spoke before I could ask her what was wrong.

"Why me?" she asked quietly.

"What do you mean, why you?" I watched her in the mirror as I finished shaving.

"Why did you pick me? Why do you love me? Of everyone, the circus girl, the girl with the spasms. All the girls you met before, why me?"

I opened my mouth to answer, but closed it quickly. How could I possibly explain the reasons when I didn't even fully understand them? I had seen that I would love her, so I did. There was never any question. I would sound like an idiot to say I believed I was born to love her, how the curse of the visions given to me was to better protect her and guide her away from insanity.

"I just... love you," I said simply with a small shrug. It was a pitiful answer. She smiled at me, and I leaned over to rinse my face and think of something better. When I stood up, she was right behind me, her hands lightly on my back.

"I guess there are no words for it, are there?" she said, looking at me in the mirror, her eyes just over my shoulder. I shook my head. She moved her hands to my waist, wrapping them slowly around my stomach and placed her head between my shoulder blades.

"I wish I could explain it," I said, running my hands along her arms in front of me. Her head rose and fell on my back for a few breaths, and then she ran her open hands over my chest, holding my shoulders, planting light kisses across my back. My skin rose up in gooseflesh, and I shivered at the soft kisses and warm breath behind me.

"We're alone," she said and something foreign in her voice caught me off guard. I turned around in the circle of her arms, and I could see something different in her eyes, too—a hint of strength or determination. I studied her for a long moment as I tried to dissect it. She looked like she was struggling with a decision and then kissed me quickly. I decided she was just nervous, took control of the kiss, and leaned her back slightly. I moved my lips to her face, down her neck and shoulder. She smelled faintly of the flowery soap we had just used. She bit my shoulder, and it took every ounce of self-restraint to hold back and enjoy this. I really wanted to take my time. I pulled her head away from my shoulder with one hand while the other found its way under the baggy gray shirt, sliding along her thigh, over the smooth, firm flesh of her bottom and grabbing a handful, pulled her firmly to me.

"Marry me," I breathed into her hair, kissing her cheek and ear.

"I already have," she said.

"We'll make it legal as soon as we can, okay?" I smiled eyes closed and smelled her one more time. She shook her head as she pulled back to look at me.

"It's just a piece of paper. What matters is what we think, what we know." She traced my lips with her finger, and whispered, "What we want. And I want you. Forever." I kissed her again and impatient hands resumed their wandering. She pulled at the towel and I held her wrist away.

"Not yet," I begged. She grunted her disapproval, and I distracted her by whispered descriptions of how she felt under my floating hands. She spoke into my shoulder in an odd voice, so softly I barely heard her.

"You know he's going to leave you."

My body froze and my eyes popped wide open.

"He'll get what he wants, and then he'll leave you."

"What?" I jerked back. She blinked twice and then focused on my face.

"Hmm?" she asked innocently.

"You said something."

"No, I didn't."

"You said I was going to leave after I got what I wanted. What did you mean?"

"I didn't say anything, Simon." I took a step back, tightening the towel around my waist.

"Yes, you did. I heard you." I tried to say more, but it stuck in my throat when I realized what it might have been. Or who. She looked like she was about to cry, and then her face contorted as if she were in pain. She bent over, pulling handfuls of hair and growled, "Noooooo!"

She was still for a moment, doubled over, breathing heavily, and then stood up slowly. When she flipped the hair from her face, she looked something between angry and suspicious.

"Elizabeth?" I whispered, taking a step back. I had the feeling she was talking to someone who definitely was not me.

"He said it didn't matter. He claims he loves you, that your cracked little mind doesn't matter to him. But I wonder how true that is." She smiled a tight, frightening smile. "Would it matter, I wonder. If he really saw?" Her voice trailed off and then changed as she whimpered, "Please, no."

Low and calculated again, she whispered. "Let's just see."

A surge of fear ran through me. I realized the other one was talking, and it made my stomach flip and my legs itch to run.

"Why wouldn't you leave?" Her voice was lower, smooth, and calm, talking to me now. "I showed you the way to the cabin. That's what you wanted." She glanced to the bed and back at me. "And you'll use me one more time and disappear."

"No," I whispered. My voice gave away my fear. "I would never do that, Elizabeth, I love you. We're going to Canada together, and we're going to get married and make a home and adopt babies."

Lightning flashed and lit the shadows of her face. She looked up at me with a thin smile.

"You're a liar."

"No. I won't leave you. You know that, Elizabeth."

"What if I want you to?" She took a step toward me, and I took an equal one back. "What if I want you to leave and never look back? What if I used *you* to get out of that place?" she sneered. Just the thought of that infuriated me.

"Bring Elizabeth back," I demanded. She lunged at me and I dodged out of the way. She crashed into the washstand and the pitcher fell, smashing into a thousand pieces. She jumped up, yelled again, and flew across the room at me. I grabbed her wrists, holding them beside her head and pinned her to the wall.

"Bring her back," I growled and gave her a hard shake. I stared, unafraid, searching for the true Elizabeth in her eyes.

"Not until I know you won't hurt her," she hissed back.

I breathed a small sigh of relief and reviewed the mental file cabinet of psychological bullshit I had memorized in the past six months.

"I know you're scared. I know that you're taking a step back and letting the other one protect you. But I love you, and I'll protect you now."

She stared at me defensively, deciding, and then slowly, the other one washed from her face. It softened, and she dropped her head to my shoulder. I felt her shudder and then start to cry. Her knees gave out, and I helped guide her to the floor in a sobbing heap. When she looked up again, I knew it was her.

"I'm so sorry," she cried, embarrassed and ashamed. "I didn't ever want you to see that." I sat beside her and hugged her close, looking for the right words. The storm outside was losing strength, and thunder rumbled low in the distance. I had no idea what to say.

"It was different this time," she said quietly, wiping her face.

"What do you mean?" I was still unnerved from the

whole ordeal and watched her carefully.

"I heard everything. I didn't just disappear like before. I could see what the other one saw and hear what it heard."

"Because you're getting stronger," I said. "You're realizing you have more control of your mind than they let you believe."

She shook her head and reached for my face. "But I couldn't stop it from saying those awful things to you."

"It doesn't matter," I said. "You're here and that's what matters. Besides, you don't believe that stuff," I said cautiously. "That I used you to get here, and I'm going to leave you? You can't believe that." Even though I knew the truth, I needed her to confirm what I just heard from her lips wasn't what she believed in her heart.

She dropped her eyes. "I worried about it at first, but—"

"What?" I dropped her hand.

"Well, it crossed my mind. I thought maybe you were picking my mind when you talked about the water, and then when I told you about the lake, it fit just enough, but you had to bring me."I held up my hand to stop her, and my mouth hung open for a few seconds in shock. "After all I went through in that hospital for you? All I've done and said and risked?" I shook my head, disbelieving.

"I know that's not the way it is now, Simon."

"It wasn't that way ever!" I pushed myself off the floor and took a few steps away. "So the other one wasn't lying when it said you used me to get out. You came with me, even though you had doubt in your mind. You suspected I was using you, but it didn't matter because I was your ticket to freedom."

"No, Simon." She held out a hand to me, but I walked away, slamming the door behind me.

I paced for a few moments and then crossed my arms, leaning against the cabinet in the dark. I set aside my anger for a moment to reflect on my first meeting with the other one.

"Jesus, that was weird," I whispered, rubbing my face. Not just weird, but unexpected. Not exactly how I thought our first night together would play out. And, after declaring ourselves married, technically, it was our wedding night. *Talk about the worst possible timing,* I thought. My mind was still catching up with my emotions. Never before had I burned through so many, so quickly—from heavenly bliss to numbing fear to protectively possessive, fighting Elizabeth for Elizabeth, then anger.

I turned away from the bedroom door with a frown. I sat on the couch in the dark, still clad only in a towel, and listened to what was left of the storm whistle through leafless trees and tap at the window and roof. She came out of the room a while later and sat on the couch near me and sniffled.

"I'm sorry," she said.

I looked at her, expressionless. "Do you have any idea how many times I got shocked for you? For us?"

She cringed. "I know," she whispered.

"And now I find out you never fully believed me. How I felt about you, the lengths I would go so we could be together."

"I did believe you. I was just afraid to trust you."

"Afraid to trust me?!"

"Well, you didn't say anything to me, and I thought maybe you were going to leave and just decided at the last minute to bring me, to help you find your way."

I sighed heavily. "I didn't need your help. David drew those maps to get off the grounds. And if I were going alone, I would have found somewhere else to stay other than here. That wouldn't have been hard. I didn't tell you until the last minute because I thought the other one was telling the doctor about us. I didn't want to risk him finding out. I had to keep it from you," I said. She nodded in understanding, hung her head in guilt. I sighed heavily and took her hand. "Elizabeth. If I were planning all along to escape alone, why would David pack me a woman's pink shirt?" I saw a smile crack and then she let out a little laugh, no doubt recalling how silly I looked in it. She seemed to grapple for words and then settled with another apology.

"I'm sorry." She crawled over to me and sat on my lap, hugging me tightly. "Can you forgive me?"

"There's nothing to forgive. It's not your fault. I just really wasn't prepared for it," I said apologetically, shaking my head.

"We don't have to let it ruin the whole night," she said, glancing at the bedroom door and back at me with a sly grin. She unbuttoned the first two buttons of her shirt and kissed me.

~ ~ ~

THE NEXT DAY, we woke at noon, or what I guessed was around noon and warmed up the last of the food David had packed.

"We'd better think about refilling before we head out tomorrow night," I told her.

"If we wait until my parents are doing chores in the barn this afternoon, we could sneak into my house and get what we need."

"That's taking one hell of a chance," I said.

"It'll be fine. Every afternoon, they work together for

a couple of hours. The barn is far enough away from the house they won't hear us if we go through the back door."

The idea made me more than nervous, but I couldn't see an alternative. We needed supplies before we headed out the next day. I held my head with one hand, thinking, worrying.

"I'm sorry about last night," I said, without raising my head. She looked up, surprised and then back down.

"It's okay."

"Just understand, it wasn't you," I tried to reassure her. "It's not that I don't want—"

She nodded quickly, interrupting me. "I know."

"I was just so distracted with everything that happened."

"You don't need to explain, Simon."

I felt like I did, and I continued to struggle and stammer for the next five minutes, trying to explain to her how my body's sudden lack of cooperation had nothing to do with her. But I couldn't explain what it really was without making her feel bad. I blamed it on being tired, raw nerves, guilt for the argument. I even tried, as embarrassing as it was, to tell her my bowels had been in a horrible state from the poor diet of the last few days, and it had prevented me from performing.

But I couldn't get the image out of my head, the scenario rather, of being in the throes of passion and having the other one join us suddenly. To look down and not see Elizabeth's eyes any longer, but to see the cold anger of the one who attacked me. That fear was enough to prevent anything from working properly.

"We should head up to the house soon," she said, cutting me off, changing the subject abruptly.

We bundled up in all our layers again, and I picked out all the bits of debris from the black wool hat before handing it to her. We walked mostly in silence, keeping just inside the thin woods, and she kept her eyes on the ground ahead of her. I didn't know if she was still upset over last night or nervous about going to her house again, possibly reawakening all the fears the surrounding farm held for her. I tried to make simple conversation that failed, mentioning things we should try to get a hold of if we could for the trip ahead.

She stopped abruptly and I looked up. The house was visible in the distance. It looked neat and well cared for, and the whitewashed boards of the house gleamed against the dreary background of winter. There was a garden on one side, surrounded by an equally bright white picket fence with a white summer swing in front of barren rose trellises.

"We'll get a little closer, and then wait for them to leave," she said. We walked a few hundred feet more, and I sat against a tree trunk. Without words, Elizabeth sat between my legs and leaned against me.

"Are you going to be okay coming here?" I asked as I wrapped my arms around her.

"Yes."

"You're not worried?"

"No. I have you," she said, twisting her head to smile at me. I kissed her briefly, and then I held her close to me while we watched the house, waiting for our moment.

Finally, we saw them leave through the back door. I fought the instinct to duck. They didn't notice us and walked toward the barn, closing the red door behind them. Elizabeth stood up and brushed off her pants, which were far too big for her. Loretta was a tall woman, so Elizabeth swam in her clothes as I swam in David's, too.

We crept nervously toward the house and made it to

the back door undetected. We slipped inside, and Elizabeth went to work right away, filling the bag with things from the pantry and icebox.

"We'll get some things from the root cellar before we go," she whispered. With the bag bursting, she turned to the stairs and I grabbed her arm.

"What are you doing?"

"Going upstairs to get us some clothes that fit and another blanket," she said. I looked around nervously, and deciding against being caught alone downstairs in this strange house, I followed her upstairs.

We went slowly, and I cringed with every creak of the old boards of the stairs. Elizabeth went on ahead more confidently.

"They can't hear us from the barn," she told me over her shoulder. From the bathroom, she took a bar of soap, a towel, and a hairbrush. She stuffed it all into a bag that she took from the closet, and then she waved me on to follow her into a room. "This is my room," she said as she closed the door quietly behind us.

It was small and smelled musty from weeks of being closed up. There was a twin bed covered in an ancient quilt. The curtains covering the window at the head of the bed were long panels of light material, adding to the airy cleanliness of the room. She opened the drawer to a small white vanity and pulled a few things out, tossing them in the bag.

"I'll be right back," she whispered and opened the door before I could ask where she was going.

She came back with a few pieces of clothes. "These are my father's, but I think they'll fit better than those you've got," she said, holding them out to me. She opened her closet door and dug through it, stuffing items in as she came across something she thought she would need.

She held up a dress in front of her and paused casually as if she were deciding what to wear to dinner. "I'm going to change," she announced and I took a step to leave the room. She stepped inside the closet and closed the door. I could hear her bumping around in the dark, and it made me nervous. I moved to the window above the bed to keep watch.

There was a small pen with pigs and a much larger one beyond that with cows as far as the eye could see. The corner of the red barn caught my eye, and I watched it intently. She emerged from the closet a few moments later in a long, cream-colored dress, flowing, and feminine.

"You really do look beautiful, but do you think that's a good idea for traveling?" I asked her, unable to take my eyes off the low cut bodice and tight waist.

"I'm not going to be traveling in it. I just wanted to make sure it still fit. You said you wanted to make it legal when we got there, so I thought I'd bring this." She looked down at herself and back up at me for approval.

"I think that's a good idea. Bring it, definitely," I said with a smile.

"You didn't change," she said, picking up the new clothes from the foot of the bed where I had tossed them.

"I was keeping watch," I said.

"Simon, I told you, they won't be back for a few hours. It's okay." She held out the clothes.

I took them, and she walked to the window and moved the curtains to look out. "I always felt safe in this room. It was kind of my sanctuary." She smiled over her shoulder and then grinned wider seeing me bare-chested, mid-shirt change. She went back to staring at the garden and swing below the window.

"This fits much better, thank you," I said as I pulled

up the pants and started in on the buttons of the shirt. I looked up, and she was there, hands over mine, stopping them.

"When I feel safe, the other one doesn't come out," she said and pushed my hands away, working the buttons back down. "I know that's what was bothering you last night," she said, watching each button as she unfastened it.

"Elizabeth, you can't be serious." I looked from her to the door and back.

"Quite." She smiled at me devilishly. She whispered in my ear and kissed my neck. "It's all right. I won't ruin it this time."

My body and mind were at war with each other and argued back and forth, allowing her time to find her way under my shirt, pushing it off my shoulders and distracting me from rational thinking with deep kisses and a playful tongue.

"I'm not sure this is a good idea—" I half-heartedly argued and then gasped as she found the waistband of my pants, popped the button and pulled down the zipper. They swooshed to the floor in a pile. She had been insistent the night before, but I could see today she wasn't taking no for an answer. As if to confirm it, her fingers dug into my arms and moved her kisses from my neck to my shoulder and along my chest. I closed my eyes and couldn't find a voice to argue.

I wasn't worried about her father bursting in with a shotgun. If he did, I would die a happy man.

~ ~ ~

I DON'T KNOW how much time passed or how we got there, but I found myself hovering over her on the twin bed, trying to get the top of her dress down and the bottom of it up, alternately. It snagged and slipped out of my grasp several times, as I frantically tried to push it up to her waist.

"Hurry, Simon," she whispered, hugging my hip with her thighs.

"I'm hurrying, I'm hurrying," I said. Too overwhelmed to be graceful, I moved my hips around, prodded blindly, searching.

"Wait!" she said, grabbing my face, one second before I found her.

"Wait?!" I gasped eyes wide open.

"I hear something." Her brow furrowed in concentrated listening. I hovered with gasping breaths, so close to heaven, writhing in agony. Then I heard her mother's voice echo up the stairs.

"Shit!" I jumped up and scrambled for my pants.

"Wait, Simon. Just be quiet!" Elizabeth whispered, adjusting her dress. I froze with my pants hanging open around my waist. We listened as they argued back and forth about something they were looking for.

"Maybe it's upstairs," her mother snapped. I heard three heavy thuds and my heart raced. I looked around and wondered if we could make the jump out the window without too much injury. The footsteps on the stairs stopped mid-way.

"No, I remember bringing it down," his deep voice called. After a moment, we heard the back door slam shut and breathed a sigh of relief. Elizabeth fell back on the bed and blew out her breath, moving loose strands of bedraggled hair out of her face.

"We should get out of here," I said while I threw on my clothes. She ignored me and held out her hand to me, wiggling her finger for me to come closer, holding an insinuating smile.

I looked down and then shrugged helplessly. All traces of excitement were long gone, and there would be no getting it back with the fear of being caught. Her face dropped in disappointment and she stood up. She peeled off the dress and quickly changed into a warm shirt and riding pants. She stuffed the dress into her bag and nodded toward the door.

"Let's go then."

I opened my mouth to apologize, but she had turned her back and was opening the door slowly. She peeked out each way down the hall before tiptoeing out. Each step caused the stairs to creak and groan under our weight, no matter how slowly we went, and my heart pounded in my ears. By the time we reached the bottom, sweat had beaded up on my forehead. All I could think of was to run back to the cabin, grab our things, and continue north to Canada.

We rounded the corner into the kitchen, and Elizabeth stopped short with a gasp. I grabbed her arm and pulled her back against me when I saw him.

"Daddy," she breathed.

An older man, salt and pepper haired, tall and work-worn, turned slowly toward us. My heart stopped, and though my instinct was to grab Elizabeth and run, my feet were frozen to the floor. His eyes fell on her first then grazed over me, and then back to her.

"Beth," he whispered and held out his arms. She yanked free from my bruising grip, took several running steps toward him, and fell into his hug.

"I missed you, Beth," he said, tears in his eyes. "I never wanted you in that place. You have to know that," his voice choked as he stroked her hair, hugging and rocking her. "It wasn't me."

"I know, Daddy," she said and turned toward me. "This is Simon, Daddy." She held out her hand for me to come closer. I took a deep breath after holding it in from shock and took one tentative step forward.

"Simon," he acknowledged me with a forlorn smile. "Thank you for helping my Beth get out of that place," he said, holding out his hand. I shook it awkwardly and told him he was welcome with a trembling voice. I didn't know him, and I certainly didn't trust him.

"You know you can't stay here, Beth," he said shakily, rubbing a hand over his eyes. "You have to get away, far away."

"I know, Daddy. Tonight we're staying in the cabin, tomorrow we're leaving for—"

"Mexico," I interrupted. "We're headed for Mexico. I have some family there," I said, praying he would believe me. He nodded and spoke to Elizabeth in a low concerned voice, and I tried to calculate how long it would take to get back to the cabin, gather our things, and get out of sight. *Only a few hours of daylight. Then we can move under the cover of darkness,* my mind raced.

"We need to go," I urged Elizabeth. I looked to her father. "I'll take care of her," I said with conviction.

He nodded and looked back to his daughter with sadness. "Send me word somehow when you get where you're going." He dug into his pocket and pulled out a small wad of bills, holding them out to me. "Here, take this. It might help," he said. Then he pulled out a vintage pocket watch on a long chain. "And this."

"You won't say anything to anyone, will you? That you saw us?" I asked. "Because they'll take us back if you do."

He shook his head, and his face scrunched up as if in

pain. "No. No, I would never send my Beth back to that place," he said. "That's a horrible place, Simon."

"Yeah. I was there," I said sarcastically.

He shook his head in pity. "For what, son? You're not split, too, are you? I have medicine." He gestured weakly to the cabinet with a look of charity on his face.

"No, thank you. I'm not split. I, ah…"

"He sees things, Daddy. Like a fortune teller. He can see stuff that is going to happen."

"You see everything? Or just some things?" he asked, fascinated.

"Just some things, it's nothing, really," I said.

"He saw us together outside the hospital, Daddy. It gave me so much strength to keep going." She looked back at me with loving eyes. "I had hope and it kept the other one away."

"Really?" her father asked in complete awe.

She nodded enthusiastically. "He saw other stuff, too, like the crash, and one of the orderlies would have died if he hadn't listened to him and—"

"Have you always been strange like that? Or was it after some medicine or shock treatment they gave you, and it just came on?" he asked, intrigued. I ignored him, thinking, *how ironic that two people with split personalities should think I was the strange one.*

"We should go," I whispered.

She hugged her father again, and he thanked me again, making me promise, again, to take good care of her. I nodded and stepped forward to take Elizabeth's arm.

"Let's go," I said softly, pulling her. She let go of her father's neck long enough to grab onto mine and started to cry. I moved her to the side of me, holding her by the waist and nodded my goodbye to her father. We slipped out the door and made our way quickly back to the cabin.

As soon as we were inside, I started throwing our things together in the bag and tried to hide evidence that we had been there in the first place.

"What are you doing, Simon?" she asked with a sniffle.

"We're leaving. Now." I hurried around the cabin.

An hour later, I sat beside her on the couch. She cried and I pleaded. "Elizabeth, we *have* to go." She shook her head in defiance. "Someone knows now, Elizabeth. It's not safe to stay. If he says anything—"

"He won't!" she yelled and I recoiled. "He hates my mother as much as I do! He won't let me go back there."

"We can't take that chance, sweetheart," I said insistently. She stared ahead of her with crossed arms, like a stubborn child. "Please." I tried taking one of her hands, but she snapped it back, tucking it under her arm against her chest. I blew out my breath in frustration and leaned back on the couch. The thick black clouds of an impending storm loomed near, and I was torn between the risk of being found and the risk of leaving during a snow and ice storm. She pouted, her body folded up tightly with crossed arms and legs, and I knew there was no convincing her.

I stood with a relenting sigh and opened the bag on the table, digging out food for dinner. She kept her back to me in silence, occasionally sniffling , and the ice rain began pelting the windows as our stew began to boil. I glanced at the small woodpile on the hearth.

"I'm going to get more wood," I said as I pulled on my coat. She nodded as I closed the door behind me.

~ ~ ~

"Simon!" I was vaguely aware of her yanking on my arm as I came out of it, blinking several times and taking deep breaths. She stood in front of me, searching my face and eyes. "Simon, what happened?" She looked shaken as I rubbed my eyes with a grimace, and then, suddenly, it dawned on her. "What did you see?" she asked ominously. I looked down at the armload of firewood that was scattered all over the porch.

"Inside," I said, looking over each shoulder before bending to gather it. "I'll tell you inside." I dumped the wood on the hearth in a messy pile and walked to the couch, suddenly tired. She followed close behind me and took my hand as I sat with my head back, eyes closed.

"Simon, what?"

"I saw more things I don't understand," I said, blowing out my breath. "Some things I did, but I didn't like it."

"Was it bad?"

"I've never seen so much at one time before," I said, sitting up and leaning over to rest my elbows on my knees, cradling my throbbing head in my hands. She rested her hand lightly on my back. "How long was I gone?" I asked.

"Several minutes," she said, moving still closer to me. "I'm sorry, Simon. I didn't mean to be so difficult. I just—"

I waved my hand and shook my head, dismissing it.

"I didn't mean to upset you. I only wanted to stay here with you a while longer. I didn't mean to cause problems."

"Is that what you think?" I turned my head to look at her. "That you upset me and that's what caused this?" She cast her eyes down and nodded. "That has nothing to do with it," I said, taking her hand. "Nothing. Being upset doesn't bring on the visions. Nor does being happy or sad or scared. They just come. I told you that, Elizabeth. I've been dreaming like a fiend ever since we got here, and that has nothing to do with you either. "The breaker rocks near the ocean. How far are we from the ocean, Elizabeth?"

"About fifteen miles," she said. "Go on," she whispered after a moment.

"My visions used to be so clear. I would see people I knew, places I recognized."

"Is it because of me?" she asked. I sat back and looked at her curiously. Throbs of white pulsating light swirled around my vision. "Why would you ask that?"

"You said ever since you met me, your visions have gotten strange. I just thought maybe I was muddling them somehow."

"I don't see how that's possible." My eyes flickered up to her suddenly

"What else? You said there were several things."

I worried our time together was growing short, and I was desperate to change the fate of my visions. We needed to leave, but the raging storm outside prevented it. We were stuck there for the night. "More things I didn't understand. Why don't we leave in the morning?" I suggested with a pleading squeeze of her hand.

"What about all the people the sheriff showed our picture to?"

I nodded with a frown. It would be hard to travel in the daytime, at least for the next few days until we put enough distance between us. *Where were we, anyway?* I wondered.

"What town are we nearest to?" I asked.

"Rockport," she said. "Why?"

I dismissed it and thought again of the disturbing

visions.

"Are you positive your father won't say anything about us being here?" I asked, rolling my head over to look at her.

"Positive." I wondered how she could be so sure. As if reading my mind, she added, "My mother put him in a place like that after he came back from the war—when she had seen he had split. He hated her for it, for a time. Nothing they did helped. It was only after he got out and the local healer gave him something that he got better."

"How did he get out then? If he didn't get better?"

"He fooled them. We had a long talk about it once after we had realized I had the same problem." She looked down self-consciously. "His works a little differently, though. It's almost like they're friends. His other one..." She took a deep breath and shot me a nervous look.

"What, my love," I whispered, pushing a lock of hair behind her ear.

"His other one is named after his friend in the war. The one who saved his life. He died over there, and I think my daddy brought a piece of him back, inside his mind."

A cold shiver went up my spine, and the hair on the back of my neck stood on end, but I tried to maintain a blank face.

"So the other one took control in the hospital and started answering to Daddy's name. After a while, they saw there was only one, so they let him go."

There was a long quiet moment, and we listened to the wind battering the cabin, rattling the windows, and the trees groaning under the strain of the gusts.

"How did the healer help him?" I asked.

"Well, she calls herself a healer. I don't know that she

is though. She's part Indian or so she says. She doesn't really look it. She wears these feathers and charms around her neck and sometimes talks in a funny language. Says it's her ancestors tongue. I think it's gibberish."

I stood and added a few logs to the fire. They caught quickly and filled the room with a peaceful glow. Nervous as I was to stay, I was grateful we were here, warm and dry, instead of out there running wet through the woods. I spooned stew into mugs, cut fat slices of the bread she had smuggled out of her mother's kitchen, and brought it back to the couch while she talked.

"Most of the locals say she's nothing more than a crazy mess herself. For someone who claims to have a healing touch, she's always going to the town doctor with this ailment or that. I heard," she gave a short laugh and continued, "the doctor was so tired of it, he told her to just start healing herself." She snorted again then wiped the smile off her face. "I shouldn't laugh. It's sad, really," she said with reproach. "Anyway, she has connections for the medicine she sells through her husband. Her third husband," she said with raised eyebrows. "The other two died from too much of her medicine." She gave a disapproving sigh and continued. "Jan is able to get hold of big enough quantities so she can sell it to others and call herself a healer. After a few days, people want the stuff so badly, they don't care what she calls herself or what she is giving them as long as she keeps bringing it." She paused to take a few spoons of her stew.

"And she brought your father medicine that helped him?" I asked.

"I suppose. It keeps the other one away, but he still wasn't quite himself. He was either really happy or really angry as if he was in pain. Like I said, he and my mother fought about it a lot at first."

"Because he wanted it more than anything," I assumed. I had seen a man brought in for a morphine habit early in my stay at the hospital, and he wanted it more than he wanted to live. I never understood how something could have that deep a hold on a body, but I felt sorry for him.

"Daddy wanted to try the medicine on me, but my mother said no." Something in her voice hung in the air heavily, and I understood that part of the conversation was over. I set our mugs of stew on the floor in front of us, both our appetites gone. I leaned back and beckoned her to join me.

"What else did you see?" she asked, leaning over on my chest. I wrapped my arms around her tightly and kissed her hair.

"I don't want to talk about it," I said quietly.

The fire had warmed the room thoroughly, and with the excitement of the day, made us drowsy. It wasn't long before I heard the soft, even breathing of deep sleep from her and rested my head on hers, closed my eyes, and drifted off myself.

~ ~ ~

I'm not sure how long we had slept, but I came up off the couch violently, spilling Elizabeth onto the floor in a confused sprawling heap, the minute the door burst open suddenly and slammed against the wall behind it. We both yelled, and it wasn't until I got to the door, fire poker in hand, ready to fight, did I see it was just a wind gust that had thrown it open. I put my shoulder to the door, closing it against the hard gust that pushed back against me and then leaned against it, panting and wiping my face. I still shook with racing adrenaline as I took a few quick steps and helped Elizabeth off the floor, apologizing. She grabbed onto me, scared and shaking.

"It's all right. It was just the wind," I said. Then holding her head between my hands, I put my forehead to hers. "It's all right, we're safe," I whispered. She looked up at me with wide eyes and short gasping breaths of lingering fear and then kissed me suddenly. Taken aback for only a second, I gripped her waist and returned the urgency of her mouth. She pulled at my shirt, demanding to be let in. I slipped an arm under her legs and lifted her up in one strong sweep and began making my way blindly to the back room, never leaving her lips.

After depositing her on the bed rather unromantically, she watched me, unbuttoning her own shirt, as I ripped mine over my head and jerked the button on my pants. The zipper snagged, and I gave a short growl as I fought with it. It gave way with a rip of fabric and my pants fell away from my waist onto the floor. I stopped breathing when I looked at her, lying on her back in nothing but an open shirt, waiting impatiently for me. I almost choked as she ran her hands down the length of her own body in silent invitation. Fighting the urges of a body that wanted what it wanted, and wanted it now, I tried to be as graceful as I could, crawling across the bed toward her. She pulled me, her hands on the back of my neck, over her, and whispered between kisses.

"No one is going to ruin this for us this time, Simon," she whispered, taking a moment to lick the outline of my lips. I let out a ragged breath and kissed her neck and collarbone, hands urgently grabbing the length of soft curves under me.

"I need you, Simon," she said, struggling to control

the tremor in her voice. "We're alone, finally." I knew what she meant—the other one wouldn't interrupt us. There was no staff to worry about finding us and the storm outside would prevent the sheriff from actively searching.

"Alone," I whispered into the hollow of her throat. "I love that word." I felt the soft skin of her inner thighs slide up along mine, and they held my hips in a vise.

"We're never going to be more alone," she whispered with a smile.

If her words were going to be completely true, then I must ask you, dear reader, to leave the room as well, and leave Elizabeth and me to each other for the next several hours. At least.

~ ~ ~

I WOKE LATE the next morning and stretched, disentangling limbs and stray bedsheets. Daylight flooded the room from the small window above the bed and warm streaks of sunlight bathed our legs in warmth from the waist down. Elizabeth lay on her side in a deep, peaceful sleep. Lifting the hair away from her face, I watched her for a few minutes. Even though we were together now, and free, I couldn't help but add the image to my mental museum of beautiful stills of her. She moaned lightly, still asleep, and rolled to her back, the last of the quilt sliding off the side of the bed. I took my time appreciating the sight, my eyes rolling down her slowly until they stopped on the dark scar across her lower stomach, and I frowned. Lightly touching the thick line, I felt her hand rest on my head.

"Does it bother you?" she asked in a rough morning voice.

"No," I said, my eyes on the scar. "Not that you have it, only that they did it." I ran my hand slowly across her stomach to her waist and then around the soft curve of her hip and thigh, resting my head on her stomach. Her stomach growled loudly in my ear and I laughed.

"Hungry?" I asked. "I'll make us something to eat," I said before she had a chance to answer. I sat up and immediately felt her hands on my shoulders, pulling me back down. Only a few seconds into the kiss, we both recoiled from each other's foul morning breath, laughing.

"Okay, maybe you should make breakfast," she said with a giggle.

I slipped my pants on and walked out to the living area. Our dinner dishes were scattered, and the last of the stew had gone bad in the black pot hanging on a hook in the center of the fireplace. Digging around for the last of the embers from the night before, I noticed there wasn't enough firewood for breakfast and slipped my coat on to fetch more and to use the outhouse.

I opened the door, and the cold winter morning air caught in my throat. I froze, prickly fear running down my spine, as I saw the small basket of eggs and brown paper package beside it, then looked up and around in panic. The neglected lawn in front of the cabin lay frozen, undisturbed, and I could see no impressions of footprints on the frost covered wooden porch. I stood in the open doorway, chilly winter air filling the cabin, watching and listening for any sign of someone being near. *Not that we would have any time to do anything about it,* I thought. Elizabeth came up behind me with her arms wrapped around herself, shivering.

"Why are you standing there with the door open?" she asked.

"Shhh!" I hissed, not fully turning toward her. She

quickly sidled up next to me and saw the gift on the porch.

"Daddy must have left these," she said casually and bent to pick them up. I almost stopped her, thinking it a trap. She opened the paper and smiled. "Bacon," she said, holding it up to me. I tried to return the smile.

"He shouldn't have taken the chance of coming down here, Elizabeth. We should leave as soon as we're done eating." I didn't wait for her to object, I wouldn't let her this time. I closed the door behind me and walked nervously to the outhouse, scanning the landscape as I went.

Coming out, I heard a noise behind me and whirled around to see a beautiful tan doe foraging for something in the thin woods beside the outhouse. I let out a relieved breath and watched her for a moment until her ears twitched nervously, and she looked up at me with wide eyes. She suddenly bound three long leaps into the woods and disappeared. I began walking toward the house, and without warning, the whole world went black.

I saw dark swirling storm clouds, howling icy wind and small light snow began falling. I heard search dogs in the distance and deep voices yelling. My heart beat with fear as I watched myself being hunted by men with guns. I saw Elizabeth's eyes in front of me, wide with fear, wet with sadness, her mouth open in a scream I couldn't hear. Felt my arms nearly ripped from their sockets as they pulled me away from her, and I fought violently.

I came to sitting on the cold ground just as Elizabeth stepped outside the door to look for me. She ran over, barefoot and shivering, and pulled at my arm. I was tired and dizzy, but I stood and wobbled to the cabin and collapsed onto the couch.

"We have to leave today," I said breathlessly, rubbing

my aching eyes.

She nodded, frightened. "What did you see?"

"I saw them finding us. Hunting us. There was a storm though." I paused to look out the window at the clear blue sky, dotted with occasional billows of white clouds. "I think it will be tomorrow. We have to be far away from here by tomorrow."

"We will be," she said, nodding furiously. "We'll leave right after dinner." She kissed and hugged me briefly before turning to the fireplace to start breakfast.

A few minutes later, I crouched in front of the fire, slowly adding smaller logs and pushing around the glowing embers. I heard her yawn behind me, and I smiled to myself.

"I guess we didn't get much sleep last night, did we?" I turned with a sly grin, and she blushed deeply to the tips of her ears.

"No, we didn't," she said, holding my gaze. "We should take a nap before we go," she suggested though the twisted smile on her lips suggested anything but sleep.

I turned back to the fireplace, still smiling and ran my fingers through my messy morning hair, leaving it worse than before I touched it.

We ate breakfast quietly, not because of embarrassment or awkwardness, but simply being comfortable enough with each other to have long periods of silence, lost in our own thoughts, and occasionally looking up to smile at the other, eager to start our lives far from here.

We cleaned up from breakfast, occasionally stopping to share a kiss or erupt in a giggling outburst of gratuitous groping. When she caught her breath, and the giggles had subsided, she pecked me on the cheek.

"I'm going to go bathe," she said. I watched her go into the bedroom with a pot of hot water, closing the door behind her.

I busied myself, gathering things from around the cabin and packing David's bag full up with supplies we would need. The cabin was enveloped in silence, and I heard one of the floorboards creak in the bedroom. Unable to resist, I opened the door a crack, unashamedly peeking in. She stood naked in front of the washstand, holding a soapy cloth under her chin. She looked at me in the mirror and smiled unashamedly back at me. Peeling off my shirt as I walked toward her, I tossed it onto the bed and reached around her for the cloth. She leaned her head forward, moving her hair, and I washed her back slowly, occasionally dipping the cloth into the hot water. Small trails of water ran down her back and legs as I squeezed the cloth over her shoulders and kissed her neck. She reached for the cloth, but I held it out of her reach until she dropped her arm, and she watched me curiously in the mirror. I bathed her hips and legs slowly, my free hand following the cloth over the slick contours of her body before turning her to face me. She watched me without any describable expression. The water was cool by the time she took the cloth from me, having taken my time bathing her, but I barely noticed the chill as she began to do the same for me. She didn't turn me around but slid wet arms around my waist and washed my chest from behind, planting light kisses along my shoulders and back. One hand bathed while the other explored, feeling the swells and creases of every muscle in my chest and arms. When she did turn me around, she dropped the cloth onto the floor with a soggy plop and pushed me back toward the bed with a demanding kiss.

~ ~ ~

Sometime later, we lay tangled, groggy, and warm in the afternoon sun. Suddenly, she let out a laugh and snuggled into my arm. "Now you're going to have to bathe me again," she said teasingly.

"That would be my pleasure," I said. "Especially if your baths end like this." I rolled toward her, grabbing a handful of her bottom. She giggled and squirmed under my hands.

"We might get stuck in a vicious cycle," she said with a false pout of disapproval.

"And the problem with that?" I asked before kissing her again. The kiss, while deeply passionate, didn't progress to anything more, and I rolled her away from me and snuggled in close behind her.

"Let's get some sleep before tonight," I whispered. She nodded, and I felt her body slowly relax in my arms. "I love you," I said quietly just as she drifted off.

"I love you, too," she mumbled sleepily.

~ ~ ~

I WOKE TO the dim glow of evening, both excited and scared to set out on our journey. As the bags were mostly packed, we would eat a light dinner before. I was eager to go. I woke her slowly with a smothering cascade of kisses on her face, neck, and shoulders. She smiled as her eyes slowly opened and she stretched, arching her back with a sleepy grunt. I looked her over, very tempted to enjoy one last encounter before leaving the comfort of the cabin. I thought better of it, though, and rolled out of bed, gathering our clothes.

We readied ourselves with a growing sense of

anticipation and ate ham sandwiches together, standing against the short kitchen counter. We dressed in all of our layers, and I filled the canteen with water and set our bags by the door. There were three now, and I lifted each one, finding the lightest one and handed it to Elizabeth. I helped her fit it onto her back and gave her a quick kiss and a nervous smile. I opened the door and she stepped out before me. I hoisted the heavy bags up, adjusting them.

Three steps away from the door, we heard them—the deep aggressive growling and barking of a dozen search dogs in the distance. I looked up and realized the dim haze was not that of early evening, but of a sunless sky. The light was mostly blocked by a wall of black roiling clouds that barreled toward us. A sudden gust of icy wind slammed against me, stinging my eyes, making my lungs ache.

Elizabeth shot me a panicked look, and I scanned the landscape quickly. I saw two cars with single red flashing lights atop racing toward us. The dirt plumes billowing behind them told me they were in a hurry to get here. I saw Elizabeth's mother out of the corner of my eye, standing silent and straight-faced, staring at me from a safe distance. Elizabeth saw her and clung to my arm, terrified.

"Run!" I jumped off the porch, dragging her behind me. We were slowed down by the heavy bags, and I took hers off her back, mid-run, and slung it over my shoulder. We dashed into the woods, whose small dead trees and short shrubs provided little cover. Jumping over fallen logs and deep pits, we dodged thorny bushes and ragged stumps until we came to a dead stop, seeing three men one hundred feet ahead of us—one on horseback, the other two holding the reins of the pack of dogs.

They spotted us, and I jerked her arm and ran to the east, and I dropped two of our bags so we could pick up more speed. She looked back at them nervously, and I pulled her along, commanding her to move faster.

As we came out of the woods, there was a clearing and her house lay beyond. Several cars were parked in the yard, and I could hear her father yelling in the distance. We ducked back into the woods and I stopped again, listening. It sounded like we would be running straight toward the snarling dogs, and my mind raced, trying to figure out which direction to go. I felt all turned around in my panic and started running blindly. After just a few moments, the cabin came into view, and I held back a fear-stricken scream. We had made a full circle. I could see them closing in on three sides.

We were trapped. I grabbed Elizabeth and hugged her tight.

"I'm so sorry," I said with a hard lump in my throat, and I watched them inch closer, now only a few hundred feet away. "When we get out again, we'll meet here," I gasped frantically and held her head so she couldn't look away. "I'll find you, Elizabeth. I promise." I kissed her, hard and desperate, and then began rattling off everything I had seen, fragments of visions I didn't understand. "You're going to be home soon. You'll be free and I'll be with you, eventually. There is going to be a man. I'm going to bring him to you, and, somehow, he is going to bring you back to me." I took a few gasping breaths. "I don't understand how, but..." I looked over her shoulder. They were so close now. I hugged her so tight she could scarcely breathe. I couldn't think in my panic and kissed her one last time. "I'll come back for you, Elizabeth. I swear I'll come for you."

I held her eyes as hands grabbed my arms, wrenching

me away from her. She began screaming and crying, fighting off the orderlies. They pulled me in one direction and her in another. I watched her, writhing and screaming. They dragged her past her mother, who took two steps back as they passed to the waiting car.

"I hate you!" she screamed, repeatedly at the top of her lungs. She coughed violently, gagging, and spit blood on the ground in front of her before resuming screaming hateful things at her mother.

I hung my head in defeat, sadness, and fear, and I stopped fighting. They threw me in the back of a small truck with metal bars between the driver and the cold empty compartment. I sat on the protruding wheel well with my head in my hands, reliving the last few surreal moments. Lifting my head, I saw the orderly on the passenger side eying me cautiously, and I turned away to hide the anger and frustration I was choking back. Out the small windows of the back doors, I saw an identical black truck close behind us and, through the windshield, I could see Elizabeth thrashing around violently—enough to make the truck often swerve a few inches to each side.

My mind raced, trying in vain to find a solution, but there was none to be had. We would go back, they would keep us apart until they transferred me and knowing what we would have to do, bide our time, play their game and endure a hellishly long separation, sent one last surge of anger through me.

The truck took a hard right turn, and I went sprawling off the wheel well, scraping my arm and slamming my head. I scrambled to my knees, holding it, growling, and cursing while the goose egg formed under my hands above my temple.

Adding pain to anger and frustration, I let loose and pounded the metal wall with both fists in rage. The driver turned and yelled something at me, but I didn't hear him and wouldn't have cared if I had.

Only ten minutes separated me from my Elizabeth, and my whole body ached—my fingers to touch her, my lips to kiss her, and my arms to hold her. I'm glad I didn't know, as the tall iron gates to the hospital grounds opened, just how long our separation would be.

ILLUSIONS

I RECOGNIZED THE two orderlies who pulled me out of the truck. They walked me through several locked doors, and I could hear Elizabeth's screams echoing behind me. The last door opened to the wing I was all too familiar with. I saw Ronnie huddled against the wall, not knowing whether to laugh or cry, and a few others stared at me in what seemed like a mix of awe for escaping and pity for being caught.

Passing the nurses station, and with the orderlies iron grips on each of my arms, I saw David's head bent over his paperwork. I could tell he struggled to compose his expression when he looked up at me, and he did a good job. Except for the eyes. It was indescribable, the look, but it was enough to make a grown man cry, and I looked away quickly. They had sedated her, or so I guessed, as her distant screams became weaker and further apart. We turned the corner, and I stopped cold.

The doctor stood with his hands behind his back, looking none too happy. A cold ball of dread formed in the pit of my stomach. It hadn't occurred to me until that moment a treatment would most certainly be in order.

The doctor gave a sharp nod toward the treatment room. With nothing to lose, I fought and kicked with all my strength, growling obscenities through clenched teeth. Two more orderlies aided in the submission, and they strapped me to the table. I prayed they would sedate me so at least I wouldn't feel the first white hot jolt. No such luck, though as the doctor stood at my head, trying to strap the prongs on, cursing under his breath as they slipped off the blood-filled lump on my head.

He leaned over my face, letting one prong slip over my ear. "We'll just talk about all this when you wake up, Simon."

And then he flipped the switch. The first shuddering pain didn't knock me out, and I vaguely remember screaming through it. The second made me feel as though my head were detached from my body, and the third brought vivid hallucinations and visions of past, present, and future events. I felt like my head was being ripped in half as one vision after another flashed in front of me, pictures passing by too fast for me to grasp their meanings or details. The last sensation before blessed unconsciousness was of my whole body being turned inside out, from the bottom up. My eyes dissolved, and the hallucinations continued in vivid colors and bright flashing lights, as I saw myself squeezing through the sockets where my eyes had once been. My body went limp, and the voices around me were distant and garbled. I welcomed the darkness with open arms.

~ ~ ~

WHEN I WOKE, I was still on the treatment table. I was unstrapped, covered, and the door had been left open. I didn't feel the pain in my head and legs until I thought about it, and even then, it wasn't as bad as it usually was. I swung my legs off the table, took a deep breath, and stood up. Peeking outside the room, the place looked deserted.

Glancing at the clock, I could see why. It was after eleven at night. I made my way down the hall to my room, passing David, who said nothing to me as I passed. I found my room locked and yanked on it in frustration. I wanted nothing more than to lie down and see Elizabeth's face behind my eyes. I walked back to the nurses station and plopped my arms down on the counter to get his attention.

"David, can you let me into my room, please?" I asked. He shook his head slowly and didn't look up at me as he spoke. "Afraid I can't do that, Simon. They filled your room."

"Filled it? What am I supposed to do?"

"You can wait in the commons area," he said with a nod, and I caught sight of his tired red-rimmed eyes. I walked into the darkened commons room and could make out the couch in the moonlight. I sat back with my arm over my eyes and summoned my images. I heard a faint sniffle and a soft moan, and my eyes popped open. I sat up, looked around, but could see nothing in the darkness. Taking long frightened strides to the door, I flipped on the light and saw her. Not my Elizabeth, but another girl with stringy light-brown hair. I could see bony shoulders sticking through the thin hospital gown, and rail thin arms hung at her sides. She hung her head and her hair fell around her face. Outlines of the knobby bones of her spine protruded out grotesquely.

"Are you new here?" I asked. She made no acknowledgment as she lifted her emaciated hands, paper-thin skin, and blue fingernails, dropping them on the table silently. "I'm Simon," I said with a shaky voice, walking slowly around the table.

Her face shocked me—sunken eyes ringed in black, skeletal cheekbones jutting out beneath tightly drawn skin, and gray lips. All the bones of her sternum and ribs protruded out from her flat chest. She stared at me with dark, hollow, hate-filled eyes. I ran out of the room, blindly through the men's hall, but couldn't find David and doubled back. I shot through the commons area, blinding my eyes to the frail terrifying girl at the table, and then bound down the women's hall, calling for Loretta. She sat at a small table, bent over a book, and ignored me. I caught movement out of the corner of my eye and followed it into a dark room at the end of the hall. I peeked in and saw another woman clad only in a surgical gown standing in the middle of the room, staring at me while clutching her stomach.

"Have you seen my baby?" she asked in an airy voice. Her eyes were sunken so deep into her skull I couldn't see the whites of them. She cried, but no tears fell from her eyes. I stood motionless, terrified. I knew her.

"I know you. You're dead," I whispered, shook my head, and stepped back into the light of the doorway. "When they took you away and sterilized you, you died during it, months ago." She watched me as if she couldn't hear me, shook her head, then slowly looked down.

"My God," I whispered. "Were you pregnant when they..."

Her face crumpled in anguished pain, and she let out an unearthly cry, bending at the knees as dark blood began to seep through the front of her gown and dripped to the floor, a thick and sticky splattering sound, forming puddles on and around her feet.

I turned and ran.

I nearly threw myself on the desk, gasping for air, trembling with fear. "David, you gotta help me," I panted. "This last treatment...it did something." I held my head in my hands and took a deep breath. "I'm seeing things. Not...not like before," I pleaded, holding my hands out for emphasis. "I'm seeing—"

"You're not seeing anything I wouldn't expect you to see, Simon," he said, finally looking up at me. His eyes were bloodshot and slightly swollen, and it dawned on me that it might be for some other reason besides lack of sleep. "Hurts like hell to come through the eyes, don't it?" he asked.

I stared at him with my mouth hanging open. "How did you know what I felt?"

"The eyes are the windows to the soul."

I waited for him to say something that made sense.

"You're dead, Simon," he said finally, his voice breaking slightly over my name. My stunned gaze didn't change, and I waited for him to say something more. He stared at me in all seriousness.

"No. No, David, I can't be dead. You can see me. You're talking to me, for Christ's sake!" I took a step back, shaking my head. "That last treatment messed up my head, but—"

"That last treatment killed you, Simon."

I was right. He had been crying.

He pointed down the hall to the treatment room.

I walked slowly and heard his footsteps behind me, surprisingly light for a man so formidable.

I looked inside without entering the room and saw

my sheet-covered body on the table. I turned and threw my back against the wall, hyperventilating. Slowly, I slid down the wall in a heap, cradling my head, trying to make sense of it all.

"You can see me," I repeated. "I'm right here. I can't be dead."

"Only by the grace of God am I not strapped to a bed in a place like this myself, Simon. If they knew about my gift, I'd be slapped crazy and locked away," he said in a low voice.

"Your gift?"

"That's what I prefer to call it," he said as he sat against the wall next to me. He pulled one knee up and laced his fingers around it. "Why do you think I was the only one here who knew you weren't crazy?" he asked, rolling his bald head toward me. "We're not so different, you and me. I can just hide mine better," he said apologetically.

He was silent for several moments, and as the shock and disbelief began to settle, I felt a thick swelling in the center of my chest, grieving for myself. It crept up into my throat, and I wanted to cry but seemed to lack the ability.

"How could I possibly be dead and not know it?" I asked.

"It's the ones who stay who don't know for a bit," he explained. "I take it you saw some of our former residents who have also chosen to stay?"

"The one who starved and the one who died in surgery," I said with a shudder. "God, I've never been so scared," I said with tightly shut eyes.

"They can't hurt you, you know," he said. "A few of them might act like they will, but you can't feel pain." I opened my mouth to argue, but he continued. "You're remembering the pain. There are emotions connected with painful moments, and that's what you feel. All you're capable of feeling now are emotions. Fear, anger, happiness, love."

Elizabeth's face flooded my mind with a fresh deep ache, stronger than when I realized I was dead.

"Can I see her?" I asked with my eyes still closed.

"You can see her anytime you want now, Simon."

I sat on the side of her bed and stared down at her sleeping face. "Does she know?"

"No. She's been asleep since shortly after she got here."

I reached out to touch her and then hesitated.

"You can," David said. "Though she can't feel it. Most she'll feel is a light breeze or a tickle, like when a fly lands on your arm." She was lying on her back with her arms at her sides, tied at the wrists to straps on the bed. I tried to touch her, but my fingers went through her hand, leaving a trail of faint golden sparks like the last traces of fireworks.

"You'll learn," David said softly.

"I'll learn what?"

"How to touch her. How to let her know you're still here."

I felt the urge to clear my throat and blink hard. I leaned forward, running a finger over the back of her hand, watching the shimmering light scatter, and gracefully slide down the contours of her hand until they disappeared.

"I thought you said I couldn't feel pain," I said in a quiet, choked voice.

~ ~ ~

LATER, I SAT in a chair next to David at the desk. I watched the second hand do a slow, circular sweep several times before I asked my next question.

"Are there many who chose to stay?"

"Five or six."

"Why?"

"They all have their reasons."

"And the ones who don't choose to stay?" I was curious if he knew what came after this.

"They leave. Though, not right away." I looked at him, confused. "It's hard to explain. It's better if you see it," he added.

"Can she hear me?" I asked after a moment.

"Not how you think of hearing. When you say something to her, it simply registers as a passing thought or a memory. Sometimes, it's a warm feeling that washes over a body when they think of something they love."

"What am I?" I asked. "Am I a ghost or an angel or what?"

"A little of both, I think," he stated simply.

"And I guess I'm doomed to walk these halls forever." I blew out my breath and looked around.

"Not forever, Simon."

"How long then?"

"Only you know when it's time to leave," he said.

"And when I know, what do I do? Knock? Ask? Pray... what?"

"You'll see," he said, glancing up at the clock. Five minutes to midnight.

"Can you see through me?" I felt stupid for asking, but that had always been my notion of ghosts. Translucent.

"No," he said. "To me, you look very much the same as you did before. Only there's a soft glow all around the edges and on everything you touch."

I looked down at my hand, turning it over and back. To me, it looked how my hand had always looked. I spent the next few minutes touching various objects, watching the beautiful traces of light sizzle over each object. There was a small chime as the clock struck midnight. I felt a small vibration all around me and looked at David with concern. He stood up slowly and nodded toward the blank gray wall of the hallway across from us.

"What's going on?" I asked, glancing at the plain wall and back.

"You wanted to know how you go, when it's time," he said, not taking his eyes off the wall. He stood up, put his hands behind his back, and lowered his head but continued to watch with his eyes. I watched the aged plaster wall across from us as the center of it began to soften, dissolve, and then slowly swirl counterclockwise. Starting with a light only the size of a pinpoint in the center, the grey wall gave way to a brilliant white burst of light, slowly stretching open wide enough for a grown man to easily walk through. The thick gray and white marbled ring around the opening churned and swelled as if straining to hold the portal open.

Craning my neck with my face frozen in awe, it seemed like the white tunnel went on forever and was almost too bright to look directly into. I watched in wonder as a man walked silently down the hall toward the portal near us. He was tall and thin and wore normal clothes and no expression. Trailing his hand along the wall as he walked, gold and silver sparks bounced against the wall, over his hand and down, evaporating before they hit the ground. He stopped at the opalescent gateway and took a deep breath as if making his final decision. Then, without a word or a look back, he stepped through. He evaporated into a sizzling shower of golden embers as he crossed from this world and then the portal collapsed.

"It's beautiful, isn't it?" he asked. David sat down slowly.

I nodded, still too stunned to speak.

"Every night at the stroke of midnight this portal opens and you have the choice to leave," he explained. "I always stand out of respect."

"That's what you meant when you said they don't leave right away," I said quietly.

"Yes. Most folks have at least a little business to take care of before they go, and they are allowed that time."

"Did you know him?" I asked.

"Yes. He didn't like to talk much. He was killed near here, but it didn't have anything to do with the hospital or the patients. He came here because, often times, they're attracted to the lights and activities of the living. He's wandered around here for the last couple weeks, but I'm glad he finally decided to go," he said.

"Attracted to lights?" I asked, almost amused. "I always thought ghosts liked the dark deserted places."

"No," he hesitated. "Not all of them." There was something ominous in his voice, but I'd had my daily allotment of bizarre already and decided to leave it alone.

"I'm so tired," I said, rubbing my eyes.

"After something as powerful as you just experienced, it doesn't surprise me," he said, shuffling his paperwork. "Mind, you're only emotionally tired. You can't feel physically tired, of course. But you can still sleep. And dream, so I'm told," he said.

I wanted to sleep and even more, dream. Relive those few days with her.

"I want you to be the one to tell her," I said softly.

"Can you do that for me, David?"

"I'll see what I can do," he said with a solemn nod.

I walked to the commons area and lay down on the couch. The starving girl was gone, but I left the lights on regardless and covered my eyes with my arm. I dreamed so vividly it was hard to identify the line between the living, the dead, and the imaginary.

~ ~ ~

THE NEXT MORNING, I stood against the wall next to David as they wheeled the stretcher past me, taking my covered body away. I rolled my head over to David.

"That's really kind of disgusting. They left me there all night."

He gave a tiny nod, and I realized he couldn't answer me now that we were surrounded by staff and residents. The place was crawling with police and state investigators and the doctor rushed past us toward his office. I pushed off the wall and followed him.

He bent over, fumbling around in his file cabinet. He seemed nervous, and as I took a step closer, I could see beads of sweat forming on his forehead. He stood abruptly and was nearly nose-to-nose with me. I looked into his wrinkled, panicked face and realized he was only concerned for his own hide, not my death, or Elizabeth's pain. I had never hated anyone more in my life. He sat down with a thump at his desk and began scribbling. I ground my teeth, realizing I was capable of a full range of feelings, fury at the top of the list at that moment.

"Do you have any idea how much I hate the sound of that pen?" I said.

He stopped, wiped his brow, and then bent his head, continuing. "Do you have any idea how much I hate you?"

I said in a low hissing voice. I saw a visible shudder go through him and hoped he'd heard me, even if he dismissed it as his own paranoid thought. "I think I'm going to have fun with you," I said sarcastically.

I leaned close to the side of his head, right next to his ear.

"*Boo!*" I said and his hand jumped, causing the end of his signature to extend further than normal. I hopped up on the file cabinet with an amused smile and sat crossed legged, looking down on him. "Well, now I know how I'm going to pass the time while Elizabeth is sleeping, don't I?"

The state investigators were growing impatient and took the doctor's written statement from his trembling hand with a jerk. They took a small file, which the doctor identified as mine, throwing an ominous, "We'll be in touch," as they left. He sat down with his head in his hands and took several deep breaths before a nurse poked her head in the door.

"Doctor, Mr. Sinclair is here to see you," she said quietly.

The doctor raised his head and inhaled deeply. He moved things around on his desk anxiously. "Send him in, please," he said.

"Oh, yeah. You have to explain to my father why I'm dead." I laughed without humor. "Boy, I wouldn't want to be in your shoes right now. That's the downside of absolute power, Doc. Having to take responsibility for abusing it."

My sarcastic harassment ended abruptly when my father walked in the door, kneading his hat between his hands. His eyes were bloodshot, and I smelled the faint scent of whiskey from across the room.

Suddenly, the doctor wasn't the only one I was

infuriated with.

"What happened to my boy?" he asked with a warbling voice. I flew off the file cabinet and was by his head in an instant.

"You killed me just as much as he did, Dad," I seethed. "You didn't believe me about Mom, and you let her go riding. I saw that horse throw her and watched her die, but you didn't listen to me. You wrote me off as crazy. Now she's dead and so am I, and you're all alone, you superstitious old bastard." He lowered his head and his clenched jaw trembled.

"Please, sit, Mr. Sinclair," the doctor invited.

"I don't even want to hear what pathetic excuse you're going to give him," I said as I walked to the door. I paused and turned back with an angry smile. "I'll be in touch."

~ ~ ~

I STOOD IN Elizabeth's doorway, watching her. She was still asleep. A nurse came in behind me, lifted her wrist, took her pulse, and then left. I spent the rest of the afternoon sitting by her bed, touching her face, outlining it in a shower of white gold. I talked to her the whole time and hoped my words would somehow materialize in her dreams.

She stirred, approaching consciousness sometime near evening. It took a long time to rise above the medicine's powerful effect. She turned her head with fluttering eyes, moaned, and then slipped back under several times. Part of me wanted her to stay there in her dream world, safe from the pain. But a selfish part of me wanted to see her eyes and hear her voice. I leaned over her, staring straight down into her face.

"Elizabeth," I whispered. Her eyes fluttered and then slowly cracked open. She stared right through me at the ceiling as reality came back to her, and she closed her eyes again, sighing deeply. Thick tears seeped from the corners of each eye, down the side of her face and onto the pillow. I tried to wipe them away, but couldn't make the connection—my fingertips sunk into her shimmering cheek.

There was a stirring at the door and I turned to see Loretta, David, and the doctor. Another nurse loomed behind them, presumably prepared with a needle in hand. Loretta's face was pained as she untied Elizabeth's wrists and helped her up to a sitting position. She sat silently by her side, rubbing a hand over her back.

"Elizabeth, there's something we need to tell you," she said. After rubbing her eyes and pushing the hair out of her face, Elizabeth looked at Loretta blankly. David sat on the end of her bed and put a hand on her shin. The doctor stood in the doorway, staring at the floor like the coward he was.

"I'm so sorry to have to tell you this, Elizabeth," she started and glanced at David hesitantly. I felt a choking sensation in my throat, and my eyes burned dry. "Something's happened, honey. Simon was taken in for a treatment, and it didn't go well," she said, misty-eyed herself.

Elizabeth waited with her hands lying limp in her lap.

"Simon is dead, Elizabeth. I'm so sorry," she whispered, and a tear slipped down her cheek despite her efforts to hide them. David's hand lifted toward his wife, but remembering, folded his arms, unable to comfort her in public.

After they had left her, Elizabeth held a catatonic stare for almost an hour. Her eyes were empty and dull, her mouth closed in a flat line. She stayed so still it was hard to see if she was even breathing. I sat in front of her and tried to put my forehead to hers. I held my cupped hands between us to catch the steady shower of golden light.

Nurses went in and out, checking on her, waiting for the break. I had stepped out of the room a while later to try to talk to David when I heard the blood-curdling scream from her room. A half-dozen nurses and orderlies went running, me in front of them. My heart ached at the sight of her, holding her head over her knees, loud sobs broken up by unintelligible screeching. David held his arm out keeping everyone away, only permitting Loretta to pass. She gathered her up and hugged her tightly, trying to quiet the screams. I slid down the wall and watched, helplessly.

Little by little, her wails subsided as Loretta rocked her, whispering what comforts she could. She rested her head on Loretta's shoulder with her hair covering her face.

Suddenly, she was silent and very still. She pulled herself away from Loretta and sat on the side of the bed with her head hanging forward. She took several deep shuddering breaths and then was still again.

When she lifted her head, it wasn't my Elizabeth's face I was looking at. The spectators in the room took a step back with an audible collective gasp. The doctor whispered feverishly to the nurse next to him.

It was rare-to-never to actually witness someone's fragile mind as it cracked, giving birth to a new personality. I shuddered with fear, anger and protective, unconditional love.

There was three of her now.

She came off the bed like a feral animal, shrieking

and flailing her fists at everyone. David watched me with pity as I turned and walked out of the room when they held her down and a brave nurse pushed her way to the front of the crowd. And then she was quiet again.

~ ~ ~

I wandered the halls aimlessly for several days with a heavy feeling of heartache and helplessness. I found myself sitting in the doctor's leather office chair, feet up on the desk and staring out the window. It was the only one in the place without bars. I looked over his bookshelf of psychology texts and a wall full of fancy degrees. My eyes fell on his ink pen, neatly arranged on the right side of the desk. I grinned to myself when I got the idea and went to look for David for help. I found him in the supply room. "Hey, Simon," he said with his back turned before I said anything.

"How do you do that?" I asked.

"What can I do for you?" he asked. He turned to me, smiling.

"You said I would learn to touch her. What about other things. Can I *move* things?" I asked.

"You can, once you learn how."

"Is it hard?"

"Not usually, but some of them never get the hang of it," he said. "We can practice that later tonight."

"Working a double shift again?" I said, sitting on top of the dirty linen hamper. He nodded and yawned on cue.

"I don't know if you noticed several of the staff have walked out, after what happened to you and then after word got around about Elizabeth. And, of course, there's the investigation no one wants any part of." He looked at me as if he wanted to say more, but was anxious about it.

"What, David?"

"Well, I don't know if you want to know." He puffed out his cheeks and blew air out slowly.

"Does it have to do with me or Elizabeth?" I asked, and he nodded quickly and looked back at the supply shelf. "Then, of course, I want to know."

He looked uncomfortable when he faced me. "Your father is burying you this afternoon," he said.

I stiffened and the light smirk fell from my face. "Where?"

"Town cemetery. That's what I heard, anyway."

I slid off the hamper and turned. "Thanks," I said as I left.

~ ~ ~

I STOOD SEVERAL feet away from my father, who cried silently as the priest performed the ritual of words, some clear, some mumbled, sprinkling water around the opening in the ground. Two strangers helped lower the box, but I didn't watch them. I stared at my father instead. His face was so anguished it was hard to hold onto my anger at him.

I said a silent goodbye, leaving him to what peace he could find, trailing my hand over the rounded top of my mother's gravestone as I went.

~ ~ ~

LATE THAT NIGHT, I sat next to David at the desk. Another orderly who kept walking by, trying to make conversation with David, interrupted our lesson several times. He was a new hire named Greg, scrawny with stringy blond hair and bad teeth. I sat back and regretted not being able to cry because I was bored to tears listening to the rambling fool try to impress David for nearly an hour with details of his sordid past.

David finally sent him away, claiming to have an overwhelming amount of paperwork. Once safely alone, he put a pencil in front of me.

"Try to push that away from you," he said. I put out a finger and tried, but every attempt ended with my finger going through it. "Concentrate on moving it, but not with the muscles in your hand. Use the muscles in your mind," he said, tapping his temple. I was still confused when I tried and failed again. David sat back deep in thought. "When you first came out of the treatment room, you tried to open your door," he said.

"And it felt the same as it always did," I said, still pushing through the pencil with a frown.

"How did you feel?" he asked, swiveling in his chair slightly.

"Tired. Sad. But mostly, I think I just didn't know I was dead."

"Play around with different emotions until you find one that works," he suggested.

After an hour of aggravating failure, I was exasperated.

"I can't do this, David," I said with a huff and threw myself back into the chair. It rolled a few inches and I looked down, surprised.

"You just did," he said, grinning. I leaned over the desk and repeatedly tried , until I found the one feeling that moved the pencil an inch away from me. Determination.

After a while, I had moved it small distances several times and felt very tired from concentrating.

"You've got time to practice," David said. I stood and

stretched.

"I'm going to Elizabeth's room," I said. He put up a hand as I walked away. Rounding the corner, I saw someone standing outside her door, peering in the small window. It was Greg, who looked over both shoulders and then opened the door quietly. I broke into a run and saw him approaching her sleeping form slowly. I jumped through him, whirled around, and stood between them.

"Stay away from her, you sleazy bastard," I seethed. His gaze went through me, staring intently at Elizabeth's face. I growled and balled my fist up, sending it through his head with an explosion of sparks. I repeatedly tried, grunting with every swing but couldn't make contact. He took a step closer, moving through me, and I ran into the hallway.

"David!" I screamed. I looked back to see Greg inching closer to Elizabeth and screamed down the hall again with all of my mind's strength. I ran down the hall to find him and ran straight through him as he came running around the corner.

"Elizabeth!" I panted, pointing to her room. "Help her!" He ran and stomped into the room. Greg froze with one edge of her blanket in his hand and looked up at David, startled.

"What are you doing in here?" David asked.

"I heard something." He dropped the corner of the blanket and squirmed. "I was just checking on her."

"That's what our female nurses are for, Greg. You should have called one of them."

"You don't believe him, do you, David?" I asked. David gave an indiscernible shake of the head.

"Oh," he said, looking enlightened. "Okay, next time, I'll just do that," he said with a bob of the head. He took a step to leave the room, but David cut him off.

"Hit him, David," I said, wishing to God that I could beat him to death with my bare hands. "Bash his head in," I growled while I paced the small room. Instead, David inched forward with a fierce expression until Greg was pressed against the wall. He put his hands on each side of Greg's head and leaned down so close I could barely see any light between their noses.

"Let me make something perfectly clear, Greg," he spoke.

"Hit him," I repeated.

"The last orderly who liked to take advantage of our patients didn't last very long here. He had a little accident." Greg's eyes widened as he tried to press himself further into the wall. David lowered his voice to a whisper. *"And they still haven't found the body."* He broke into a sadistic grin. "And they won't find yours, neither." Sweat popped up on Greg's forehead and he nodded silently.

"Please, David. Just once. You know what he came in here to do!"

Without warning, David planted an iron fist in the pit of Greg's stomach. He slid to the floor in a gasping heap, and David pushed him roughly with his foot.

"Get out of here," he said. "And don't you never let me catch you in here again."

He continued to *help* Greg down the hall with his foot while I waited by her door.

"Thank you," I breathed when he returned, glancing back at Elizabeth in the bed. "I don't know what I would have done if you hadn't been here," I said, running a hand over my face. "I have no way to protect her." I looked away, angry at my helplessness.

"Practice," he said firmly. He held out a pencil. "So you can protect her." I held my hand out and pictured myself beating the degenerate that almost had his hands on my Elizabeth. He slowly set it in my hand, and it didn't fall through. I could learn this, after all. I found the emotions that controlled objects. The part of me that was protective of her and possessive of us. I looked up at David with a triumphant smile. I rattled off a list of things for David to bring me, and I sat at the desk the rest of the night practicing and perfecting the skill.

I lay down next to Elizabeth just before dawn. I blew and the ends of her hair scattered over her shoulder. I smiled and rested my head next to hers. "I'll kill anyone who tries to hurt you," I promised her for the second time and closed my eyes.

She stirred just before lunch, swaying slightly as she sat on the side of her bed. I touched her arm, this time feeling soft skin instead of sinking through it. She scratched at the spot lazily and then stood, knocked on her door and waited with her head against the wall for someone to let her out. I followed her out of her room, waited outside the bathroom and then walked next to her to the commons area. She sat with a thud, sprawling her arms out on the table in front of her. The nurse put a tray of food down, and she picked and pushed, but didn't eat.

"You should eat," I said. After a moment, she put a small bite in her mouth and chewed in slow motion.

~ ~ ~

LATER, I SAT next to her in the doctor's office. He paced behind his desk a few lengths before speaking.

"Who am I speaking to?" he asked politely.

"Elizabeth," she said, gripping the arms of the chair and staring straight ahead.

"I'd like to talk about when you escaped with Simon,"

he said.

"I don't want to talk about that," she said with a stone face.

"I need to know how you got out," he explained.

"Don't tell him. Don't, Elizabeth. No matter what he says."

"I don't remember," she said calmly, raising her eyes to him.

"I think you might not be telling me the truth, Elizabeth. Now, I understand you've gone through quite a shock recently." He looked down and fumbled with the edge of his white coat. "But in order to protect the community, we need to know how you got out."

"I told you, I don't remember," she said, then smiled. "I wasn't born yet," she said calmly.

The doctor looked visibly rattled. "I thought I was talking to Elizabeth," he said.

"You are."

"But if you were just born recently?"

"My name is Elizabeth," she insisted.

"Can I talk to the other Elizabeth?" he asked.

"No."

"Can I talk to him?" he asked.

"No." Elizabeth smiled slyly. I felt panic roll through me. For a moment, I thought the doctor meant me. But he meant her other one. The original other one. I had suspected it was male from our brief encounter at the cabin. The deep voice, eager to fight, but I wasn't sure.

"Please?" the doctor said as if talking to a stubborn child.

"You can only talk to me," she said with a teasing grin and a tilt of her head. "The others can't come out and play right now."

"Where are the others right now?" he asked,

scratching at the notepad in his lap.

"Sleeping," she said, dropping the smile. They had sat in a silent standoff for several minutes before he dismissed her. The nurse escorted her out, but I stayed.

"This is all your fault, you know," I told him. "Did you know the other one only came out once the whole time we were together? Of course, you don't, because you shocked the shit out of me before asking any questions. She was normal out there with me," I said, staring out the window. "You ruined everything and now she's worse," I said, feeling the sudden urge to throw something at him, now that I had the ability to. But David had warned me to be subtle. I walked to the wall directly across from his desk. A crucifix hung in the center, surrounded by his degrees and awards.

I leaned one shoulder against the wall and watched him for a moment. He was certainly stressed, visibly affected by what had recently happened. I wondered how much was remorse and how much was self-preservation. I reached up and touched the bottom tip of the cross. I pushed it an inch away from me then let go, letting it swing lightly against the wall. The doctor stopped writing and looked up just as it came to a stop. I pushed again, harder this time and it scraped against the wall several times like a pendulum, and then slowed to a stop, centering itself. He watched it with a gaping mouth, then gathered his papers hastily with shaking hands and ran out of the room.

"Might wanna ask for something to help with those hallucinations, Doc," I called out after him and then walked to his desk, randomly pushing his perfectly arranged things around with the tip of my finger. My hand hovered over his annoying pen and I smiled. I opened the top drawer, took out all the pens, and systematically drained each one of its ink, right into the seat of his chair. *Not very ghoulish, but fun,* I thought to myself with a shrug.

~ ~ ~

The days quickly fell into a dull and familiar monotony. I stayed by Elizabeth's side much of the time and talked to her as she drifted asleep, hoping to bring her to the surface, even just for a few moments. It became clear, day after day in the doctor's office, a stronger fraction of Elizabeth held control now, and she would not relinquish it for anything. She was very powerful, determined, and calculated. She rarely lost control physically and talked the doctor in circles until he was so confused, he dismissed her.

She was in the office the morning he sat in the puddle of ink in his chair, his white coat wicking it up into a black spot on his backside. She laughed uncontrollably, and when he confronted her as to whether she had anything to do with it, she simply flashed a wicked smile and raised her eyebrows. It unnerved him to no end.

I *almost* felt sorry for him. But not enough to keep me from sitting in his office every day between patients to remind him of all the destruction he had caused in the name of mental health. Every now and then, I would move something so subtlety he assumed his mind was playing tricks on him.

After about a week, I watched him pull out a small bottle from his bottom drawer and pour two pills into his shaking hand. He threw his head back with the glass of water and then waited with head on folded arms for the pills to take effect.

"I think I'm really starting to get to him," I told

Elizabeth with a laugh as I lay next to her that night. "He's on edge all the time. He deserves it, the controlling bastard. I saw him taking pills, and I heard one of the staff say he will be turning in his resignation." I watched her face as it stared blankly at the ceiling. "Don't worry about the next doctor," I told her, ever so lightly moving a few strands of hair out of her face. "If this next one isn't good to you, I'll scare him away, too."

She took a deep breath and sighed, rolling over toward me. "Close your eyes," I whispered. After a few seconds, she did. "I wonder if that's just coincidence," I said with a light laugh. She opened them again, staring through my head. "Close your eyes," I repeated. She did. "Can I talk to my Elizabeth?" She made a light noise with a small headshake, snuggling deeper under the covers. "I'm not trying to take you out of control, Elizabeth. I just want to talk to her. Just for a minute, please?" I touched her face and she felt it, scrunching up her nose. When she opened her eyes, they were soft and familiar. Her face shifted to sadness and pain. Tears welled up in her eyes.

"I miss you," she whispered aloud, closing her eyes quickly. Her face dissolved, and I watched her go back to the safe recesses of her mind.

"I miss you, too." I wanted more time with her, but I wanted to gain the stronger Elizabeth's trust. I put my arm around her and watched her as she fell asleep.

Unable to rest my mind, I walked the halls later. I passed a few other lost souls, and even though I knew they couldn't hurt me, I put as much distance between us as the hall would allow. A few of them looked at me curiously, but most of them ignored me. I had counted six, so far.

Walking down the men's hall, I passed by Ronnie's door and heard him whimper. With nothing better to do,

I stepped inside and just when I thought things couldn't get any more bizarre, I saw him cowering in the corner on his knees. A man loomed over him, shimmering with a dull silver glow. He was dressed in tattered colonial clothing with a pistol on one hip and a long sword on the other. Except for a high red velvet crown, he looked like he might have been nothing more than a high-ranking soldier during the Revolution.

Well, I'll be damned. There really is a king, I thought. I caught a glimpse of something shiny at his feet just before he kicked it toward Ronnie. It made a metallic scrape on the floor and then came to a stop against his knee. Ronnie looked down at it and shook with fear. The self-proclaimed king turned to me abruptly.

"Go away," he ordered. "This is none of your concern." His accent was definitely from a time long ago, as were his graceful movements.

"What do you want with Ronnie?" I asked. He glared at me silently. "Can he see you?" I asked, taking a step closer. "I thought David was the only one who could see us."

"He can hear me," he said with a grin and turned back to Ronnie. "Open it, Ronnie," he commanded. Ronnie, sniveling and crying, picked up the razor that rested against his knee. "Now, put it to your throat," the king said, a smile spreading across his face.

"Hey! Now, wait a minute! What the hell are you doing?" I yelled. My eyes darted between the king and Ronnie, who now had the blade pressed against his throat. Ronnie trembled with tightly shut eyes.

"Ronnie, don't do this!" I yelled.

"He can't hear you. He can only hear me."

I walked over and stooped toward Ronnie. "If you can hear him, you can hear me. Put it down, Ronnie," I said.

The king laughed behind me, loud and cold.

"*Pull it, Ronnie. Do it now!*" he seethed with anticipation. I saw a hard shiver roll through Ronnie, and I put my hand over his.

"Don't," I commanded. Using every bit of concentration I had, I got a grip on his hand and slowly pulled it away from his neck. He looked down in confusion as he watched his own arm being pulled away from his body. I pried his curled fingers away, the razor fell to the floor with a clink, and Ronnie balled himself up, crying hysterically. I turned around to confront the king, but he was gone.

The next day, I found David and told him what happened.

"I know. That one is a menace," he said grimly. "He tortures poor Ronnie."

"Well, what can we do about it?" I asked.

"Nothing, except wait till he decides to go."

"Ronnie almost killed himself last night," I said. "We can't just let this continue and hope one day he'll decide to go through. From the looks of him, he's been here for a while. Or at least he thinks he has."

"He's been here longer than you or I, Simon. This hospital was built on a colonial cemetery, and he's not too happy about it. He thought very highly of himself—"

"I noticed," I interrupted dryly.

"He thought a shrine should be built over his grave to honor him. When he found out the shrine turned out to be a nuthouse, he thought it was personally offensive, and he's been wreaking havoc ever since." He shrugged his shoulders and bent his head. "I'll try talking to him again," he offered.

I sighed and rubbed my hand over my face and through my hair. "I gotta get us out of here," I said.

The next day, I started working on a plan. I sat in the doctor's office and casually put my feet up on his desk.

"You need to let Elizabeth go home," I said, getting right to the point. "She is as stable as she's going to get, no thanks to you, but she would do better at home and you know it."

He muttered to himself, flipping through a thick psychology text.

"She might talk," I said. He stopped and stared at his desk. "She might let the other Elizabeth tell them how we escaped on your watch and wouldn't that make you look incompetent?" He rose quickly, threw the book back on the bookshelf, and dug in his drawer for his pills. "And she might tell them about the pills and bottles of booze in your bottom drawer. And about the nurse you're a little too friendly with." I had seen no evidence of this personally, but I had heard the whisperings of the staff over the months of a quiet affair with an older nurse. "Wouldn't your wife love to know about that?" I laughed. "You should let her go home," I said, dropping back down into seriousness. "Besides, you have many more serious issues to deal with than a harmless girl with a broken mind. The investigation won't stop with me, you know. They are going to look into the deaths of every one of your patients."

I had figured out the weaker a mind is, the easier it is for them to hear my words as their own thoughts. And the good doctor was growing weaker by the day. I stood and leaned over his desk.

"I won't leave you alone until you send her home," I promised him grimly with a low voice.

The following day, I returned as promised, but this

time, I brought a friend. The starving girl stood behind me, terrified.

"He can't hurt you," I promised her. "He can't see you or hear you." I looked at the doctor, who stood near the window, staring intently. "Tell him what he did to you," I urged. "Tell him he's responsible."

"I thought he couldn't hear me," she said in a high-pitched ghostly whisper.

"He can't hear us directly. But our words come across as his own thoughts. Didn't David explain this to you?" I asked. She shook her head, and her wispy hair fell around her face. "I'm afraid of him, too," she whispered.

"Who? David? You shouldn't be afraid of him."

She looked up at me with caution. "He won't tell them I'm here? That I don't want to go?"

"No, he won't," I said and then curiosity got the best of me. "Why won't you go?" I asked, sitting on the edge of the desk.

"I don't know. I just don't feel like I can."

I looked at the doctor. "You should talk to the doctor," I said with a sarcastic smile. "It'll make you feel better."

Eyes down, she sat nervously wringing her bony hands in her lap.

"My stomach hurt all the time. That's why I couldn't eat," she said softly. "I tried telling him—"

"Talk to him, not me," I said, nodding to the doctor.

She looked up at him like a frail mouse. "I tried to tell you the medicine you gave me made my stomach hurt. You told me I was trying to get attention. Day after day, I sat at the table so very hungry. But I couldn't eat. You wouldn't listen." She sighed and looked down. Suddenly, she came up out of her chair and stood next to the doctor, breathing heavily through her nose. "I couldn't eat because you wouldn't listen. And even as I wasted away to nothing, you accused me of doing it on purpose," she said through her teeth. "You killed me."

"Send Elizabeth home," I added.

"You killed me," she fumed.

"Send her home."

The doctor held his head and grunted, squeezing his eyes shut.

She turned away quickly and sat down as if she were exhausted. She hung her head for several moments and then looked up at me slowly.

"Thank you," she said. "I do feel better." She looked at the doctor, who was taking a long drink from his flask. "I'm not done, but I feel better for now." She smiled. By reflex, I put a hand on her shoulder and was surprised it felt semi-solid. I squeezed lightly and could feel the mass of bones under my hand. "That feels good," she said, closing her eyes. I dropped my hand quickly.

"I'm glad you feel better," I said with a smile and turned to leave.

She followed me down the hall to Elizabeth's room. It was empty and I sat against the wall, waiting for her to return.

"What's your name anyway?" I asked the girl as she sat in the opposite corner and drew her legs up in front of her.

"Anna," she said, looking around the room. "Is this where you hide?" she asked.

"Hide? No, this is where I like to be," I said.

"Near her," Anna assumed and I nodded. "I watched you, you know. When you were alive. I saw how you both looked at each other, how much you loved her. It made me sad."

"Why did it make you sad?" I asked.

"It made me miss my beau. He was waiting for me." She glanced up at the barred window. "Out there."

"You can go see him," I said. "Like I see Elizabeth. I don't know if it will make it better or worse. Sometimes, I'm torn."

She nodded slowly, thinking it over. "It never occurred to me that I could leave," she said. "I knew I couldn't go through, but he lives far away," she said sadly.

"Well, something David told me is that you simply have to concentrate on something or someone and you are there. Just like that," I said.

"Really?"

I was taken aback at how some of the dark had lightened around her sunken eyes, and I could see they had been blue.

"I haven't tried it, but that's what David says. You really should talk to him," I suggested and then looked up at her gratefully with a thought that hadn't occurred to me. "It's been really nice talking to you. I almost forgot what it's like to have a two-way conversation." She returned my smile as Elizabeth walked through the door, humming. I stood up with a relieved smile on my face. Elizabeth stood in front of the small desk, picked up the brush and began running it through her hair. I leaned over, kissed her cheek, and whispered in her ear. She brushed over my kiss with the back of her hand, a faint smile on her face.

"She really can hear you," Anna said in amazement as she turned her face away with an expression that mingled with longing and embarrassment and then left.

~ ~ ~

ANNA RETURNED THE next day and waited for me in the

commons room. She sat with her hands in her lap, head hanging down, letting her hair hide her face. Elizabeth was asleep. So heavily sedated, I knew there would be no chance she would hear me as one of her own thoughts. This was the only time I felt like I could be close to her. I took the time to wander the halls, peeking in on people I knew. I checked on Ronnie often. Not that I liked the bastard. Even in death, I couldn't bring myself to like him after what he did to Elizabeth. But I did feel sorry for him. David had worked out some sort of temporary truce with the king who haunted Ronnie, and he had yet to be seen by anyone, alive or dead, in a few days.

David had told me the day before the ghost who haunted Ronnie had actually been a soldier from the Revolutionary War. He had died on the battlefield, quite possibly because his inflated ego made him so easy to pick off, even from a distance. He was buried where he fell by his soldiers, who didn't take much time out of their day to grieve for him. He had watched and listened after he'd died to crude remarks made at his expense. It made him angry, and he chose to stay to seek revenge for the disrespect. The company of soldiers had no idea their less-than-liked dead comrade stayed very close to them. They only knew about the strange things that started to happen. Eventually, every last soldier was driven to madness by the stresses of war and deprivation and the constant unseen, unheard taunting echoing deep in their minds as a memory or a harassing thought. Or a very malicious suggestion.

When the hospital was built on the patch where the self-proclaimed king was buried, he thought it was being built as a shrine to immortalize him. When he found out it was a lunatic asylum, he was more offended than when his fellow soldiers mocked and ridiculed him in death. He had been there ever since, torturing different patients of his choosing since the place had opened. I sat on the far end of the couch in the commons area.

"Hey, Anna," I said. I felt tired but knew that it was only an illusion. The memory of being tired. She made a small noise of acknowledgment and crossed her arms. "What's wrong?" I asked. She looked up. The area around her eyes again darkened several shades.

"I found him," she said.

"Your beau?" She nodded, clearly not happy with what she had found. "It's harder in a way, isn't it? Seeing them, hearing them, and yet unable to touch them or talk to them. Not how we're used to, anyway."

"It's not that," she said and suddenly, her face stiffened. It made her cheekbones stick out in a grotesque and unnatural way. "I found him, but now he has a new girl. He's getting married," she said, low and angry. I watched her as she recounted the first few moments of seeing him again.

He had sat in the living room with his parents, talking of serious things. Marriage and military. Honor and country. She had been elated, relieved, and overwhelmed by the love she remembered. And then a young woman walked in. She sat next to him on the couch and he took her hand, turning it over to show his parents the diamond ring on her left hand.

"I know it must have been hard seeing how he had moved on," I said.

"If only they hadn't thrown me in here. If they hadn't given me that medicine." She glanced back to the table. "If only I could have eaten," she said. "I hate them. I hate every single one of them."

"Anna, I know this is hard. But he's still living. Of course, he moved on, but it doesn't mean he didn't love you. Or that he doesn't still love you and think about you." She shook her head in disagreement. "You have a choice, Anna. You can stay near him, or you can move on at midnight. You can wait for him on the other side if it's too hard to wait here." She looked as if she were deciding or at least thinking about deciding.

"Or..." she said. Her eyes flashed with an idea, dark and sinister.

"Or what?" I asked, trying not to sound wary.

"Or I can make him pay."

"Anna. He hasn't done anything wrong. He's doing what anyone would do, you included. If you loved him, then you wouldn't want him to be sad and alone. You'd want him to find what happiness he could."

She listened to me patiently and then smiled, tight and malicious. "Not my beau. Not Matthew. The doctor," she said with venom and stood, gone before I could blink.

I sighed, leaning my head back and closing my eyes. I felt bad for her, and I had a fairly good idea of what she intended to do, but thought she could do little harm since she had never grasped the ability to move things. She seemed to have a strong vocal impact, however. She had agitated the doctor much more than I had. Or he could simply feel more guilty over her death, I supposed with a slight shrug.

I found Elizabeth in my mind and relived the happier memories from the cabin.

My head came up off the back of the couch with a snap, and I stared ahead in disbelief. I held my breath, unsure of what had just happened. Woven into my memories of Elizabeth, a vision had begun to swirl and form in front of me. It startled me, and for the first time, I was able to stop it simply by opening my eyes. I was hesitant, not wanting to be held a captive audience as I had been in life, but closed my eyes, directing my thoughts again to the vision. It picked up right where it left off. After a few seconds, I opened my eyes, mid-vision. I gave a short disbelieving laugh. I was in total control.

I concentrated again, this time with eyes open, and clearly saw a man with white blond hair and eyes black as pitch sneaking along a pier. He held a box far out from his body as he walked, peering in the early evening darkness at the painted name of each moored boat he passed.

I moved my eyes, breaking the concentration and sighed. I was relieved I had control of the visions but was frustrated that it was another I didn't understand. Mostly though, I was amazed how they had followed me after death.

~ ~ ~

I FOLLOWED ELIZABETH into the doctor's office. He really looked like he was falling apart—dark eyes, limp, greasy hair, a disheveled white coat. He popped two pills discreetly as my love sat down across from him.

She, on the other hand, looked wonderful. Her skin was smooth and bright, her eyes clear and lively. She had an air of vibrancy about her. She smiled at the doctor, and much to my amusement, she took control of the visit.

"So, how have you been, Doctor?" she asked, crossing her legs and then folding her hands across her lap.

"I'm—I'm fine, Elizabeth. And you?"

"Just lovely." She smiled sweetly.

"Well, let's get started, shall we?" he asked, opening her file and searching for his pen.

"We already have." She grinned and added, "You

don't look so well, Doctor. Have you been sleeping all right?"

He looked slightly surprised and then very distracted. "Ah, no, actually, Elizabeth, I haven't. Is it that apparent?" he asked, his voice wobbling slightly.

"Yes," she said with a pitiful expression. "What seems to be troubling you so much that you can't get a restful night's sleep?" she asked, tilting her head in the same way he did when he was waiting for an explanation.

"Well, now, it's just a touch of insomnia, really."

"There are medicines to help with sleep," she said helpfully.

"And they do help somewhat."

"Are you taking anything for the stress, Doctor? This has to be a very stressful job. Especially, after all that's happened."

He nearly looked relieved—grateful to have someone finally recognize the weight he carried on his shoulders of trying to mend broken minds.

"I am and it helps somewhat. I just feel like—" He stopped abruptly, remembering which side of the desk he was on and straightened in his chair. "That's not important," he said, trying to regain control of the conversation.

"But it is important, Doctor. After all, how can you help me if you are in need of help yourself?" She smiled sweetly, and I couldn't help but laugh.

"God, I love you," I said with an amused smile. Something flashed in her eyes.

"Today, I would like to talk to the others," the doctor said. She shrugged her shoulders as if she didn't know what he was talking about. "I understand you go by the name of Elizabeth, but I want to talk to the real Elizabeth. The *original* Elizabeth.

"Ah," she said, seeming to understand. "Go right ahead. What would you like to ask me?"

"W—wait," he looked slightly lost. "You are not the original Elizabeth."

"Oh, I'm quite certain I am," she said. "Go ahead, ask me anything." She smiled confidently.

"All right. If you are indeed the original Elizabeth, there are things you'll know the others wouldn't. For example, how did you and Simon escape?" he asked with a curious, almost teasing tone.

Her smile dropped and she looked upset. "I don't want to talk about Simon."

"Because it upsets you? Or because you are not the original Elizabeth and don't know."

"I know," she said quietly. "I just don't—" She looked away, toward the window where I stood near. She looked as if she were about to cry.

"The gate was open," she started. "Someone opened the door for us just at midnight—"

"Elizabeth, don't! Don't tell him about David!" I yelled.

"Who opened the door?"

"Damn it, Elizabeth, don't you dare!"

"It was Greg," she said. Greg, the pervert who had tried to sneak in her room before I learned how to move things.

"Ah. I see," he said, scribbling on his pad. I wondered how long it would take him to figure out Greg had been hired after we had been caught. "Where were you going to go?" he asked.

"Mexico," she said and I stood a little straighter. I began to think it really might be her. Only stronger. More confident. I would have given anything to kiss her. And all I owned was my soul.

"And what after that?" the doctor asked, trying to hide excitement at the breakthrough.

"We were going to find work, a little place of our own. Maybe adopt children one day." As her voice broke, I felt my throat begin to close a little. "That's all we wanted."

The doctor stared at her, hints of victory vanished, replaced with visible regret.

"I am sorry for your loss," he said finally. I had the overwhelming feeling he truly was.

"I want to go home," she said, raising her head after discreetly wiping her eyes.

"Well, let's not get ahead of ourselves. I need to know you are cured. And it's curious how you do appear to be in control of yourself despite any change in therapy."

"She's better. Let her out," I interrupted. "Write it down. Now. That she'll be monitored for two weeks, and if there are no signs of another personality, then she will be released."

He rubbed a hand hard over his stubbly face and sighed. "I will see what I can do, Elizabeth. To see you home as soon as I am sure you're well enough." She smiled again and rose to leave without waiting for his signal. After she had left, I watched over his shoulder as he scratched out his progress notes. I smiled as I left the room.

Patient is to be monitored over the course of two weeks.

~ ~ ~

A WEEK OR so passed and things seemed to settle down. I rarely saw the other ones, and that was fine with me. Only, I worried about Anna making daily visits to the doctor's office. She would walk in slow circles around the desk, glaring hatefully and constantly talking . I knew he could hear her, deep in the recesses of his own damaged mind, and he looked like he was unraveling at the seams. I tried to get Anna to stop, or at least, back off a little. Not for his sake, but because I still needed him. Just a few more days' worth of progress notes and Elizabeth would be able to leave. She ignored my pleas. Her hate had intensified, feeding off itself and growing into an uncontrollable monster. She grew more creative in her torture by bringing others to help her.

I watched helplessly the next afternoon as she and the woman who died during sterilization chanted together, circling the desk. He was really cracking now— digging in his drawer and taking pills, chasing them with a long drink from a flask. He covered his ears and made pitiful whimpering noises. He knew he was losing his mind. I hated feeling sorry for him. I spent my time talking to him about letting Elizabeth out. I no longer blamed him, out loud anyway, figuring Anna was torturing him enough for every lost soul in this building.

I was so happy when he finally wrote the words.

Patient is to be released the end of the week.

I walked back to Elizabeth's room to tell her the good news. I knew what was going on with her now. She was using the same trick her father had used when he was released. She let the stronger Elizabeth take over long enough to convince them she was stable. When she got out, there would be no need for her to hide behind the stronger one and she would be all right. I looked forward to seeing my Elizabeth again.

Late the next evening, I walked the halls. David was out sick, and I was bored with no one to talk to. Passing the doctor's office, I noticed light coming from under the door and stood close to it, listening. I wondered why he was working so late. I heard several voices—six, at least. I stepped past the door and found Anna, along with several others, circling the desk like sharks. All of them had their eyes fixed on the doctor, who looked nearly dead himself. He was drunk, slumped over his desk, and looked as though he had been crying.

He struggled with writing his progression notes in the open file in front of him, stopping periodically to give a desperate growl and bang his fists on his head. He wasn't working late. He couldn't leave. They wouldn't let him.

"Anna, that's enough," I said. I was all for justice, but there was no need to go this far. She ignored me. "Anna, I said that's enough. You guys need to leave now," I said, taking a step inside the circle of hate that took on a translucent dark glow around the doctor's desk. It was cold, and I could feel their hate. It crackled like electricity and swelled like the ocean's tide.

I instantly felt scared, hollow, and I very much wanted to run. I stepped back, outside the ring of revenge and the cold nauseous feeling went away. I called to Anna again. Her eye sockets had returned to their previous black-as-night hollow state. She was so caught up in the witch-like proceedings that she ignored me. I looked at the others as they passed in front of me. They were chanting together now with heads low and never taking their eyes off the doctor.

Besides Anna, the woman who looked for her baby and the self-proclaimed king walked with them, plus a few new ones I didn't recognize. One a young man in his early twenties with dark scorch marks on his temples. I assumed he died as a result of too much voltage as well. Another young man with no visible marks chanted in a foreign language. Another woman, older and slightly pudgy with long, stringy gray hair. She looked more sinister than the king with deep-set dark eyes and no teeth. Wringing her hands in front of her chest, she grew more and more excited. As I watched them, I realized something was about to happen. And it wasn't good.

The doctor rose from his chair with a start, his face decided and his fists clenched on the desk in front of him, the circle around him stopped abruptly, silently watching. They all smiled. He swayed slightly where he stood as he wiped beaded sweat off his forehead with his sleeve. As he moved from the desk, the circle dissipated, allowing him to pass. They all filed out behind him. They whispered now, a chorus of diverse hissing mumblings that I couldn't understand. I watched in confusion as he turned down a darkened hallway of supply closets instead of toward the exit.

After fumbling with a ring of keys, he opened a heavy door that led to stairs. I moved to the front of the crowd, standing beside him as he began his slow climb.

"What are you doing, Doc?" I asked. I glanced up the winding staircase and back at him. The whispering continued in a constant volume behind him, echoing through the empty stairwell, broken only by the occasional outburst of sadistic giggling from the woman with no teeth.

At the top of the stairs, he unlocked the door that led to the roof. Suddenly, I knew what he was going to do.

I tried to reason with him, shouting above the others who had clustered in a vibrating hive of excitement behind him. I screamed at them to stop, begged the doctor to stop as he made his slow, steady march toward the edge.

He closed his eyes. *He heard me*, I thought.

The others kept following him, chanting whispers of

encouragement, and he neatly walked off the edge of the building.

I yelled as the others howled in victory.

I looked down where he lay, twisted and broken, on the front steps of the hospital in the bright glow of the winter moon. Everything was silent again. The others dissipated to wherever it is murderous spirits go to while I went down to the front steps. I stood by his body, staring at his relaxed face. I did hate him, but not this much. Hearing a noise behind me, I turned quickly.

The doctor looked down at his body, his face frozen in surprise. I watched it relax after a moment, and he appeared deep in thought. He sat down hard on the steps next to his body and nodded calmly.

"I deserved it," he said finally.

"No, no one deserves this. You didn't even choose to do this, you were driven to it."

"I thought I was going crazy," he said with a rough laugh. "But they really were talking to me." His mind now free from pills and booze, he saw everything clearly for what it was. "I always thought I was doing the right thing. I really thought I was helping. It's what all the books, all the schools, all the great doctors told us to do." He shrugged helplessly.

I stared at the ground in front of me, unsure of what to say.

After a moment, he looked up at me.

"I'm sorry for what I did to you. I shouldn't have shocked you with that hematoma on your head. I should have known better." His eyes begged forgiveness, but I wasn't entirely prepared to give it to him. After all, I was still separated from my Elizabeth. The thin veil of life kept us apart, and it wouldn't be until she died that I could truly hold her again.

"What happens now?" he asked with a curious expression, giving up on my forgiveness. "I always thought when you died—poof—you're in heaven or hell."

"You can choose to go or stay. It's up to you."

"And if I choose to go?"

"You can. At midnight."

He nodded, deliberating. As if on cue, a chime echoed twelve times from somewhere distant, and the wide wooden doors behind him began to dissolve and swirl.

He heard the low noise, like wind and water, quietly churning and turned toward the open portal gleaming with pearly streaks of bright light ringed in gold.

"What if I don't go right now? What happens to me?" he asked.

"You have the choice at every stroke of midnight," I told him. He looked relieved. "I'll stay. Just for a bit then," he said and the gateway collapsed, suddenly yet gracefully.

"Why?" I asked him when he finally turned away from it.

"I need to make amends," he said quietly as he stood, turning away from his body and walking back into the hospital.

To say the spirit world was upset by the doctor's decision to stay would be a massive understatement. In fact, the hospital had become loud. Very loud. So disturbed by his presence, two had even chosen to go on. One, the one with burnt temples, ran from him. Only the young man with the foreign accent talked to him. Anna chose to leave and follow Matthew, still pining for him. I had only one objective and it was to see Elizabeth home.

Her release was delayed by the new doctor's need to review all of the files and meet with each patient a few times before writing up a new treatment plan and approving discharges.

He was young with black hair and brown eyes. His mind was strong. When I tried to talk to him, I quickly realized he couldn't hear me at all. His heart seemed to be in the right place, though. He seemed kind. I overheard him telling the nurses he had much more humane treatment options in mind for the patients.

~ ~ ~

ELIZABETH WAS FINALLY allowed to leave the end of the first week of February.

David had returned from a bout of severe pneumonia and walked Elizabeth, small bag in tow, out of the ward to the front of the hospital where her father waited. I talked to David though he couldn't answer me.

"I'll come back and see you," I said. He blinked.

"Take care of Loretta," I added. Small nod. He looked at me, and to the others it looked as if he stared at the picture on the wall behind me.

"You take care of yourselves," he said.

Her father ended a long, relieved hug with Elizabeth and nodded.

"We will. C'mon Beth, let's get home," he said, a wide smile revealing several missing side teeth. Throwing one last glance at David over my shoulder, I gave him a nod and then followed them out.

Elizabeth said little on the ride to her house. Her father talked up a storm, though. He was overjoyed at having his daughter home again. As we rounded the tight curve in the dirt road before her parents' home came into view, her father broached the subject of her mother.

"You're not mad at her, are you, Beth? She didn't mean no harm. She thought she was helping you."

Cold eyes turned on him with a glare that made him uncomfortable. He pulled up to the house and cut the engine. Digging under the seat, he pulled out a small bottle.

"Here, Beth. Have some of this," he said, holding it out to her.

"Your medicine?" she said, eyes gone soft.

"It helps, Beth. I think it will make things easier, just at first," he said.

She took it, stared at it, and then spoke to her father, eyes still on the bottle. "This keeps your other one away, right?" He nodded, looking away as if ashamed. "And it might do the same for me?" she asked hopefully.

"Maybe. I don't see why not. You can at least try it."

She smiled and drank from the bottle. She wavered slightly as she took the stairs, her father babbling on about cleaning her room and the fact that everything was just as it was when she had left.

The bedroom door swung open, and she stood on the threshold, gazing slowly from right to left. It smelled heavy of cleanser, and the billowy curtains and antique quilt gleamed white.

"I don't want this room anymore," she said firmly. She stared at her father with a neutral glassy-eyed expression.

"Why not, Beth? It's all nice and clean, just for you. And I bought you this new vanity, so you can sit and brush your pretty hair." He glanced from it to her, waiting for her appreciation. She turned away and walked down the hall.

"So much has happened. I'm just not the same person anymore, Daddy. Besides, that room has too many memories. I want this room," she said as she opened the door to an old bedroom full of stored items from years gone by.

"This old dusty room?" he asked, running a wrinkled hand through his thin white hair. "Well, if that's what my Beth wants."

"Yes, Daddy. It's what your Beth wants."

He smiled, nodded, and turned to go downstairs. "I'll just go clear a space in the barn for all that old stuff," he said. She watched him until he was out of sight and then walked back into her old room. She pulled something out of her bag and took it to the new vanity. I stood beside her as she placed the clay heart I had given her near her hairbrush. She touched it with her fingertips and sighed lightly before leaving, closing the door behind her.

~ ~ ~

I WAITED FOR Elizabeth, my Elizabeth, to return. I followed her around the house and whispered to her of our memories. When she slept, I talked to her, hoping she would dream of me, and it would help bring my Elizabeth to the surface. Occasionally, she talked in her sleep, and once, she said my name. When her eyes opened, however, it was always the strong one with her chilly disposition and arrogant insistence on getting her way.

After a few weeks, I began to wonder if it would ever happen. If she was ever going to surface or if she would stay trapped in her own mind beneath the stronger one, under its control.

I watched her father bring her medicine morning and night. She slept a lot and ate little. When she was awake, she dealt mostly with her father, who had begun to teach her the business of tanning cowhides. Her mother avoided her, and when close proximity to each other was unavoidable, Elizabeth would simply stop talking and glare at her. Elizabeth grew distant and more hostile; her mother grew introverted and more fearful.

She walked around with glassy eyes, speaking with a slight slur. Her behavior became odd and erratic. One minute she was soft-spoken and gentle. The next, she would fly into a rage, cursing and throwing things in a violent display of her fragile temper. She would change into her father's clothes and write letters at the vanity in her old room. She would return later, having changed back into a dress with freshly washed hair, and sit and read the letters and cry.

She needed the medicine now, and her body would revolt whenever dosed weakly or late.

It was on a night like this when I watched her pace nervously alongside her father, both sweating and twitching as they waited for a delivery.

I recognized Jan from Elizabeth's description. The one who claimed herself a healer. She wore charms and Indian feathers around her neck and dressed oddly, sort of like an old world gypsy. She would only deal with Elizabeth's mother, however, when she made her monthly rounds to make her deliveries, she would never step inside. She stood on the porch with nervous eyes swaying sideways and chanting something in another language. A package wrapped in brown paper and secured with twine exchanged hands on the front porch for cash and leather. Elizabeth's mother closed the door and held out the package to her husband without looking him in the eyes. He grabbed it and took it quickly to the kitchen where he opened the package and poured out a small pile of pills onto a plate. He showed Elizabeth how to grind the tablets and mix them with water over heat to make a syrup. He made a weaker mixture for her and a much stronger one for himself.

When it was finished, they anxiously self-medicated. Elizabeth measured and her father gulped. I watched as her eyes dulled and her pupils contracted. She smiled in relief and stood slowly, turning to the doorway where I stood.

"Has it been helping you, Beth? Does the other one stay away?" her father asked, slumped in the chair as the opiate mixture eased his pains. I could have sworn she was looking right at me. That she could see me. I held my imagined breath.

"She's never coming back," she said with a cold smile. My heart sank, and I knew she was right.

~ ~ ~

I SAT BESIDE her bed for a long time, deciding. I didn't want to leave her, but I couldn't stay and watch her do this to herself. I wanted to stay and protect her, but what she needed protection from was herself. I was powerless against both the stronger one and the opiates. Between the two of them, my Elizabeth was lost.

I stood and turned away before I could change my mind. I left and didn't look back.

I had resolved to leave her, but hadn't yet decided whether I would leave it all behind and cross to the other side. Staying here but staying away, I could console myself with the fact I could always look in on her if it became too painful to stay away. Once I crossed, however, I would be separated from her until she died. At least that's what I thought, and I hadn't heard otherwise.

I don't know how long I walked, but as the afternoon sun began to sink low on the horizon, I could smell the heavy salt air as the calls of the seagulls grew closer. I heard the low roar of the ocean in the distance. I turned, drawn toward it and walked along the breakers, wrestling between guilt and relief. I already missed her and had the sudden urge to turn back. I stopped and thought for a moment. I loved her enough to stay and wait. I wanted to help her in whatever way I might. And I selfishly needed to be near her. *But it isn't really her*, I reminded myself. I began walking again with a heavy heart. I ended up walking along the edge of a small town. Feeling the need for some kind of human contact, I ventured into the town.

The whole town seemed to be congregating at a little chapel near the ocean. Black Model-T Fords, old and new, lined the street and filled the small parking lot. I stood across the street from the Pigeon Cove Chapel and watched as what appeared to be half the town filed in, dressed in black with heads hung low in grief, holding onto each other, giving and needing support. Glancing to my right I saw a man standing with his back to the chapel, staring out toward the open ocean.

He wore a thick, yellow-tinted sweater and rugged, black wool pants. The black knit cap pulled low over his ears matched the scarf wrapped under the round neck of his sweater. His shoulders shrugged with a deep sigh as he gazed out over the open blue.

"Is this for you?" I asked, somewhat awkwardly, interrupting his private reflection.

He nodded and scratched his chin through his thick beard, brown sprinkled with white.

"I was in there for a bit, but I couldn't see them so sad. I'll wait here," he said.

"What are you waiting for?" He knew he was dead, obviously, but I wondered if he knew what he was waiting for.

"There's someone I haven't seen in a while. I wanted to see him one more time before I go. I think he'll come," he said as he looked over his shoulder. The chapel door was open to accommodate the overflow.

"You were well liked," I said, impressed by the number of friends and family at his memorial.

"I suppose." He shrugged and gave a rough laugh. He turned to face the chapel, and I turned with him, hearing the distant echo of the pastor's voice from inside.

"Aryl Sullivan was loved by many."

"I thought I'd stay for the whole thing." A shiver ran through his chest and shoulders. "It's sort of creepy, you know? Standing there at your own memorial," he said with a smile, his brown eyes twinkling. He looked to me for confirmation.

"I went to mine," I offered. "And yes, it was strange. It was only my dad and a priest, though." It suddenly made me sad that I had been laid to rest with only two people to witness and one to grieve as the plain pine box was lowered into the ground. This man was liked and loved. He would be missed. I wondered if Elizabeth missed me, somewhere deep in her mind. He turned back to the ocean and stared intently. "Is your wife in there?" I asked. "Or has she gone on ahead?"

"Don't have a wife."

With so many bodies in the chapel, I found it hard to believe this man with the mischievous grin had never found someone special. "You never fell in love?" I asked.

"Oh, I did. A few times." He laughed as his eyes scanned the horizon. "But none held the power that she did."

"Who?" I asked.

"Her," he said with a nod to the sea. "That's the only place I want to be. I have no idea what's on the other side, but I hope it's big and blue with an endless horizon."

We were quiet for a few moments and listened to different voices echoing from the chapel, dotted with reverent laughter. He glanced back, slightly amused. "I wonder what they're saying about me."

"How long ago?" I asked.

"Four days. Ticker gave out," he said with a thump of his fist on his broad chest. "Always thought I would die at sea. I was on the pier. Close enough, I guess."

"Have you decided to go?"

"Tonight, I think. After I see him."

"Who?" I felt I was being nosey now, but I enjoyed talking to him. My soul was beginning to feel lighter for the contact.

"Him," he said with a backward nod of his head.

A young man stepped up beside him just then and standing with an identical posture, shoved his hands into his pockets and took a deep breath, blowing it out slowly. "He's my nephew. They named him after me. A good boy. We did a lot of fishing together when he was younger. He's been off in the big city for a while now." He spoke to me but watched the young man. We were quiet for a few moments and let the ocean have her say in the distance.

"I'm sorry we never got to go to Madeira," he said softly to his nephew. Whether he heard him or not, I didn't know. He didn't look weak of mind, but then, he was grieving. He blinked quickly and focused on the hypnotic rolling ocean waves. The old sailor pulled off his cap, and I noticed the family resemblance in the longer, curly brown hair, as well as the eyes. But I noticed something more and it startled me. The younger one. I knew him. I stared, trying to place the face.

"I want you to go," he said. "Go and take Claire with you. Do everything we talked about doing when you were young. You can tell me all about it when you talk to the stars at night, all right?"

The nephew sighed, glanced up at the sky, then down at the sandy shore, and that's when it hit me.

With his head down and the curls of hair resting on his forehead, I recognized him as the man I had seen in some of my visions—the ones that held no meaning or reason.

After the old sailor had said everything that he needed to say, there was a look of peace about him. A woman stepped up beside the nephew.

"It's over," she said quietly. He put an arm around her and they turned away.

Old sailor watched them as they got into a car and pulled away, watched until they were out of sight.

"I'll go tonight. After they had put my ashes to the sea," he said aloud. I couldn't tell if he was enlightening me to his plans or confirming them to himself. "What about you?" he asked, turning to face me. "You going?"

I shook my head. "I won't go, not just now. But I can't stay where I was."

"Why not?"

"I just can't watch her. It's complicated."

He smiled and turned toward the beach. I followed, and we walked for a while in silence before he spoke.

"When my nephew came to me and told me he had fallen in love and was going to be married, I have to admit, I was saddened. We had made many plans to travel the world together, and a wife wouldn't fit into those plans. I told him if this woman called his heart stronger and louder than the adventure, the freedom of the sea, more than anything else in the world, to go to her and never look back. He did and I'm glad for him. I never found what he has. But then again, he never found what I have. My adventures and memories, my heart and soul lost to the sea." He stopped and smiled at me. "Aryl will never be lost to the sea like me. His heart will always beat for Claire, and not even all this," he paused, swept his arm across where the ocean met blue sky on the horizon and said, "could ever keep them apart." He looked at me with amused suspicion. "But you knew that," he said. "You're more of the angel type, aren't you?" His eyes narrowed, looking me up and down.

"I don't know what you mean," I said. He grinned beneath the beard, his brown eyes danced, crinkling at the edges.

He said no more, just turned and began to walk away.

"Where are you going?" I called out after him.

"I'll wait by my boat. That's where I want to be when I cross over," he said above the crashing ocean waves. Suddenly, he stopped and turned around. "If this girl, your girl, calls to your heart more than anything else, go to her and never look back," he said. And with a small nod, he turned in the direction of his boat and never looked back.

I selfishly wished he wouldn't leave. I wanted to tell him about Elizabeth and my visions. Most of all, I wanted to ask him if he knew why his nephew clouded my dreams all the time. And, if he didn't have a life on the ocean, why I saw him amidst a storm that tore a boat in two. The old sailor likely had no answers. I decided if he had, I had a feeling he wouldn't have shared them. I thought of his advice and wondered briefly of my alternatives if I didn't return to Elizabeth. I resigned myself to the inability to ever really leave her. He called it as it was. She was my heart, and I couldn't abandon her, even in death. Not even for the pain of watching her being destroyed by the others who controlled her mind. I would stay with her and protect her.

I had vowed that much to her in life, in not so many words, when we declared ourselves married. I turned toward the direction of her house. Hard as it was, I would stay.

Until death do us reunite, I vowed silently as I made my decision.

~ ~ ~

IT WAS WELL after dark when I returned to the house. Elizabeth, her father, and her mother sat at the dining room table, set semi-formally. Her mother said little and stared at her food as she ate. Her father smiled with hazy eyes as he asked questions about a young man, a strapping-looking fellow, though a little skinny.

"You ever do much sugaring, son?" he asked, shifting the food in his mouth to compensate for a few missing teeth.

"Back on my parents' farm, we did a lot before they died. Got a sister who lives in Georgia, she grows cotton with her husband. Ain't heard from her in a while. Got another sister in the big city. We haven't talked in years neither."

"What brings you here?" Elizabeth asked. The way she smiled at him made me uncomfortable. She sized him up appreciably and made sure he noticed.

"Well, ma'am—"

"Call me Elizabeth," she said.

He smiled back, and his eyes said enough to make me want to knock him out of his chair.

"Well, Elizabeth, I just been working my way slowly up and down the country. Not a lot of jobs around the small towns, but farms always need some extra hands. I'll be saving just enough to get down to my sister in Georgia. Stay on with her for a while, I suppose." The sudden hint of courteous southern accent caught me by surprise.

"What's your name?" she asked with a tight smile.

"Daniel, ma'am," he said with a teasing emphasis on *ma'am*.

"Well, the sooner you can start, the better," her father interrupted. "All my other chores have kept me busy. There's a room set up in the barn. You're welcome to use that. Meals are at seven, noon, and six while you're here. There are a lot of buckets out there. Afraid they aren't all together, maple syrup not being our main crop. They're dotted all over the farm. Then, of course, we gotta boil it all down, get it bottled. Gonna have to work fast, the sap season's winding down. I can pay you a fair percentage when it's sold."

"Sounds fair to me," Daniel said to her father but kept his eyes on Elizabeth.

The next day, I followed Elizabeth out to the barn. She wore her father's work pants with a plaid shirt, her hair tucked up under a man's hat. She hadn't said much of anything to her father all morning, but helped him care for the animals, and then helped him stretch a new hide on a large wooden frame.

They stopped together and sipped from their bottles. Her father sighed heavily, leaning against a pole inside of the barn.

"I better go check on our new hire," he said. "Can you handle the rest of this?" He gestured to the back of the barn where two chickens waited to be slaughtered in a small wire cage.

"I can go check on him," Elizabeth offered. Her voice was lower, more insistent. Her father shrugged his indifference, tucked the bottle in his back pocket, and picked up a small hatchet. The edge of the blade caught the light, and it flashed brightly as he twirled it, over and over, in his large hand. "Here, chickie, chickie, chickie," he called as he walked toward them.

Elizabeth stepped into the mudroom and slipped out of the work clothes, which were covered with bits of hay, mud, manure, and slimy bits of flesh debris from the freshly scraped hide. She stepped out of the pile nude and made her way upstairs, lacking any modesty. She returned a few moments later in a dress and a black wool coat, her hair brushed and her face washed. She hummed to herself as she came down the stairs, smiling.

I walked with her into the thin woods, following a string her father had tied between trees leading to every productive maple on the property. She came upon one, peeked in the empty bucket and went on to the next, still humming.

Daniel stood in the distance pouring the contents of a bucket into a caldron sitting in a wheelbarrow and then placing it back on its hook.

"Hello," she said, as we got closer.

"Well, Elizabeth, ma'am. Hello to you, too. How are you this fine day?" He smiled with shining dark brown eyes.

"Just fine. And yourself?"

"A lot better now," he said and grinned.

"Daddy sent me to check on you," she said, beginning to walk a circle around the tree and glancing to make sure his eyes followed her every move.

"Well, I assure you I'm working hard. Got about twenty trees done just this morning. Getting ready to take this load to the fire pit."

He stood behind the wheelbarrow and picked it up by the handles, flexing his muscles with a little more added show than was necessary.

"Daddy was wondering if you needed any help," she said, still circling, still watching him. It suddenly reminded me of the patients who circled the doctor's desk. Hunting.

"No, I'm doing fine. But the company sure is nice. Gets lonely out here all by myself. No one to talk to but the trees. And they don't say much back." He flashed another smile.

"I'll stay and talk to you," she said.

"I'd love that. Your father's paying me good money for this job, though, so I'll work while we talk if you don't mind." He smiled and started walking the wheelbarrow over the uneven terrain of the natural forest floor.

"So your first name is Daniel. What's your middle name?" Elizabeth asked.

"Don't have one," he said and then grunted over a few rocky bumps, trying not to spill the sap.

"Everyone has a middle name," she said. She walked slightly ahead of him, swaying her hips a little too graciously.

"Well, I don't. My family was sort of cast out. My parents eloped against both the families' wishes, so they were disowned I guess you'd say. I guess they figured there weren't any names they wanted to keep the tradition of." He attempted to shrug while holding up the handles of the wheelbarrow.

"I'll give you one," she said. "Everyone needs to have a middle name." A slow smile spread across Elizabeth's face.

He stopped and carefully set the wheelbarrow down with a grunt.

"All right then," he smiled, mopping his brow with a handkerchief, slightly out of breath. "What is it?"

"Stewart. Your middle name is Stewart," she said with an intoxicated grin.

"All right, ma'am. I suppose that'll work. Daniel Stewart."

"You won't mind if I just call you Stewart, will you? In honor of me giving it to you and all," she said and swirled her skirt around her legs.

"I'd be honored." I walked behind them back to the house, rethinking again, my decision to stay. I thought of Anna, how upset she was when she found out Matthew had moved on. I was torn, stuck between my vow to stay by Elizabeth's side and watching her move on and find happiness in someone else's eyes. *It's not really her,* I thought. *The stronger Elizabeth is still in control, and she is the one making advances toward Daniel,* I reminded myself. That helped a little, but not much, because it was still Elizabeth's eyes that shined and flirted. It was still her lips that smiled, still her blood that flushed her face, though the blushing did seem to be on cue.

When the house came into view, I had talked myself fully in circles, deciding twice to leave and a last time to stay. He said he would be leaving and if I could hold out until then, I would have Elizabeth all to myself again. He set the wheelbarrow down and tossed a flirty grin Elizabeth's way. As he stepped away, I stuck my foot out and he went sprawling, quite ungracefully, landing on his face in the mud.

"Oh, Stewart, are you all right?" Elizabeth rushed over and held his arm, helping him up.

"I'm fine. Tripped over my own feet," he said, looking back over the flat ground. "Mama always said I was clumsy as a newborn colt," he said as he stood, slightly embarrassed.

My little prank backfired in my face as Elizabeth stood very close to him, brushing bits of dirt and small twigs from his shoulder. She lingered too close for too long with an alluring smile, and I threw a tiny pebble at his head to break their concentrated stare. He rubbed his head and went back to his work.

"Tell me about your family," she said, as he dumped the sap into the boiler.

"Not much to tell," he said, frowning slightly.

"You said you had sisters."

"And I said we don't talk much."

"Why?"

"You're a nosy one," he said. His teasing grin lingered and so did her question. "We're just real different. One's a real homebody. She doesn't like me wandering around like I do. The other one is real uppity. We never did get along."

"Why?" He shot her an amused look with a hint of frustration and ran a hand through his dark hair. "C'mon. I don't have any brothers or sisters, so I don't know about this stuff," she said.

"We just don't get along is all. It isn't much different with siblings than it is with other people. Isn't there anyone you didn't get along with, no matter how hard you tried?"

"Yes, now that I think about it. A couple of people," she said with a tight smile.

"Why don't you get along?"

Her smile dropped, and her fists slowly curled into balls at her sides. "Because they interrupt. They keep trying to yell over me, and they won't..." she paused, looked up, took a deep breath, and said, "...play along. It's very frustrating."

"Well, that sounds like my sister. Like I said, she's the

uppity type who can't stand it if everyone isn't looking at her, talking to her, talking about her. The whole world had to revolve around her, and there was hell to pay if it didn't. I can't stand her and she can't stand me."

"Why can't she stand you?"

"She says I'm a habitual liar."

"Are you?" she asked curiously.

"If I gave you an answer, how would you know if I was telling the truth?" he teased.

"I wouldn't. But you don't have a reason to lie to me," she said.

"True. You seem harmless enough." She didn't answer but stared at him, her face void of emotion. "Okay, maybe I'm a bit of a liar," he said with a laugh.

"How so?" She folded her arms over her bulky coat and stepped out of the way, as he continued to work.

"Well, what I told your father at dinner about my folks, that was a lie. Sort of."

"You said your parents died."

"I did. And they did. Sort of. They're dead to me, so I guess that's the same thing. I took off years ago, and I haven't been home since. My one sister who still lives in Georgia has written to me, begging me to come home. She misses me, and her husband could use the help with the farm, so I told her I would. I've been working my way south for a few weeks now. But I'm taking my time about it, you see. Not real anxious to see my folks again."

"Why not? Were they bad to you?"

"Not directly, I guess. My dad's had some problems with women. He ran his business and our family into the ground with his habits, and my mom stuck by him the whole time. When I left home, they had lost just about everything. I hated him, and I couldn't watch my family suffer, so I just took off."

"So it's been a while since you've been home?"

"About six years."

"Do they know where you are now?" she asked.

"No. Last I wrote them, I was in Connecticut." I watched Elizabeth closely and could see her mind turning furiously behind her eyes.

"How long do you think you'll stay on here?" she asked over her shoulder as she started to walk away.

"Till the work is done," he said and then stopped, bucket mid-air, looking her up and down with obvious meaning. "Unless I find another reason to stay," he added with a suggestive grin.

She smiled, blushed, and turned toward the house.

Later that evening at dinner, I stood against the far wall of the dining room, glaring at him. I had tried talking to him while he worked, but he had a strong mind. He didn't hear me, he only saw Elizabeth.

I watched as they peeked up to steal glimpses of each other, much in the same way Elizabeth and I had in the hospital, and it made me furious and mournful of our time together.

A few days went by, and I swallowed my anger and heartache for the sake of staying near her. Glances turned to stares, smiles turned to giggles, and innocent brushes turned to lingering touches.

She brought his lunch to him every day and stayed to talk, never minding the winter's wind and sticky mud. She stopped wearing her father's clothes and stopped working with him in the barn. He protested slightly, mostly missing the company and small talk, but she brushed him off and disappeared into the woods for hours at a time. I noticed neither of her parents argued with her. No matter what she said or did.

On a bitterly cold Monday toward the end of

February, I realized where this was going with Elizabeth and Daniel. She stood against a tree to watch him work. Something in the way the two of them acted told me something had changed. The stakes had been raised, and this was more than casual flirting out of boredom.

He leaned in to kiss her after a steady buildup of glances, giggles, teasing, and suggestive looks that morning. I closed my eyes and turned away. It was time to visit David, I decided.

~ ~ ~

STEPPING BACK INTO the halls of the hospital was slightly unnerving and uncomfortably familiar. Not much had changed. A few new faces. The new doctor walked by, holding Sobbing Susan's hand and talking quietly. Three resident ghosts followed close behind him. Not menacingly, but curiously.

David couldn't contain his smile when he saw me. He motioned with his head toward an empty room, and I followed him as he paused along the way to grab a stack of clean linen.

"Simon, how are you?" he asked in a whisper as he started to make the bed.

"All right."

"How's Elizabeth?"

"It got to be too much. I had to take a break." I shrugged, looking down.

"What got to be too much? Is she getting worse?"

"No, not really. She's not better, either. The stronger one is still in control. But she's, uh, found a new interest," I said and crossed my arms, leaning against the wall.

"You had to know that would happen," David said.

"I know. But it's still hard to watch."

"You're not messing with him, are you?" David grinned.

"Well, you know." I smiled and shrugged.

"Simon, that's not nice," he whispered, his teasing smile lingering, his eyes dancing. "What did you do?"

"I tripped him. And threw a pebble at his head. Nothing too ghastly."

"You're not the ghastly type," he said as he smoothed down the flat white sheet. "Speaking of that, though, the king went on, finally. Ronnie's been doing a whole lot better for it."

"That's good. I'm glad to hear it. How's Loretta?"

He paused and peeked out the door to be sure we were alone.

"She's expecting," he said with a grin when he turned around.

"Congratulations! That's great."

"It is, but it's also complicated. She'll have to leave here when she starts to show to avoid questions."

"Where will she go?" I asked.

"North Carolina. I've got some family there. She'll pretend she's a widow and find work there until it gets close. Then she'll go to my parents in Georgia and have the baby there."

"It's awful that you guys have to do things like this."

"I'll head down there when it gets close." He frowned as he went about his work. "I hope I make it this time. I missed little David Jr. by two days. Hardest part is bein' away from them for so long."

I watched him work for a moment, unsure of what to say.

"Anna's been back a few times," he said, breaking the silence.

"Oh, yeah? How's she doing?"

"Not that well. I keep talking to her about going. It's eating her alive watching her beau with another girl. I think she's tormenting both of them."

"That's not good. But I can understand how she feels. It's hell to watch."

"But I think she's doing more than a little trip here and a pebble thrown there."

"Like what?"

"Not sure exactly. Maybe you could stop in and talk to her? She's mentioned you a few times. I think she misses you."

"I can do that," I said, glad to have something else to do before going back to Elizabeth. "Give me directions, and I'll go after I leave here."

"Still doing things the old-fashioned way, I see," he said. I gave him a curious look. "I told you early on, all you have to do is focus on a person, and you're right there. That fast."

"You sure know a lot about being dead for someone with a pulse."

"Comes with the job." He plucked at his white uniform shirt.

"So," I said, sitting down on the stool in the corner, "catch me up on hotel le manic. What's been going on?"

"New doc seems to be fitting in well. He's young and got a human side to him. Some of them are getting better."

"What about the old doc?" I asked with one eyebrow raised. I wondered if he had shown himself to David.

"He's still here. He still tries to do his job. Said he won't leave until all the souls who died under his care cross over."

"I guess that's good of him."

"Thing is, I don't know if he'll cross over himself after

they have gone. He feels a lot of guilt about what happened. To all of them, but mostly over you," he said.

I sat quietly, staring at the floor. I wasn't in a forgiving mood just after having left Elizabeth in another man's arms, and I pushed from my mind what might be happening at that moment. "I hope he can help the others," I said, unable to give more than that.

David opened his mouth to say something as the metal door to the room swung open wide.

"They need your help in the commons. Got an unruly one," a young, thin orderly said with a hint of panic. David glanced at me, and I nodded, following them out to the hall. There was a crash of shattering glass, and David broke into a jog.

I called out after him, "Just another day in the happy factory."

He threw one hand up in a wave, and I turned and left.

Outside on the front steps, I looked in all directions before deciding what to do. I had known all along I could be somewhere with a focused thought, but I did enjoy doing things the old-fashioned way. Thinking deep thoughts on long walks was something that made me feel as if I was actually alive. It reminded me of our walks around the courtyard, our long nights of walking when we escaped together. It seemed to keep me closer to the life I left behind. Suddenly, my life seemed like a distant memory as thoughts of Daniel and Elizabeth crept into my mind. I closed my eyes and thought of Anna.

When I opened them, I was standing in a dining room. Anna was there, perched high in the corner. She watched over the room with a scowl. Her eyes had grown very dark, sunken further into her emaciated skull. Her eyes were fixed on one girl at the table. I assumed the girl was the offending fiancée. She seemed nervous, fidgety, and unable to concentrate on eating or maintain eye contact.

"Now, look at that, Anna, you've got this girl scared out of her mind," I said.

Her eyes jerked toward me and then softened. "What are you doing here, Simon?" she asked as she slowly sunk down to the floor.

"Just dropped by to say hi," I said. "Let's go for a walk."

She shook her head and glanced back at the table where Matthew and Nicole sat with both sets of parents.

"They aren't going anywhere," I promised. "Come walk with me." I held out my hand, and she looked at it to Matthew and back.

Matthew laughed at something his father said and looked at Nicole.

"Relax," he leaned over and whispered, taking her restless hand in his on the tabletop.

"I was a nervous wreck before I married your father," Nicole's mother offered with a sympathetic laugh. Anna looked in her general direction and hissed.

Anna walked over and stood behind Nicole's chair. She blew on the back of her neck, and Nicole shivered hard as goose bumps rose up on her arms.

"He's mine," Anna whispered close to her head. "Leave and don't come back."

Nicole blinked and shuddered, putting down her fork and crossing her arms. Matthew looked over at her rigid posture and uneasy expression and leaned close to her.

"What's wrong?" he whispered. Nicole adjusted in her chair.

"I just don't feel well."

"Are you getting sick?" he asked, the parents'

conversation going unnoticed in the background. She shook her head again and then excused herself, nodding for Matthew to follow.

"If you're not sick, then what's wrong with you?" he asked somewhat impatiently in the far corner of the living room. "We're having a nice dinner party in there, and everyone is having a great time, and you act like you don't even want to be here."

"I don't like it here," she said. "In this house."

"What's wrong with my house?"

"I don't know. For the last few weeks, there's been weird things happening whenever I come over here. There's this feeling here." She paused, looking around. "It's unnerving."

"I think you're just nervous. There's a lot going on, and I think maybe you're getting a case of the wedding jitters." He took a good look at the dark circles around her eyes. "You look like you could use some sleep, too."

"I can't sleep. I've been having nightmares and—if I tell you something, do you promise not to be mad?"

"No."

"Then I'm not telling you."

"Fine, I won't be mad, what is it?"

"I did some research at the library. Apparently, someone was killed in this house twenty years ago. Right there in the kitchen," she said and glanced nervously around. "I think that person is still here. I think your house is haunted, Matthew."

He stared at her straight-faced and then broke into a laugh.

"Don't laugh at me!" she said indignantly.

"You only said I couldn't be mad. You didn't say anything about laughing."

"I'm serious. You can ask your father. I'm sure he

knows about it."

"I'm sure he knows, and I'm sure he doesn't believe in ghosts or spooky things that hide under the bed. You've got one imagination," he said with a grin.

"I'm being serious."

"And so am I. There is no ghost of someone killed in our kitchen haunting this house or you. You're nervous and you're tired. It'll all be over soon, and things will settle down, I promise." He gave her a quick kiss on the forehead and returned to the dining room.

"Everything all right, son?" his father asked.

"It's fine," Matthew said with a smirk. "Nicole's under the impression the house is haunted."

Everyone at the table laughed, and Nicole shot Matthew an angry look as she slipped into the chair beside him.

I looked at Anna and nodded toward the door. She followed me out with a satisfied grin on her face.

"So when are you going to ease up?" I asked as we walked.

"When she leaves."

"Anna, that's not fair," I said. I felt guilty in chastising her. I wouldn't be satisfied until Daniel left, and I often thought of ways to help encourage that.

"Why are you here?" she asked.

"David was worried," I said honestly. "And I needed a break from Elizabeth."

"I thought you loved her." She squatted, a skeleton folded into thirds.

"I do. But she's interested in someone else right now, and it's a little hard to watch."

"Then you know how it feels!"

"Yes, and it's terrible."

"And you haven't done anything?" she asked

suspiciously as she slowly rose to stand.

"Well." I grinned and looked away.

"See! You have done something to him! What did you do?" she asked excitedly.

"It was harmless stuff, Anna. And I don't take pleasure from it. It got to be too much so I took off for a bit. I think you should do the same thing."

She stared at me, unwilling to negotiate. "What if she doesn't leave?" I asked.

"Oh, she will," Anna said and turned away from me, taking slow, deliberate steps back toward the house. I caught up with her, stood between her and the porch.

"Anna, please. Leave them be. Just go on to the other side, or travel or something. Please."

She bent down, and when she came up, she had a blade of dead brown grass between her fingers.

"You're learning to move things," I said, not hiding the sinister annotation. Anna was a vocally powerful ghost. To combine that with the ability to move things in the real world held the possibility for her to become a very troublesome entity.

She smiled with satisfaction, blew the blade of grass off her fingers, and I watched it float to the ground.

"That's all I can do right now. But I'm working on it," she assured me.

Back in the dining room, Anna stood behind Nicole and reached atop her head, holding up one strand of hair and then snapped her wrist.

"Ow!" Nicole yelped as her hand flew to her head.

The whole table stopped to look at her. "I think my headband's too tight," she said, self-consciously adjusting it.

"As I was saying," Matthew's father continued to the waiting audience at the table, "we're certain we're looking at just one or two men. They've all been petty crimes so far. Break-ins and thieving along the outskirts of Rockport. I've got two deputies on it. Most likely a drifter that'll move on."

"How long did you say this has been going on?" Nicole's mother asked.

"Started getting reports a couple of weeks ago."

I immediately thought of Elizabeth and then Daniel and closed my eyes.

When I opened them, I was in Elizabeth's bedroom. She was alone, reading a book by the window. She paused every few moments to look out the window at Daniel, who was working below in the yard, and I moved to sit against the wall so I could watch her and not see him.

"I miss you," I said. She stopped reading and sighed. "I don't like him, Elizabeth. There's something about him. You should stay away from him." She glanced out the window at Daniel again. "He's not going to stay, Elizabeth. He's going to move on. And he's going to break your heart when he does." Her smile dropped. "He isn't who I see you with." I had scrunched up my face as if the words tasted bad. "I see you with someone else, Elizabeth. The one who will bring you back to me. Remember? I had told you all about it before we got caught." I stared at the side of her head while she stared at Daniel below. "I wish you could hear me," I said with a heavy sigh.

I closed my eyes and thought of all the visions that included her and this man I would bring to her. I didn't know how or when it would happen, and all I could do was wait. Wait for a sign, wait for a cue or a vision... I didn't even know what I was waiting for.

After getting a taste of what it would be like to watch her with someone else, I began to think of abandoning my vow and crossing over after I found the one I needed to bring to her. The visions I had of them together were hard enough. I didn't think I could stand to watch it firsthand. I opened my eyes and decided.

"I'm going to leave after I bring him to you," I said. "I know I swore I'd stay, but I just can't, Elizabeth. I know he'll take care of you. And it's okay because you'll be a different person for him. You won't be my Elizabeth for him. I just can't watch you take the medicine and wrestle with yourself." I glanced at the window. "And I can't watch you love anyone else. I'm sorry." She closed her book with a snap, tossing it on the floor and suddenly left the room. I followed her to her old room as she slowly sat down at the vanity. Leaning against the doorjamb, I watched her as she stared at herself in the mirror for a long moment before dropping her head. She reached for the clay heart.

"I miss you," she whispered as she rested her fingers on it lightly and sighed. As quickly as she had appeared, she was gone again. Her head rose and her smile reappeared. She pulled up her hair and tucked it under a man's hat that hung from the corner of the mirror. She reached into the top drawer, pulled out a journal and began writing. I stayed frozen for a moment, reliving the brief instant my Elizabeth had surfaced. It was enough to give me the smallest shred of hope.

"All right." I surrendered with my eyes closed. "I'll stay."

~ ~ ~

I HAD REGRETTED that decision before the next day was over. I couldn't watch them together—kisses and handholding, ducking behind trees to snuggle and grope.

The urge to hurl a bucket of hot syrup at him was getting too intense to resist. I went on many walks, getting to know the townsfolk of Rockport by eavesdropping.

I returned to watch Elizabeth sleep at night and talk to her when I thought she was most likely to hear me. I heard the barn door creak on one of those late nights. The window was left open for a breeze, and the noise had echoed across the yard. It was darker than usual from a thick cloud cover, which blocked the moonlight, but much warmer than usual for March.

From Elizabeth's bedroom window, I could see Daniel crouching out from behind the door, clad in a black wool coat and cap. I thought of him with contempt and was by his side instantly.

"Where ya headed?" I asked as I walked next to him. He walked quickly, but carefully, trying to be as stealthy as possible. I stepped on a few twigs, and he jumped at each snap, stopping to look around him with a gasp. I followed him, this time allowing several feet between us. He walked to the very edge of Rockport. He stopped at a small, whitewashed farmhouse and walked around the side, peeking in windows all around before stepping lightly to the backdoor. He opened it without trouble.

These people don't lock their doors. In fact, most doors probably don't even have locks on them, I thought. He slipped inside, lit the stub of a candle for light.

"So you're the one committing the robberies," I said. "Wouldn't Sheriff Vincent love to know about this?" I closed my eyes and opened them in Vincent's bedroom. I shook the bedpost lightly and he stirred but didn't wake up. His mind definitely was not weak, and he had no way of hearing me.

"You might want to get up and get over to the McGregor's," I said anyway. "A guy named Daniel is in the process of robbing the place right now." He jumped, snorted, rolled over, and farted. I grimaced, waving my hand in front of my face. "Nice, Sheriff. Now get up and go get that lowlife out of mine and Elizabeth's life!" He grunted and mumbled in his sleep, but still didn't wake.

I walked downstairs to his kitchen and found paper and pen. I hadn't written anything since David taught me how, and I struggled with gripping the pen and the wording. My handwriting looked ragged and childish. But hopefully, it would be enough.

Daniel is the thief.
Elizabeth William's house.

I knocked over a chair, making a loud crash in hopes of waking him up. Hearing nothing from upstairs, I blew out my breath, closed my eyes, and returned to the McGregor's.

Daniel was stuffing silverware and a few pieces of crystal into a bag. I thought to physically stop him, make a noise, or do something to scare him, but I worried for whoever lived here. If they were to wake and find him here, well, I didn't know whether this degenerate was beyond murder or not. I was helpless to do anything but watch.

I followed him back to the barn and watched as he put all his spoils into a crate, which he had hidden in the corner of his room in the barn. When he lifted the lid, I knew without a doubt that I had been right about him all along. He was the one responsible for the break-ins around Rockport.

The crate was full of silver, jewelry, and crystal— quite a tally for a little town.

The next day, I was ecstatic to see the sheriff pull up,

knock on the door and step back, waiting for some kind of reply. Daniel was out working in the field and her parents were in the barn. Elizabeth came out onto the porch, wiping her hands on her apron.

She had taken to cooking and other things domestic and devotional since Daniel had arrived. A gold cross with a diamond in the center hung from a gleaming gold chain around her neck, a gift from Daniel. Stolen, no doubt.

"Can I help you, Sheriff?"

"Hello, Elizabeth," he said stiffly. He unconsciously took a step back and surveyed her warily. "I was just wondering if I could speak to your pa for a moment." Her father was in the barn cooking up another batch of medicine, and Elizabeth made excuses that he was too busy with work and asked if she could help.

"Well, I hope so. Did your pa happen to hire some help recently?"

"He did, why?"

"Well, I was wondering if I could speak to him."

"You want to speak to Stewart?"

The sheriff straightened and looked slightly confused. "Well, I was looking to speak with someone named Daniel."

"No one here named Daniel," she said, shrugging. "Not now, anyway. Daddy did hire a man a few months ago, his name was Daniel. But he's gone now. There's only Stewart."

"Hmm. When did he leave?" The sheriff scratched his head. He tried not to look at her suspiciously, but he knew her history.

"A few weeks ago."

"All right, probably just a prank."

"What was a prank?"

"It's not important, Elizabeth. You have a nice day." He sat in his car for a moment thinking before sputtering away.

On the long dirt road leading away from the house, he passed the field where Daniel worked. The smug bastard threw a cordial wave with a smile at the sheriff as he drove by.

Elizabeth met Daniel in the field with a small lunch basket just after noon. The sun was trying desperately to break through the rain clouds.

"What did the sheriff want?" he asked as he bit into a thick shredded beef sandwich. I wondered why he didn't even look concerned. He sat on a bench of two hay bales, close to being arrested for burglary, and he munched as if it were just another day. Elizabeth snuggled next to him, a chill in the air.

"He wanted to talk to Daniel. I told him Daniel wasn't here anymore. There was only Stewart."

"I think you giving me a middle name was about the best thing anyone has ever done for me." He smiled.

"Stewart, why would the sheriff want to talk to Daniel?" she asked casually.

He shrugged just as casually and then pretended to be suddenly concerned. "I hope my sisters are okay," he said, worriedly. "I hope he wasn't here to bring bad news to me."

"Maybe you should telegraph them?"

"I think I'll go into town tonight after supper and do that."

"I could go with you," she offered, but he shook his head hard.

"It's supposed to get cold tonight. I wouldn't want you catching a chill. It'll be a long walk, besides."

"I don't mind long walks. In fact, I wanted to ask if

you wanted to take a walk with me tomorrow afternoon after you get done with your work."

"Sure. Where to?"

"My family's cabin down by the lake."

"There's a lake around here?" he asked with a mouthful of food.

"It's a good twenty-minute walk, and it's not much of a lake, but it's quiet." She gazed at him. "Private and very romantic."

That was my cue to leave, and I turned on my heel. I wanted to hear no more of what she had in mind for the cabin. I considered that our place. It was our refuge, and the last place I saw the true Elizabeth. I bristled at the thought of her taking him there.

Her next statement, thrown out nonchalantly amidst a long-winded description of the cabin, caused me to stop.

"We should get married, Stewart."

He choked, but much to my disappointment, managed to swallow and breathe.

"Hey, hey now, I'm real fond of you, Elizabeth, but we've only known each other a few weeks. That's moving a little fast, don't you think?"

"Maybe. But I love you, Stewart. I want us to be together for always. You said you would stay if you had a good reason."

"Well, yes, but—"

"And I'm planning on giving you plenty of reason, if you'll meet me down at the cabin tomorrow evening."

I turned away again. Even if he agreed to marry her, I would find a way to stop it. I'd get Anna to help me if needed, and we'd scare him right out of there. Or find a way to get him caught. The thing was I knew he wouldn't marry her. He was a drifter and a thief. He had no intention of settling down. I purposefully stayed away for three days.

I wandered for a while and then decided to check in on Anna at the end of the third day. I closed my eyes and was surprised when I opened them in front of the asylum. Anna stared at the building with an evil smile.

"Am I late for a reunion?" I asked, walking toward her. She glanced my way, but she didn't drop her strange smile.

"Welcoming party is more like it," she said and began up the steps to the front door. She paused at the door and turned to me. "Your eyes," she said, her face now somewhat concerned, "they're so dark, Simon."

David must have noticed, too because he did a double take when we walked onto the ward floor. Still not sure why Anna was here, I simply shrugged as we passed him.

"I hope they give her my old cell," she said, stopping at it.

"Who?"

Just then, there was a loud shriek and the muffled rustling of struggling. I whirled around as the door crashed open, and two orderlies were half-carrying, half-dragging Nicole in. She was wearing a straitjacket. Her parents, Matthew, and his parents stood outside the door, and all of the women were crying.

"What the hell did you do, Anna?" I turned to see her grinning as they walked past her, and it took a great effort to get Nicole onto the bed in Anna's old room. "She's not crazy, Anna. How could you do this?"

"I wasn't crazy either!" she hissed. She glanced back at Matthew through the small window of the ward door. "He'll get over her, just like he got over me," she said.

"This is mean, Anna. To torment her until they thought she was crazy! This was an evil thing to do."

She glanced around at the souls who walked through the halls—the old ones and a few new ones, all crying desperate wails, bleeding from wounds that would never close and speaking in strange languages. "Evil is all around us."

I raced back to the nurse's station. David was standing by, checking to see if the orderlies could handle the situation.

"David. This is a mistake. Nicole isn't crazy. Anna tormented her—haunted her. She may be a basket case because of it, but she's not crazy."

David nodded discreetly.

"How can we get her out of here?" I asked. He shrugged slightly. "Damn it, David, this isn't right!"

"I'll do what I can," he whispered.

"Keep the others away from her. She can hear them and once they figure that out, they'll finish the job."

A familiar nurse with a needle rushed past, and Nicole's screams subsided gradually. I grabbed Anna by her scrawny arm and the contact surprised her. "You'll leave her alone so help me God, or I'll push you through myself the next time the hole opens up."

"Why are you even here, anyway?" Her eyes narrowed at me.

"I came for your help." I glanced guiltily into Nicole's room as the focus shifted to my problem at hand. *There is nothing more I can do for her right now,* I told my conscience.

"Help with what?" she asked warily.

"I need some help getting rid of someone."

"So it's okay for you, but not for me?" She laughed loud, ugly.

"It's not the same. This guy is bad news for Elizabeth."

"So was she. Matthew was thinking about not joining the military and just settling down instead. Being a salesman or something. His father will be happy she's gone, and so will he, eventually."

"No, Anna. This guy is a thief and a liar. He's dangerous."

"And he's sleeping with her, right?"

I rubbed the back of my neck and frowned. "I don't think they're doing much sleeping, but it's not just that. He's going to lead her on by saying he'll stick around and marry her, and he isn't going to do that."

"How do you know?"

"I just know. So will you help me?" I waited rather impatiently for her answer, anxious to get rid of Daniel and to get her away from Nicole before she could do any more harm to the poor girl.

"Sure."

"He's got a strong mind, it won't be easy."

She beamed at the challenge.

We approached the cabin at dusk, and I could see flickering candlelight through the small window. They were still there. Or back again.

I stopped about thirty feet from the porch. "You go in. I'll stay here." She glanced at me and nodded. I waited by the lake, picking at the brown grass that was slowly turning green in the early spring. I looked around and saw a few trees struggling to bloom, tiny buds of flowers and leaves dotting the ends of branches.

A flock of birds returning from their wintering called from overhead and then swooped low, the leader guiding the group to a smooth, graceful landing on the mirror-like surface of the lake.

The water broke into dozens of small ripples that met and then merged, stretching into two or three wide ripples. I watched the wrinkles lap against the muddy edge. The whole lake top seemed to shift side-to-side in one slow fluid motion. Something caught my eye in the water, working its way to the edge. It looked like cloth, and I pulled it out.

It was a scarf, brown with black edges. I tossed it away to the muddy edge.

"They're just talking." Anna sat down beside me and stared at the ducks. "He looks like the shifty kind," she said.

"Is that supposed to help?" I gave a dry laugh.

"Well, no. I just see what you mean, wanting to protect her. I've told you this before, but I think she's lucky. To have you, I mean. Then and now."

"Thanks." I attempted a smile.

~ ~ ~

THE NEXT EVENING, Anna stood in the dining room with me.

"We have to be careful. Elizabeth will be able to hear you, too. You have to do most of your talking when he's alone. In the barn and when he's working."

She nodded, understanding. Cecile glanced around the table with a look of suspicion bordering on anger and approached the subject on her mind.

"Daniel, the work is almost done, so I suppose you'll be moving on soon. Do you plan on heading down to Georgia to your family?"

Elizabeth whipped her head toward her mother, glowering.

"Actually, Mother, Daniel and I have some wonderful news. We're getting married."

Her father looked at each of them several times as

thick tension hung in the air. Daniel pulled at his collar as if it were a constricting noose.

"Is that so, Daniel?" he asked, staring at Elizabeth.

"Well, sir, we were thinking on it," he said, his voice wavering.

"Did you think to talk to me about it first? I am her father, after all."

"Well, er, it came up sort of sudden-like. We haven't made any plans or anything. We just thought about thinking about it." Daniel hadn't raised his eyes from his plate the entire time, and Elizabeth had shifted her glare to his head.

"Well, I suggest we do some talking over the next few days, son." Her father seemed suddenly jovial and went back to his dinner with enthusiasm.

~ ~ ~

WE TALKED LATE into the night, coming up with a solid plan, and Anna began work the next day. Accustomed over the last several weeks to pestering the living on a daily basis, she had become very good at it and began using her verbal power to break through Daniel's strong mind.

I walked with her out to the field where he worked the next day. The Williams grew all their own feed corn and planting was supposed to be the last task for him to complete before he was free to go. He was alone. Elizabeth was working in the kitchen garden next to the house.

It was sunny and warm for March. I carried a silver spoon and a ruby necklace that he had stolen at some point during the last few weeks. My ability to grasp and move things combined with Anna's vocal influence was the perfect combination.

He stumbled around in the lumpy field, struggling to control a horse drawn plow. I stayed behind him, out of sight so to speak. He couldn't see me, but he would be able to see the items I was carrying. I laid them on a patch of unbroken ground in his direct path when he got the stubborn old animal turned around and started working his way back. Anna walked behind him, loudly talking to Daniel incessantly.

"The sheriff knows it's you, you know. He has proof. It's only a matter of time before he comes back here to take you away."

Daniel didn't look phased at all, just stopped to mop his brow and then slap the reins on the horse's rump to get him moving again. He plowed over the spoon and necklace and I grumbled.

"What now, Anna?" She stood and I waited, sitting down in the freshly plowed earth. It smelled wonderful. Wet and heavy with the sharp scent of trace minerals and it reminded me of home. I pushed the thoughts from my mind and looked up at Anna, staring directly into the horse's eyes.

"Daniel's mind is too strong. We have to break it down a little." She reached up to pet the horse and looked sad when it didn't quite work. The horse whinnied and tossed its head away nervously. I thought I saw its large eye following the cascade of golden sparks that fell from where her hand met his forehead.

"Bring the necklace here." I rose and brought it over. "Tuck it under the strap of the bridle." I smiled and did when Daniel's back was turned. I added the spoon to the other side, sliding it between the leather strap and the coarse brown hair. "Now, put your hand on his forehead," she said.

I did, waiting for her to begin talking to the horse.

"You better be nice," I warned. "This horse didn't do a damn thing to you."

She smiled. "Of course. What do you think I am? A monster?"

I glanced sideways at her and thought of Nicole wrapped up in a straitjacket and high on medicine that would make her forget her own name.

"Don't move," she told the horse. "There's danger up ahead. You can't go any further or you could get hurt." The horse whinnied loudly, showing all of its teeth and shook its head wildly. Daniel cracked the reins down on its rump and yelled for it to move. It threw its head and dug its feet in where it stood. A few more cracks of the reins and he reared up on his hind legs with a whinny so loud and insistent that I took a step back, startled. When his head reared back, the necklace swung into view, glinting in the sunlight.

"What the—" Daniel set down the reins and circled the horse.

Anna took a step back, speaking to the horse with a soothing and sweet voice.

"Calm down, boy. Yeah, you're a good boy. Everything's all right. There's no danger. You're okay."

Immediately, he settled and stood still, the necklace swaying by his jowl. Daniel lifted it off the bridle with wide eyes, breathing shallow and quick. He looked all around nervously before stuffing the necklace into his pocket. Then his eyes caught the spoon and he snatched it with a gasp. He looked around again and seeing no one, mopped his brow with his handkerchief.

Anna smiled and spoke in a sighing tone, her voice like a cold night wind forcing its way through rough tree branches.

"They're onto you, Daniel. They're going to come for you any day now. You're no good, a thief and a liar, and you're going to get caught."

I watched a shiver run through his whole body, and then he scratched the horse on the forehead. "I think it's about time to move on," he said aloud.

~ ~ ~

ANNA AND I went up to Elizabeth's room after dinner and waited for her there. She liked my idea of talking to Elizabeth, too, trying to convince her that Daniel was bad news and to let him go without a fuss. Maybe she'd break it off with him before he left, so she wouldn't feel sad and abandoned.

"Tell me something." Anna sat on Elizabeth's bed, and I watched the hypnotic trail of glitter roll gracefully off the bed. "If this guy was a good guy, would you be doing this right now? Running him off, I mean?"

I hesitated. I wanted to say no. But I knew I was jealous as hell and absolutely couldn't stand the thought of watching Elizabeth with anyone else.

"I don't know," I said honestly. "It's so hard."

"You don't have to tell me. I know it's torture."

"The thing is, Anna, we don't have to stay. We don't have to watch, but yet we do. We damn ourselves to suffering. Are we just too stupid to cross over and wait there?"

"I just can't let go," she said with a shrug. "Every day, I think this is it. I'm going to go. And every night at midnight, I change my mind. I still can't decide if it's harder to watch or to be away from him? What if time is slower there? What if it just drags on forever?"

"What if time moves faster? What if we were to cross

and then it just seems like moments and they're with us again?"

"What if someone he falls in love with crosses first and we're both waiting for him. Or what if he crosses first and he wants to wait for someone else. How awkward would that be?"

"We could speculate all day, I suppose. There's only one way to find out."

"Are you thinking about doing it? Once Daniel is gone?"

I shrugged sloppily and sat down on the floor. "I think about it every day. But I can't go just yet. Even if I wanted to."

"Why not?"

"I'm waiting for something."

"You're not waiting for her to go with you, are you? That could be a while."

"Not as long as you think. But no. I'm—" I hesitated, cleared my throat, and avoided her gaze.

"C'mon, Simon. You can tell me. After all, I'm about the only one you have to talk to... besides David."

"True. I almost forgot how nice it was to have a two-way conversation." I smiled. She rose off the bed and sort of half-walked, half-floated over, sitting much too close for comfort. "So tell me. I won't judge you." She tried to take my hand, but it sank through and just produced sparks.

I froze, debated, and then took hers. She sighed heavily and she closed her eyes. "This is what I miss." We sat quietly for a moment, and then, with a look of deep concentration in her eyes, she slowly leaned her head over onto my shoulder. It made contact and she laughed lightly.

We were quiet for several moments listening to the

sounds of early evening outside. "Talk to me, please? I miss talking." I suddenly became concerned over Anna's perception of our situation.

"You know we can't. I mean, I love Elizabeth and you love Matthew. I wouldn't want to make you think..."

"We're just friends," she said plainly, but not without a hint of disappointment. "I know that. I won't lie, though. It did cross my mind. That we could ease each other's loneliness for the time being, but—"

"But we love other people."

"That's just it. They're people. What are we? Ghosts... spirits... blobs of energy... angels?"

"I think it's safe to count out angels," I laughed. "Honestly, I don't know what we are."

"Neither do I. So what was it you were going to tell me?"

"I was hoping you'd forget," I said with a smile and a squeeze of her gaunt hand.

"Nope. Tell me. You've got me curious now."

"I guess it won't do any harm. Well, you know I see things. Visions of things that come true." I thought of David. "Well, most of the time they come true. Anyway, I have seen things regarding Elizabeth's future and her coming to me."

"You mean crossing over to you?"

"No, I don't see her crossing. Or dying. I just see someone I'm supposed to bring to her."

"Who?"

"I have no idea. I saw him in my visions a few times, and then I met an old sailor in Rockport, who had died a few days earlier. I recognized his nephew as the man in the visions. I have to save him. I don't know why or how, but I'm waiting to bring him to Elizabeth. And somehow, he will help her get back to me."

She stared at me for a long moment.

"Gosh, you really are nuts, aren't you?" she said. Then she broke into a big grin and I exhaled in relief. "You know I'm kidding. But what do you mean you have to bring him to Elizabeth? You don't have a choice?"

"That's what it feels like, anyway. It doesn't make sense. It's hard to think about, and it will be harder than hell to actually go out of my way to bring her someone who will take my place. I can't explain it. It's like I can't refuse, you know?" I dropped my voice to a whisper out of habit, hearing someone coming up the stairs. "I have to do it. I feel very compelled to find this man and save him so he can save Elizabeth."

"And you don't see any way out of it?"

"There was only one time I was able to change the outcome of my visions. And I think that one was more of a warning to protect David. So I was able to change it. But I don't think I can change this." She nodded, trying to understand. "I think that's when I'll cross. When I know he will take care of her."

We listened for a few moments to Elizabeth as she drained her bathwater and readied for bed in the bathroom next door.

"I feel bad," she said suddenly.

"For Nicole?"

She nodded.

"Then why don't you do something about it. Go make it right."

"It sounds real noble when you talk about leading someone else to Elizabeth to take care of her, but for some reason, I just don't know if I can do it. You're a lot stronger and kinder than me." She squirmed uncomfortably.

"Nah. You're just the jealous type," I teased. "Just

give it a thought, okay? You know she doesn't belong there. Won't you feel guilty if something happens?"

"I didn't belong there either." I couldn't tell if it was guilt or retribution I heard in her voice.

Elizabeth walked in then, smelling of rosewater and soap. She took off her flannel robe and hung it by the door.

"I'll leave you two alone," Anna said and slipped out of the door.

~ ~ ~

"GREAT!" ANNA SAID as she practiced plucking grass near the lake's edge where we sat a few days later. I figured they would end up here, as they did most days after the work was finished. "This isn't going to be nearly as hard as you made it sound. What am I going to do when he leaves in a few days?" She looked serious, but her voice teased.

"I didn't think it would be this easy. And he's not gone yet."

"He will be. I talked to him late into the night. I think he's convinced the law is onto him and he'd better leave soon."

"I hope Elizabeth gets over him quickly. I hope it's not too hard on her." I stared out at the ripples started by a bird taking flight off the lake's surface and watched as they rolled slow and steady toward the muddy edge.

If Anna said anything else, I didn't hear it. I was pulled into a vision and I tried to relax, taking in every detail I could.

I saw the marble statue of a man fall and shatter into a hundred pieces, and as each piece shattered, it erupted into flames. I saw crying and desperate people running in and out of the fire, and I saw him again. The man I was going to save. He walked straight into the fire without fear or hesitation. I saw the chaotic scene in deep swirls from far away. Suddenly, a dozen people were running in every direction, screaming and crying. I didn't see him come out.

I heard the loud ticking of a hundred pocket watches. They hung from the house, the trees and lay all over the ground. Each one of them read six-fourteen. I batted my eyes and refocused on the world around me.

"What did you see?"

"I have to save him from a fire," I said and stood up. "I need to find the house I saw. Can you keep working on Daniel and keep an eye on Elizabeth? I have to go to this house. I saw six-fourteen, I don't know if that's morning or night, but once I get there, I can check back in every day."

By concentrating on the house in my vision, I opened my eyes to find it in front of me. I saw a barn to my right and recognized it. Elizabeth and I had spent the night there when we ran from the hospital. I pushed aside painful memories and walked toward the house.

Inside the kitchen, a largely pregnant woman stood ironing shirts with a determined crease in her brow and an older woman at the stove stirred a massive steaming pot.

"Would you be a dear and call Hubert in for lunch, Ahna?"

The younger woman stopped her ironing and arched to stretch her back. She walked with a slight waddle as she left the kitchen. Hubert walked through the kitchen door a moment later. I recognized his face as the one etched into the marble statue that shattered, exploding into flames. I looked around, nodding, knowing I was in the right place.

A knock on the door made me jump, and Ethel opened it to an older woman with short, curly gray hair. She stepped in and hugged Ethel, said polite hellos to Hubert and Ahna, and then invited Ethel to a get together at her house to play bridge. Ethel smiled, nodding excitedly and walked to the calendar on the wall and circled the date to remind herself. When she stepped away, I glanced at the calendar and froze. In thick red pen circled three times was the date June 14.

"Six-fourteen," I whispered to myself. *"It's a date. Not a time."*

~ ~ ~

WHEN I RETURNED, Anna was waiting for me in the yard, looking displeased.

"What's wrong?"

"Elizabeth invited him to the cabin again." I made a small grunting noise of disgust, rolled my eyes, and put my hands on my hips. "The sheriff came by again while you were gone. He said there was another break-in close by, and he wanted to talk to whatever worker Charles had hired."

"What did Daniel do?"

"He hid. When no one could find him, the sheriff said he would be back this evening."

"Where are they now?"

"At the cabin."

"All right. Let's go. I have an idea. I think this might be the last push. He's sure to leave now."

I sent Anna inside and waited by the lake's edge. I had spent so much time sitting here, staring out, thinking, and trying not to think, I had memorized it in detail.

"They're just talking," she called from the porch after a moment. I lumbered up, still hesitant to see them in our cabin together.

When I got to the porch, I touched Anna's arm and said, "Here's what we're going to do. You're going to talk to Daniel while I talk to Elizabeth. If anything starts to happen, I'm going to have to leave, but I want you to keep working on Daniel." She nodded and we stepped inside. Elizabeth stood at the small makeshift kitchen, her forehead creased with worry, her arms crossed tightly over her chest.

"Why don't you start a fire?" she asked, glancing at the cold stone hearth. I pushed away thoughts of Elizabeth in the firelight. All of the beautiful features of her face softened and glowing when she had smiled at me shyly over dinner.

"It's blazing hot."

"It's romantic."

"I thought we were here to talk," he said impatiently.

"We are. But that's not all we have to do," she said suggestively with a wry smile.

"Elizabeth," he exhaled hard and ran his hand through his hair. "I have to be going. I have to leave here."

"Let him go, Elizabeth."

"You should leave before the sheriff returns. He knows it's you and he's coming to arrest you."

"Why does the sheriff keep asking to talk to you?" she asked suddenly and suspiciously.

"I don't know. This has happened before, Elizabeth. A few months ago, I had the law on my tail thinking I did something I didn't do."

"He did do it, Elizabeth. He's a thief and he's been

stealing from your neighbors. He's a liar and he's been lying to you."

"They're coming for you. Tonight." Anna looked at me with exasperation. "This is boring. I can only tell him so many times that they know it's him, and they're going to arrest him."

I nodded toward Elizabeth knowing Daniel had set his mind on leaving. I decided to have us concentrate on convincing Elizabeth to let him go. Anna smiled and walked over and stood next to Elizabeth, mimicking her posture and facial expression.

"Then take me with you."

"I don't think I can, Elizabeth."

"He never had any intention of taking you anywhere. Or marrying you. He used you, Elizabeth. He used you in every way. He's a tramp. Let him go. Push him out. Make him leave. You deserve better," Anna hissed, and the effectiveness of her words showed on Elizabeth's face.

"Don't you love me?" she squeaked. "Don't you want to marry me?"

"Look now, Elizabeth. You're a great girl. I've really enjoyed my time with you. But I really don't have a lifestyle that fits with marriage and a family. I'm a wanderer. That's no life for a woman." He turned to see her staring at him, mouth open with shock and hurt, tears welling up in her eyes.

"I ought to kill you for hurting her, you bastard," I seethed, glancing at the iron fire poker with longing.

"I need to leave tonight," Daniel said with finality.

"You said you wouldn't leave me."

"I never said that."

"Yes, you did, Stewart. You said you'd always be with me. Always be a part of me." Her voice cracked, wavering with emotion.

He shook his head and sighed with an extremely uncomfortable look on his face.

"My name's not Stewart, and I can't stay, Elizabeth. I can't take you with me," he said softly. She walked slowly to the back of the sofa and put her hands lightly on his shoulders. I took a step back as if repelled. Her face had changed, no longer hurt and heartbroken, but resolved and accepting.

"All right," she said in a whisper. He turned his head to look at her, slightly disbelieving of her sudden understanding. "I guess I knew all along this wouldn't work out. Not for the long term anyway. Deep down, I knew you'd leave someday."

He faced forward again, and I was disappointed to see some remorse and poignancy on his face.

"I'm sorry, Elizabeth. I didn't mean to hurt you," he breathed. She nodded and looked away.

"I'm sorry, too." She hesitated and then faltered a little as she spoke. She slid her hands from his shoulders up his neck into his hair. I looked over at Anna.

"I have to go." I turned to the door and then looked back quickly. Elizabeth had a handful of his hair, gently pulling his head back, leaning down to meet his lips.

"Try to ruin it for him or something," was all I could think to say before I hurried out the door.

~ ~ ~

ANNA SOON BOLTED from the cabin and ran to me at the lake's edge. She was shaking all over, the whole image of her vibrated, and her mouth hung open, unable to speak for a moment.

"What's wrong?"

"Simon, I have to leave," she breathed and looked back at the cabin with an unexplainable look. "I can't. Please, Simon, think about crossing. You need to leave here. Elizabeth isn't right. She's really messed up. She—"

"Is she okay?"

She stared at me with a straight face. "Physically."

"Look, I don't want to know what they're doing."

She straightened—her face blank and suddenly void of any emotion. "No. You don't."

"You didn't have to watch it all, you know. Just pop in at the last moment and ruin it!"

"They weren't doing anything. Not like what you're thinking."

I turned to ask what it was that had spooked her, but she was already gone.

I stared at the scarf that had washed up on the lake's edge, now buried half under the thick mud, feeling very alone. I glanced at the cabin. It was quiet, thankfully. I heard the chirping of birds overhead and went back to the house to wait.

~ ~ ~

I WAS ON Elizabeth's bed on my side. The pillow smelled like her. I closed my eyes and inhaled deeply, hoping she would return soon, wanting to see her. I was a fool to think I could ever leave.

The sheriff, making good on his promise to return, interrupted the night's supper. I hadn't left the house since leaving the cabin. I only followed Elizabeth around when she was inside, refusing to pass the threshold when she stepped outside.

Sheriff Vincent removed his hat as he stepped in, making apologies for interrupting their meal.

"I'd still like to talk to your hired man if you don't mind, Charles."

"Well, I don't mind at all if you can find him. I looked for him to give me a hand earlier this afternoon, and I couldn't find him."

"He left." Elizabeth stared at her food as she spoke. "He told me earlier today that he had to go." Her voice was solid and cold.

"He's gone for good?" Her father asked, offended. Elizabeth nodded with a tear slipping down her nose. The sheriff looked at her oddly and then glanced at Charles.

"They were engaged," Cecile said flatly.

"I take it he broke the engagement, Beth?" Elizabeth nodded again. Charles reached across and put a work-weathered hand over hers. "I'm so sorry, dear."

"Do you mind if I have a look around where he was staying?"

"Sure." Charles led the way out of the kitchen. "I'll show you."

Cecile and Elizabeth sat in silence for several moments.

"This is your fault," Elizabeth said, raising cold eyes to her mother. A look of shock and fear had rippled through her before she mustered enough courage to speak.

"I don't see how this is my fault," Cecile said, weakly defensive, focusing on her dinner.

"You didn't like him. You didn't like the idea of us getting married. He was uncomfortable around you because he knew you loathed him and that's why he left me. That's two now," she growled, glaring at her mother, who exhaled in relief when Charles and the sheriff re-entered the kitchen.

"Well, I think we found our thief," he said, holding up

several gold chains and an armload of semi-valuable trinkets.

Elizabeth pushed away from the table violently and ran out of the room, stomping upstairs. I lay beside her while she cried, clutching the clay heart in her hand.

~ ~ ~

THE DAYS QUICKLY settled into monotony as Elizabeth fell into a new routine. She dressed in overalls with her hair pinned under a hat and worked with her father in the barn and in the fields. Her mother spoke little, and I got the distinct impression she was genuinely afraid to speak out of turn to either Elizabeth or her father. She went about her domestic chores in silence, rarely speaking without having been spoken to.

Elizabeth always wrote in her journal before changing out of her work clothes. I watched her as she wrote—her face hard and determined as she wrote with a heavy hand. She gripped the pen so hard her knuckles turned white as she poured out her feelings and frustrations to the red leather bound book. I had been tempted to read it on many occasions, but thought that would be a terrible invasion of privacy.

I longed to read it, though, praying I would see my name written and know that she remembered me. Or possibly read of some of our memories, if she were writing them out. If she hadn't, I wondered how well she could hear me, and if I recounted our memories and our time together, whispered them to her, she might possibly feel compelled to write about them. For some reason, it seemed if I were able to read them, written by someone else's hand, it would make them real again. I could live them and feel them again. And neither of us would lose them. We had already lost so much.

The heat of June bore down, and Elizabeth had stepped only a few feet from the porch before sweat sprang up on her forehead. The air was muggy and oppressive. She and her father complained as they worked. Elizabeth hadn't spoken of Daniel in the months that had passed, and I had seen no witness of her pining for him after the first night. She simply slipped back into who she was before he ever came. She did start to take a lot of medicine again, dipping into her father's readily available supply several times a day.

"Opiates," her mother would grumble resentfully under her breath. Most of the time, it was just us, and I would talk to her while she worked. Sometimes, she would answer, hearing me as her own thoughts and it would always make me smile. I had enjoyed our time together, but that particular morning was bittersweet.

~ ~ ~

IT WAS THE fourteenth of June.

When I arrived at the house in the late afternoon, all looked well.

An auburn-haired man with a sturdy build paced the floor with a bounce, a tiny baby on his shoulder. He whispered soothing words and then attempted a terribly off-key lullaby that just seemed to make the baby more upset. I smiled at his loving fluster over his disconcerted child. I sat down and watched them, nothing more to do than wait until I was needed.

"Maybe she doesn't like her name? Ever since we gave it to her, she's done nothing but cry."

"Don't be silly. Try holding her the other way."

"I've held her every way there is to hold a baby.

Nothing helps." He began pacing again, patting her back with a bouncing shuffle. A little boy with black hair and big, brilliant blue eyes sat on the couch with a worried look and both fingers in his ears.

"It's colic." I recognized Hubert as he leaned on the doorjamb with a look of sympathy on his slightly reddened face. "You had it something awful when you were about this age. Seems to be when it starts. I think you cried for two months straight, didn't get a wink of sleep." He shook his head, reminiscing.

"Well, I'm sorry I was such a difficult child, but how do you fix it? There has to be something we can do." He looked down anxiously at the baby whose little red face was quivering with one piercing cry after another.

"Well, if I remember correctly, the only thing that quieted you down was a ride in the wagon. Damn near drove two of my best horses to an early grave from exhaustion."

"Again, sorry I was so much trouble," he said sarcastically. "Maybe I could try that."

"Can't. Got rid of the wagon last year. Maybe you could take her for a horse ride, though." Hubert wiped the sweat from his brow with his sleeve. "Sure is getting hot," he mumbled.

"You feeling okay, Dad? You don't look so good."

"Just getting a cold." He lumbered back to the kitchen. "Maybe I'll turn in early tonight," he called.

"Mom's not back yet?"

"You know how she gets when she and the other hens get together, Caleb." He flapped his fingers to his thumb several times and I laughed. "The gossip alone could go on for hours before they ever get to playing cards. I'm just glad they have their meetings over at June's house." Caleb stood at the back door, staring out through the screen.

"Maybe a walk outside would calm her down. We've got that old pram."

"I'm willing to try anything. You want to take her or do you want me to do it?" his wife asked.

"Why don't both of you get some fresh air. I'll stay here with Jean and Samuel," Hubert offered, leaning over the table to light the oil lamp.

The wick took to light and then faded as Hubert lowered it. The amber light from the small flame brought out the shadows and sallow color in his face. "C'mon, Jean, I'll show you where Ethel hides the cookies," he said.

Hubert reached to the top of the pantry and pulled out a jar. He smiled with effort, his face glistened with the sheen of cold sweat, and his breath was hard and short. The sky darkened as storm clouds gathered overhead.

"Here you go. I think I better sit down," he panted while groping for the chair in front of him. "Think you can manage the milk from the icebox?" Jean nodded and skipped to the icebox, having to move items around to get to the round milk pitcher.

"Jean."

Jean turned toward his grandfather's empty whisper. Hubert's mouth was open in a silent scream, his hands clutching his chest. He was rigid and silent, exactly like the statue I had envisioned. I watched the statue free fall onto the table, tipping it over. He landed on the floor with a meaty thud, eyes wide open, but perfectly still. The oil lamp skidded across the room, spraying oil in a circular pattern as it spun on its angled side. The fire quickly jumped from the wick and chased the oil in all directions. I looked back at the little boy, who stood frozen in fear for a moment, and then we both turned our heads at the sound of an infant's cries coming from upstairs.

Fire, a foot tall in some places, stood between him and the stairwell. He watched frantically as the fire jumped to the curtains of the back door, and the kitchen quickly filled with black smoke. He still held the ceramic pitcher of milk, petrified. I knelt in front of him and put my hands over his, guiding it up, dumping the milk over his head, hoping the wetness would provide some protection from the fire.

"Go. Get upstairs to the baby!" I told him. I saw the thought register in his eyes, and he ran, jumping over the fire in spots as he raced up the stairs. I followed Jean as he stood on tiptoes to reach him in the crib. He could barely touch him, so he dropped to his knees to reach through the bars and pulled him close to the edge. Back up on toes, he grabbed two fistfuls of Samuel's sleeper and pulled, but wasn't quite strong enough to lift up the well-fed baby. The fabric of his sleeper slipped out of his grasp and he cried out in aggravation, his little face scrunched in fear as the baby slipped out a second time. Without looking to see if the parents had returned to search for their children, I reached into the crib and put my hands under the baby, supporting its body as Jean pulled it up and over the railing. He nearly dropped him as the baby came over and landed in his arms. I kept my hands under the baby as Jean shifted him, trying to get a good hold.

"Get out of the house," I told him. Locking one of his little fists onto the other to hold the baby in his arms, he walked quickly but couldn't run as he struggled with his heavy little burden.

I followed him outside and watched as the mother grabbed them up, sobbing with relief. I looked around for the man, but he was nowhere to be seen. It was only this small family, crying with relief and fear, horror at watching their home burn. Shortly, neighbors appeared to help battle the blaze.

"You there!"

I didn't think anything of it when I turned to look at who was calling. Hubert stood, staring at his body, confused. When I acknowledged him, he began toward me, scarcely taking his eyes from the barn where the children were accounted for and safe.

"What happened?" he asked. There was sadness and pain in his eyes as he surveyed the scene. He knew. But he needed confirmation. He glanced around with a helpless look on his face as his family and friends raced, trying to save the house. Two cars tore into the muddy drive and swung to a stop. One man jumped out of each, wearing no protection from the rain, and I recognized one as the man from my visions. What did the old sailor say his name was? I struggled to remember. *Aryl, that's right.* The old sailor had called him Aryl. He didn't walk into the burning house, though. He picked up a bucket to join the effort. He wasn't the reason I had been called. This time. I glanced at the baby in its mother's arms and smiled, feeling peaceful for the first time in ages. I looked back at Hubert.

"Let's go for a walk," I suggested with a friendly smile. "I'll explain everything."

He nodded, still looking dizzy and confused, and I took him by the elbow, leading him away from the scene into a patch of trees.

~ ~ ~

TWO WEEKS LATER, I woke with a start next to Elizabeth

from the most vividly colored and detailed dream I had ever had. I looked over at Elizabeth's peaceful face, deep asleep and safe. I sighed, brushing the hair from her face and kissed her lightly on the forehead.

"It's time," I said. "After this, I have to go."

Charles was already awake, sipping a cup of coffee at the table, reading the newspaper. It was early and light outside, warm already, and I knew deep down I had little time to spare.

Feeling driven to the meaningful work of saving another life ahead of me, I felt energized, almost jovial.

"All right, Pops. You don't mind if I call you that, do you, Pops? Since your daughter and I are soul mates and all." He cleared his throat and adjusted his paper. "So I'll get right to the point. I know you have a weak mind, so I know you can hear me. I need your help. I have to do something today that I can't do without you."

He continued to read, seemingly unaffected by my words. I wished briefly that I had Anna's help. "What I have to do is for Elizabeth. You have to help me help her." His eyes flickered past the edge of his paper. I felt a surge of excitement at his acknowledgment. "I knew you could hear me! Now get up and get your raincoat." He rose from his chair and walked slowly to the hall closet. Opening it, he rummaged through several coats and started to pull one out.

"Not that one. Your raincoat." He shook his head with a frown, put it back, and pulled out a dark raincoat. "Now tell your wife you're going into town. You'll be gone for a while."

He walked to the washroom and opened the door. "Cecile, I think I'm gonna meander into town for a while. I'll be back by supper."

She stood by her pile of laundry, looking puzzled.

"But what about the work today, Charles?"

"I'll get to what Elizabeth can't do tomorrow," he said casually. He just stood there, sort of lost and staring at the floor.

"Now, go get in your truck," I said.

When we were in the old beast, sputtering down the dirt road toward town, I told him, "Drive to the beach access about a mile down from the marina." He hummed a tune to himself with a light smile, quiet and serene. The wind was picking up, and the distant sky, thunderheads black and purple with deep green veins, threatened a vicious storm.

Once he parked, he settled back with his hands in his lap as if waiting for instructions.

"All right. Normally I'm not one for stealing. In fact, I just did my part in running off that thief you had hired. But we can't do this without a boat."

"I wonder where Daniel went," Charles wondered quietly, looking out the window.

"It doesn't matter," I said.

"It doesn't matter," he repeated.

"We're going to have to steal a boat. Not steal, really," I corrected myself quickly. "Just sort of borrow it. We'll give it back."

"Need a boat," he mimicked, almost childlike.

"If I had known you were this easy to talk to, I would have started talking to you long ago."

"I get lonely," he whispered, looking down into his lap. I had a surge of pity for him then, at his life and how broken his mind really was to hear me so clearly. I imagined him leaving years ago as a strong young soldier, returning with a damaged mind, carrying the personality of the best friend he couldn't bear to part with. Heavy sadness filled the car, and I sighed and looked out the window.

"We just wait, Charles. That's all we need to do right now is wait." He settled back and closed his eyes.

When the rain began tapping the window, and the sky had grown several shades darker, I had an urgent feeling that it was time.

"Let's go, Charles. Time to find a boat." He exited the car and began walking down toward the beach.

We had walked a while before we found a small rowboat tied to a short pier on someone's beach house property. Without instruction, he jumped in, untied it from the pier, and rowed with a blank expression.

"Toward the storm, Charles. We need to go straight into the storm."

After a long time rowing, Charles' extreme sweat was masked by the driving rain and mist from the waves crashing all around us. He panted with exertion and stopped to wipe the water out of his eyes with his sleeve. I wasn't sure what time it was, but it was as dark as evening as the storm intensified with every passing minute.

Before long, I had to yell for Charles to hear me over the wind, and his eyes squinted against the storm.

"We wait here!" I yelled. After a moment, he pulled the oars in and set them on the floor of the boat, leaning over his knees to catch his breath. I stood and could barely make it out in the distance. Maybe one hundred feet away a fishing boat was tossed violently, helpless against the power of the squall. I could see two figures running about. *Any minute now,* I thought to myself.

"Charles, we have to get closer." He either didn't hear me or ignored me, keeping his head bowed between his knees, taking deep breaths. Suddenly scared and frustrated, I grabbed the oars, and it took every ounce of concentration I possessed to use them. Charles didn't notice the oars suspended in midair, working autonomously. After some strokes, a flash of white blinded me. When I turned my eyes toward the boat, I saw it was partially on fire with no sign of the two sailors. I rowed furiously, the oars slipping out of my grasp due to lack of concentration. I could barely make out the name *Ava-Maura* painted on the side of the boat.

"Charles! You have to row! Elizabeth needs your help!" He snapped his head up, took the oars, and rowed against the force of the powerful waves. Looking over him, I realized telling him to get his raincoat had been pointless as he was soaked to the bone. I heard a rumbling roar and turned my head slowly toward it. I stared in awe and fear at the largest wave I had ever seen barreling toward us. I closed my eyes as the edge of it lifted the small boat and pushed it along before engulfing the *Ava-Maura* just as a second explosion ripped the boat in half.

I saw him thrown off the deck into the water. A moment later, a large wave threw debris over both men.

"Charles, stay right here," I said and went into the water. I came up to find Aryl gone. I looked around wildly for him and put my head down into the water.

He was sinking slowly, unconscious with his arms limp above his head, gliding toward the bottom of the sea.

"Oh, no, you don't," I said, diving. I grabbed his hand, stopping his sinking, but pulling him up was a struggle as he was dead weight in the water. It took every ounce of concentration. I fought my way to the surface, towing him away from the murky depths of the ocean that wrestled fiercely to claim him. My head broke the surface and I screamed for Charles. I was barely holding on to Aryl, still trapped under the surface, dying. I reached the edge of the rowboat and yelled for Charles again. He snapped out of his daze, and I pulled Aryl's arm up with all my strength and concentration, holding the tips of his fingers above the surface of the water for Charles to see. His eyes opened wide, and he groped wildly for the lone hand, gripping it, and pulling with all his strength.

Leaning far over, he managed to get under Aryl's arms but struggled with getting him over the edge and into the boat. Finally, Aryl landed in the small rowboat with a soggy thud, unconscious with water pouring from his mouth and nose.

Now in the boat, I helped Charles roll him onto his back. With his hands on Aryl's stomach, he pushed hard, causing him to spew an enormous fountain of seawater from his mouth. Charles was shaking, terrified and looking very lost.

"Start rowing! Get to shore!" I yelled over the storm. I looked back just in time to see the bow of the Ava-Maura disappear beneath the crashing waves. Just beyond that, a fishing vessel's sailor hoisted the other man up and over the edge of their boat. I could make out his arms, flailing and pointing toward the depths, begging for his friend, I assumed. I couldn't hear his screams over the wind and the rain.

When I looked back down at Aryl, I realized he was very badly injured. Blood was flowing from wounds on his head, chest, and back. It mixed with the seawater, sloshing back and forth around him. It was a gruesome sight.

He coughed and sputtered, but never regained consciousness. Charles started rowing madly, and I held my head in my hands, the memory of emotional taxation engulfing me as I pondered what I had just done.

~ ~ ~

Cecile watched in mute surprise as Charles burst through the kitchen door. He gripped Aryl under the arms, pulling him across the threshold, the deadweight of his legs dragging the floor, leaving a wet, muddy trail.

"Grab his feet," Charles said, panting for breath. Cecile, confused and slightly scared, did as she was told, and they both grunted with the exertion needed to lift him off the floor. It was a slow and clumsy climb up the stairs, but eventually, they got him into the vacant bed of Elizabeth's old room.

Charles sat down hard in the small chair in front of the vanity, breathlessly wheezing. Small pools of water formed under the chair from his soaked clothes.

Elizabeth burst into the room, looking from her father to the stranger in the bed. A loud, wet gurgle grabbed everyone's attention, and Cecile moved to roll him onto his side.

"Elizabeth, help me," she said, and they gave a great push, rolling him to his side where a steady trickle of water ran from the corner of his mouth. Cecile rubbed her forehead and her hands alternately, visibly shaken and fretting.

"Where did you find him, Charles?" she asked finally.

"The ocean. He was drowning. Something happened to his boat. I pulled him out. I couldn't think of what to do besides bring him here."

"What were you doing out on the water in a storm like this?" she asked as a loud clap of thunder rumbled overhead, shaking the house. The lights gave a hearty flicker. "You'd best get the lamps," she told Elizabeth.

"What were you doing out there, Charles?" she asked again.

He shook his head pitifully and shrugged. "I don't know."

The lights went out and it was pitch dark. Elizabeth returned a moment later, an oil lamp illuminating her way into the small room.

"A lot of good it did spending all that money to wire the house for the lighting. We have to use the oil lamps every time it even threatens to storm," Cecile huffed with irritation. Charles and Elizabeth ignored her, staring at the unfamiliar person in the bed. His short and erratic breathing was interrupted by the last wet bubbles of the seawater.

"Well, what are we to do with him?" Cecile asked.

"Nothing, until the storm passes. Just try to keep him alive, I suppose. You can make him better, can't you, Cecile?" His voice was juvenile, like a child asking a mother to repair a teddy bear. She looked bewildered and stammered for words, finally uttering a meek, "I'll try."

"I'll get him some dry clothes," Elizabeth offered as she left the room. Her mother began to strip off his waterlogged clothes, covering him discreetly as she dropped each piece on the floor.

Elizabeth returned with a pair of her father's pajamas and set them on the bedside table. She helped her mother roll him from one side to the other, placing dry bedding underneath him. She towel dried his hair, making it stick up in clumps of curls from his scalp. When it came to dressing him, Cecile turned to Elizabeth but avoided her eyes.

"This is nothing for a young girl's eyes," she said discreetly. Elizabeth stayed motionless for a moment, and then turned to leave, holding her hand out for her father's as she went.

When the door latched softly behind them, Cecile crouched down and fished out the man's wallet from his pants. Fingering through the contents, she found identification and a few pictures, wet to near ruin. She slipped it all into the front pocket of her apron.

His eyes fluttering now, he coughed and sputtered, uttering a low and raspy moan.

"What is your name?" Cecile asked. His eyes lolled, unable to focus, and he grunted something before slipping back into unconsciousness.

Cecile joined Charles and Elizabeth at the table and served herself a cup of coffee. She shivered with a chill despite the soft warm glow of the oil lamps set all about the room.

"How is he?" Elizabeth asked.

"He's badly hurt. Besides lungs full of water, he's badly cut on his back and chest. He'll develop pneumonia, no doubt. I'll do my best to keep an infection at bay. I'll need another jar of honey from the cellar, Charles." He nodded and hesitated to look up from his food.

"What'll we do with him then?" he whispered.

"You did a good thing, Daddy. You're not going to get into trouble. You saved a man's life. You're a hero."

His eyes lit up and he smiled slowly. "I do hope he'll be okay."

"We'll aim to see him better. After the storm passes, and if he wakes up, we'll call the sheriff to help him find his way home."

They sat vigil through the night as the storm eased, trying to coax him to. A fever set in by morning and Cecile had a deeply concerted look on her face as she worked. She sponged him with cool water to bring down the fever and changed out the dressings on his wounds, smearing them with a light coating of honey before covering them with boiled strips of cloth.

"He needs something to help bring up the sickness," she said, wiping her face with her sleeve. His body radiated so much heat it made the room hot. His breathing was irregular and labored, his face flushed with red splotches. "If it were winter, we could pack him with snow. There's not much to do for summertime fevers."

"What about Jan?" Charles suggested. "She might have something that would help. Perhaps she could make a concoction... a remedy."

Cecile scoffed and stiffened. "There's only one kind of medicine that woman specializes in, and I doubt it would do the young man here any good." She eyed Charles and his addiction accusingly, and then gave a passing glance to Elizabeth.

"It's worth a try, Mother," Elizabeth said. With their eyes on her, and no other option to save the man's life, she nodded her agreement to go to Jan for help.

She returned by mid afternoon with an amber bottle and went silently up the stairs to the young man, Elizabeth following closely behind. With a cool cloth, she talked to him, trying to stir him awake. After several moments, his eyes fluttered and opened slowly, revealing bloodshot brown eyes.

"Where am I?" he croaked weakly.

"My husband pulled you from the ocean. Your boat sank. You're very sick." She put a hand to his head and recoiled from the searing skin. "I have some medicine that might help," she said, raising the spoon in offering. He looked confused as only his glassy and tired eyes moved about the room.

"Where am I?" he repeated.

"What's your name, young man?" she asked, touching a cool cloth to his head, making him jump.

"That's freezing," he whispered.

"No, you're burning up with fever. Now, open your mouth, take the medicine." He did and grimaced at the foul liquid. "The worse it tastes, the better it works," Cecile said with a glance at Elizabeth, who stood by the door, intently watching.

"What's your name?" Cecile asked as she commenced a cold water sponge bath that quickly sent him into violent shivers, on the verge of losing consciousness again.

"It hurts," he whispered as his eyelids slowly sank.

"Who are you, son?" Cecile asked, shaking his shoulder to rouse him.

His eyes opened a slit, and he looked as if he were mustering every ounce of concentration he could.

"I don't know," he breathed and then slipped unconscious again. I heard Elizabeth's quick draw of breath and looked over at her. Her eyes had narrowed, her mental wheels turning at full speed. I watched her as she intently deliberated something in her mind. She moved quickly and opened the bottom drawer of her vanity, pulling out her leather bound journal. Clutching it to her chest, she spun around and left the room. I followed her as she closed her bedroom door and sat on the side of the bed, hunched over the journal. She began writing furiously, concentrating intently. Her body rocked, and I could hear the rough scratching of the heavily pressed pen tip on the paper. I was instantly irritated, taken back to bad memories of the doctor's office.

"I don't know why I had to bring him to you," I told her. "And now that it's done, I need to leave." I leaned my head back on the wall. She finished a hasty writing session and then rose, seemingly at peace again, apparently having gotten something off her mind. I still thought about reading it, but something always stopped me. Having my privacy invaded so many times had left me with a deep respect for the privacy of others. Still, I longed to know what she was writing, what she was thinking. Were thoughts and memories of me anywhere in that journal? She pushed the journal under the edge of her mattress and left the room. I stared at the spot for several moments, then sighed and followed her out.

~ ~ ~

ARYL WOKE SEVERAL times over the next two days, delusional with fever, weak and dehydrated. Cecile managed to get him to take a few sips of water whenever he woke and ask him, yet again, what his name was. Each time, he answered the same.

A whispered, almost anguished, "I don't know."

I spent time sitting at the foot of his bed and talked to him when no one else was in the room. I didn't know if he could hear me or if he would remember my words as a fever induced delusional dream, but I talked regardless. I told him all about Elizabeth and me, and how I had seen him in visions for months. I admitted I didn't know how he was supposed to help Elizabeth, but he would, and I was grateful for it. Even though he was well-built and attractive, I didn't feel the violent jealousy I felt with Daniel. I explained I would leave, and I would have to entrust Elizabeth to him.

Cecile entered the room with a tray of medicine and clean cloths, and Elizabeth quickly appeared.

"Tomorrow I can go into town and talk to the sheriff

and the newspaper—"

"No, you won't," Elizabeth said calmly. She sat on the side of the bed, placed a hand softly on his knee, and watched his face adoringly. "He's mine. I'm keeping him."

"He belongs somewhere, Elizabeth. He must have a family, people who miss him. Your father told you we would only see him recovered."

"I want to be here when he wakes up," she said with resolve, ignoring her mother.

Elizabeth's narrowed eyes suspiciously watched her mother leave the room. She turned to the young man, pulled his hand out from under the covers, and held it, stroking the back of it with her fingers. The gold band on his ring finger caught her eye, and she played with it, spinning it around his finger while deep in thought. She decided quietly as she worked the ring off.

"I'm sorry. I need you more." She held the ring up to examine it in the dim light. She placed his hand on his stomach, noticing how the white strip of flesh gleamed in contrast to his tanned and work-weathered finger.

The band was wide and gold, thick and of good quality. She slipped it onto her own finger and caught sight of an engraving. Walking over to the lamplight, she tilted her hand until she could see it clearly. The extra width of the band accommodated the engraving. The outline was that of a lighthouse with two hearts engraved on each side of it—an A set in the center of one heart and a C set in the center of the other.

I didn't understand why I was to deliver Aryl to her, and I didn't understand the odd way she claimed him as if he were a lost and hungry puppy. I only had the sense that there was nothing left for me to do. Having completed my task, I knew it was time. When the portal opened tonight at midnight, I would leave.

~ ~ ~

I WAITED UNTIL after dark to say my private goodbye to Elizabeth. The house now hushed and settled for the evening, I watched her hunch over her journal again in her room. She wore overalls and boots, her hair tucked up under her father's hat. She occasionally laughed , low and gruff as she scribbled. Curiosity was driving me mad. What was she writing while she was dressed in her father's work clothes? Was it different than when she wore the dress she tried on for me, the one she wanted to wear for our wedding? I walked over behind her, staring at the back of her head.

"Mind if I take a peek?" I asked politely. She moved her arm over her book, protecting her writing in answer. That made me even more curious. I craned my neck and peeked over her shoulder. I could see the center of the page above where she was writing. I read a few sentences and then froze. My eyes wide, my breath caught, and fear ran in cold prickles up and down my spine.

Daniel wouldn't play along. Daniel had to die. Tangling my fingers in his hair, I pulled his head back and kissed him, caressing the side of his neck, feeling for the pulse. It was quick, the pull of the knife across the skin, much like trimming the hides with Father. I held his head back and put my hand over the wound, feeling the life drain from him. It was different from the last time. I was in control.

This one is a blank slate. This one will be who I want him to be. And if he won't—

"My God, Elizabeth, what have you done?"

I looked back toward the bedroom where Aryl lay helpless. *"What have I done?"*

I knew now I couldn't leave. I had to save them both.

READING THE SERIES IN ORDER

1929 - Book One
Elizabeth's Heart - Book Two
1930 - Book Three
Drifter - Book Four
Purgatory Cove - Book Five
1931 –Book Six
Purling Road: Season One
A 1929 Serial

OTHER BOOKS BY M.L. GARDNER

Simply, Mine
Short Stories from 1929
A Homespun Christmas
Sayan Knights

ABOUT M.L. GARDNER

M.L. Gardner is the bestselling author of the 1929 series. Gardner is frugal to a fault, preserving the old ways of living by canning, cooking from scratch, and woodworking. Nostalgic stories from her grandmother's life during the Great Depression inspired Gardner to write the 1929 series—as well as her own research into the Roarin' Twenties. She has authored eight books, two novellas, and one book of short stories. Gardner is married with three kids and three cats. She resides in northern Utah. www.mlgardnerbooks.com